# Desperate Measures

Once she'd dragged the man to the sand, she put her ear to his lips and listened for breathing. There was none, so she undressed him. Back at her small makeshift bed, Emer groped around for the crucifix. Then she returned to the naked body, and, with the cross, said a few words in Gaelic above him for their combined sins.

Then Emer walked out to the surf. Starting with the man's blouse, she began to rinse out her new clothing, not knowing if there were bloodstains or holes in it that needed to be patched. She scrubbed the fabric together furiously, as if the sea could wash away what a dead man had seen and felt.

When Emer returned to the cave, she laid the clothing out to dry on the rocks and picked up the cutlass again. She felt its edge, and then tested its sharpness by clutching several strands of her long hair and pulling the cutlass through them, cutting the hair at chin length, away from herself. In a trance, she continued to do the same with the rest of her hair—clump by clump—until it was all relatively the same shape around her face, with an uneven boyish fringe at her forehead. She gathered up the pile of hair and walked it to the sea, throwing it as far away as she could and holding back tears.

*Sometimes, to defend your honor, you have to do awful things, Emer,* her mother said.

## OTHER BOOKS YOU MAY ENJOY

*The Accident Season* — Moïra Fowley-Doyle

*The Alex Crow* — Andrew Smith

*Exit, Pursued by a Bear* — E. K. Johnston

*The First Time She Drowned* — Kerry Kletter

*I'll Give You the Sun* — Jandy Nelson

*The Impossible Knife of Memory* — Laurie Halse Anderson

*Kids of Appetite* — David Arnold

*Mosquitoland* — David Arnold

*Rebel of the Sands* — Alwyn Hamilton

*Schizo* — Nic Sheff

*Still Life with Tornado* — A. S. King

# THE DUST OF 100 DOGS

## A.S. KING

speak

SPEAK
An imprint of Penguin Random House LLC
375 Hudson Street
New York, New York 10014

First published in the United States of America by Flux, an imprint of Llewellyn Publications, 2009
Published by Speak, an imprint of Penguin Random House LLC, 2017

THE LIBRARY OF CONGRESS HAS CATALOGED THE FLUX EDITION AS FOLLOWS:

King, A. S. (Amy Sarig), 1970-
The dust of 100 dogs / A. S. King.—1st ed.
p. cm.
Summary: Cursed to live the lives of 100 dogs, a seventeenth-century pirate finally returns
to life as a human being and has only one thing on her mind—to recover the treasure
she has buried in Jamaica three hundred years before.
ISBN 978-0-7387-1426-4
[1. Pirates—Fiction. 2. Reincarnation—Fiction. 3. Dogs—Fiction. 4. Blessings and cursing—Fiction.]
I. Title. II. Title: Dust of one hundred dogs.
PZ7.K5693Dus 2009
[Fic]—dc22    2008034369

Speak ISBN 9780425290576

Printed in the United States of America

1 3 5 7 9 10 8 6 4 2

*For my fierce daughters, until the end of time.*

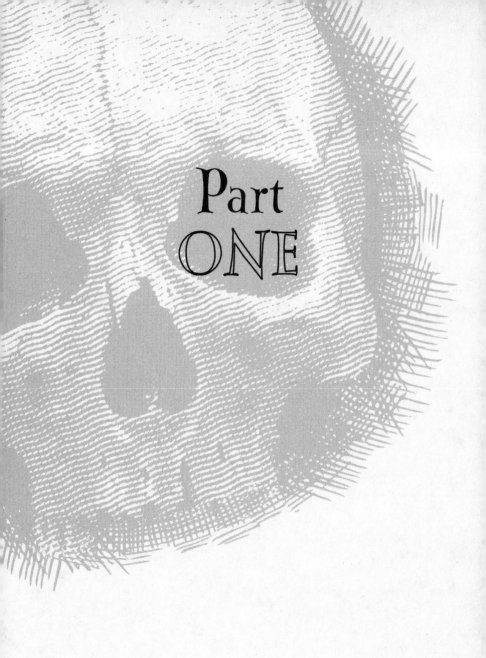

Part
ONE

*Live it up, live it up, live it up, live it up!*

ROBERT NESTA MARLEY

# Prologue

With one last, almighty roar, the Frenchman fell to his knees and died. When the smoke cleared, Emer kicked him to make sure he was dead. Bent on one knee in the moonlight, holding his head with her left hand, she took a marlinspike and removed his right eyeball with relative ease. She rolled it in the sand next to his head and shoved the spike deep into his empty socket.

She placed her pistol gently into her waistband and looked toward the sea.

"I curse you!" she screamed at the dark water. "I curse you for all you gave me and for all you pilfered! I curse you for the journeys you begin and the journeys you end! I curse you until I can't hate you anymore! And I scarcely think I will ever hate you more than on this wretched day!" Her fair hair stuck to her face, wet with sorrow and surf, and her hand-embroidered cotton blouse clung to her, stained with her lover's blood.

Turning again to the two dead bodies, she retrieved the shovel from underneath Seanie—Seanie, her first and only love. She limped back to the clearing. Looking around to make sure no one was watching, she sat down on the edge of the hole and talked to herself.

"There was only one reason to stop all of this poxy business." She turned and looked at the distant dead. "What worth is a precious jewel now? Damn it! In all these years, over all this water! And I end up a fool with a lap full of precious nothing."

She dragged the two crates into the hole and began to cover them quickly, concerned that the Frenchman's reinforcements would arrive at any minute. She buried the shovel last, on top, and used her hands to fill the remaining depression, covering the sand with sticks and dead leaves.

Returning to the scene of the dead men, she lay down beside Seanie, placed her head on his chest, and sobbed.

"It's like two different lives in the same bloody day."

Through her sobs, Emer heard footsteps. A voice boomed from the darkness, making her jump. She scrambled to her feet and reloaded her pistol.

"Foul bitch!" he began, in island-accented English. "You have meddled in my life for *too many* years! I'm sure you didn't know every whore in these islands heard him scream your name a thousand times! And me, too! Now look at him! Dead!"

Emer saw the man emerging from the tree line, his hands hidden. She had seen him before, on Tortuga and on board the *Chester*. The Frenchman's first mate.

"You will *see*!" he yelled, jumping from the brush. "You will see how true love lasts! You will *see* how real love spans time and distance we know nothing of!"

He rushed forward then, shaking a small purse toward her. From it came a fine powder that covered Emer's hair and face. She reached up and wiped her eyes clear, confused.

"What are you at?" she asked, spitting dust from her lips.

He stood with his arms and face raised to the night sky. "I curse you with the power of every spirit who ever knew love!" he screamed. "I curse you to one hundred lives as the bitch you are, and hope wild dogs tear your heart into the state you've left mine!" He began chanting in a frightful foreign language.

Still brushing the dust from her hair, Emer took aim with her gun and fired.

As she watched the man fall, she felt a burning prod in her back and stumbled sideways—long enough to see that the Frenchman had miraculously not been all dead, and long enough to see that he was covered in stray pieces of the strange dust his first mate had thrown at her.

She tried to fall as near to Seanie as possible, and managed to get close enough to reach out and grab his cold hand. She took her dying breath lying halfway between her lover and her killer, covered in the dust of one hundred dogs, knowing she was the only person on the planet who knew what was buried beneath the chilly sand ten yards away.

# .I.

# Isn't She Sweet?

Imagine my surprise when, after three centuries of fight-ing with siblings over a spare furry teat and licking my water from a bowl, I was given a huge human nipple, all to myself, filled with warm mother's milk. I say it was huge because Sadie Adams, my mother, has enormous breasts, something I never inherited.

When I was born into a typical family in Hollow Ford, Pennsylvania, in 1972, my life was finally mine again. No more obeying orders from masters, no more performing silly tricks, and no more rancid scraps to eat. Within seconds of my birth, I was suckling like no other child in the local maternity ward, in order to grow strong quickly and return to a life cut short by the blade.

A puppy can walk and wander and whine from the minute they leave the amniotic sac. There is a freedom in that which I learned to appreciate during those first years as a human again. Lying on my back for hours in a crib, wearing a diaper, and drooling made me feel like an idiot. I first tried to walk again at five months old and promptly fell over onto the linoleum floor, wailing from pain and frustration.

I was the youngest of five children born to Sadie and Alfred. Being the last, there was no wonder for them in my first steps or mutterings, and only a sigh of relief when I started to use the toilet by myself.

I don't know if my parents saw it then, but they certainly noticed later that I was completely different from other children. When I first began talking, I sometimes spoke of places I'd never been, and they would look at me, confused. When I started school, my kindergarten teacher arranged a meeting with them and asked where I'd gotten so much knowledge of history and language. They shrugged and figured I was going to be the genius in the family—so I didn't let them down.

In all fairness, they needed a genius. As I grew up, I started to notice that life in the Adams household was less typical than it appeared on the outside. My father suffered horribly from the side effects of his tour in the Vietnam War and my mother had never recovered from her childhood. Their lives had been lived on the edge of poverty and emotional instability. In me and my superhuman intelligence, they saw a way out of their troubles and shame, and so they rarely questioned any of it.

But after a meeting with my first grade teacher, they had to sit me down and ask a few things.

"Saffron, how did you know so much about the second world war?"

"I guess I saw it on the TV," I answered, trying not to sound coy.

My father frowned. "You couldn't have seen it on the TV. They don't say that much on the TV."

"Must have read it in a book, then."

"Sweetie, we don't have any books like that. Did you read it somewhere else?" my mother cooed.

"I must have."

"Hmmm."

"Saffron, we know you're a very clever girl, but do you think there's a way you could stop showing off in class? Mrs. Zeiber is concerned that you're making the other children feel bad," she said.

"Then why don't they put me in a higher grade?" I didn't like Mrs. Zeiber, but now I had reason to like her even less. I pictured myself liberating her eyeball from its socket and tossing it onto the merry-go-round in the first grade recess area.

"But we thought you liked being in Mrs. Zeiber's class."

"I do, but I'm pretty bored. I'm sick of counting to a hundred," I whined.

They looked at me, and shrugged at each other. Two weeks later, after winter break, I was enrolled in the district's gifted program—the ultimate place for showing off knowledge that no other first grader could have. I blabbered about everything—the goings-on in the Truman White House, the main tenets of Hinduism, the political complications of Central Africa. My peers envied me, even the teachers envied me. I was like a miracle kid or something, and people started to talk.

The next year, I realized that life as Saffron Adams would have to be far more inconspicuous. I couldn't go around claiming to be a genius, and I couldn't go telling stories from history that I shouldn't know yet. I guess I realized that the more I said, the more chance I had of ruining everything I was working toward.

It was then, in 1980, the year I turned eight years old, that I forged my plan to return to the Caribbean Sea. Most of the other kids in my class were toying with being rock stars or President of the United States, but I had something much more appealing in mind. Finally done with my one hundred lives as a dog, I would one day reclaim my jewels and gold, hold them close to my heart, and live happily ever after.

So from that day forward, in order to seem my age when people asked me what I wanted to be when I grew up, I answered accordingly.

"I want to be a pirate," I would say. And they would smile and think, "Isn't she sweet?"

# .2.

# My Mother's Lament

Growing up where I did, it was kind of funny for a kid to want to be a pirate, I guess. There wasn't a spot of water for miles. Three hundred miles, to be exact, to the New Jersey shoreline. My mother liked it that way. When we took our weeklong vacation in the summer, we always went west or north or south, but never east.

"I've spent enough time near the sea for this life," she would say. But still, all my sister's friends spent their vacations walking the boardwalk eating ice cream and salt-water taffy, while we took historical outings. Sometimes, if we would whine too much about the mosquitoes or the boring Civil War battlefields of Virginia, she would scare us with lies: "Children your age go missing every summer on the boardwalk," or "I won't have you running around half naked in front of old perverts." She would turn her eye to my teenaged sister and whisper, "Especially you, Patricia."

It wasn't until I got older that I learned what she had against the sea.

Once Patricia had moved out and Darren was packed for college, my mother began to need me more. I used to talk to her on the rare nights when, feeling lonely, she would sit at the kitchen table with a bottle of Irish whiskey. On a night in 1985, she told me what happened to her family back in the 1950s. I was thirteen.

Her brother Jim had called from Ireland that night, which he often did since he'd found us six years earlier. They'd talked for about an hour and, when my mother hung up the phone, she turned off the lights in the kitchen and lit a candle. She fetched a glass from the cupboard and sat down with her bottle. (She would sip minute amounts of drink and never get tipsy, but seemed to get some sort of familiar relief from it.) Teary eyed, she made me sit down, and poured herself another short measure.

"Saffron?"

"Yeah?"

"Do you know the story of my brother Willie?" My mother spoke in a mixed Irish-English accent, the kind that sounds like a question all the time.

"Willie?" I asked, having never heard her mention him before.

"The second youngest?" She pulled her fattening fingers through her black mop of dyed hair, which seemed more like a wig than real hair. Maybe it was the stark color or the three-day-old hair-spray consistency that made it seem fake, but somehow it suited her. She pulled her bangs from her face and tried to tuck them behind her ears.

"I don't think you ever told me about him," I answered.

She got up from the table and poured me a cup of weak tea from the hot kettle. "He was some little dote, that one. I think it's time you knew."

"Is that what you were talking about with Uncle Jimmy?"

"That and the rest," she answered, sighing and sitting back down. Her eyes had sunk deep into her head recently. I noticed near-black circles hidden behind her out-of-fashion 1970s glasses. She looked a lot older than forty-one, which was how old she told us she was. Her stray bangs continued to make her face itch, and she continued to try to plaster them back somehow.

"I thought there were eight of you," I said, "but I never heard of Willie."

"There were nine of us—well, ten if you count the baby that died our first winter out of Wexford town. Four girls and five boys. Poor as this," she said, holding out her empty hand. "Willie was the most stubborn of all of us. He'd do whatever my Mum told him not to."

I nodded.

"And you know, my father was an awful man who sold every last scrap we had for the drink." She wiggled the bottle. "This shite. That's how the nuns got my sisters and me. That's how the brothers got your Uncle Jimmy and the boys. Willie never made it past the docks in Dun Laoghaire.

He was drowned there, before we all got on the mailboat to England with my mother."

I was doubting that my mother was sober at that point. She'd never spoken of her father so roughly before. "What do you mean, Willie 'was drowned'? Like someone killed him?"

She nodded her head and continued her story, looking all the while at her glass and the Formica table. "Yes. Last I saw him he was crying, calling for our mum, and a nun was giving out, telling him to shut up. He must have talked back, because she slapped him and he ran to the edge of the dock."

I stopped sipping from my cup and sat completely still, wondering what she would say next.

"When he jumped, I don't know. I saw him from the stairway to the boat—thrashing around for a few seconds and then going under. I tried to stop and go back down, but there were too many people. My mother watched from close by, but was stuck in the crowd the same as I was. I remember her yelling his name over and over. Before I knew it, I had lost all sight of my brothers and never saw them again, until your Uncle Jimmy came to see us in seventy-nine."

"Didn't anyone dive in after Willie?"

"No," she answered, still looking at the table, now firmly holding her misbehaving bangs at the sides of her temples. "No one."

"What did the other people on the dock do?"

"They just stood there. The nuns turned their back on him and told everyone to go back to what they were doing."

"Wow," I answered, trying to act as if I had no idea life

could be so cruel. But I had seen worse. I had done worse. I had done far worse.

"That's just how things were, pet. My mother had signed the papers, and we became property. My knees were bloody for five years, slaving for those nuns in the south of England. I never saw my mother again and only heard she was dead, surely, when Jimmy came."

"How old was Willie when he died?"

"Four or five."

"How did they get away with that?"

"They got away with whatever they wanted to," she said matter-of-factly. "Still do."

"Is that why you left Ireland?"

"No," she answered quickly. "My mother would have never left Ireland if she didn't have to. But since my Da left, she was desperate. We lived for a few months on land belonging to old neighbors in Kilkenny—that's when the nuns caught up with us and told my Mum that we'd all have a better life in England. My mother refused. After a few weeks, the nuns came back again. 'Ten healthy children and you won't take the trip to England? Why not?' they asked her. She said she couldn't and wouldn't go—she was an Irish woman and belonged to Ireland."

I nodded. This was a feeling I could relate to—more than my own mother would ever know. Maybe more than my own mother had ever herself felt.

"You know, in the autumn, those nuns brought us milk and bread every single week. But once winter came, the deliveries stopped. By Christmas, two of the kids were so sick from hunger and cold they had to go to the local children's infirmary. That's when baby Avril died. After Christmas, the nuns came back and my mother agreed that we would all go to England, where there were free houses for people like us and good jobs. Ha!"

She poured a little whiskey into her glass.

"Ha!" she repeated. "Good jobs. Free houses! What a fool she was to believe it! Although I don't think she really did. Then to see little Willie drown like that? I think she must have pretended that it was some other mother's boy. That it wasn't Willie. That was how I got by, anyway," she whispered, confession-like, as if it were a sin to pretend. "Any faith she had left would have been all for naught, had she seen us battered and worked like slaves, digging frozen ground for vegetables to feed ourselves! For Christ's sake, it was 1958. But like the Dark Ages."

As I sat patiently, my mother refilled my teacup and poured herself a last measure of whiskey. She patted the bottle and put it back into the cupboard by the sink.

"You know, it's not just about Willie," she started, "or the way they lied to us and used us. It was the fear—" She stopped and shook her head as if trying to believe this was really her story. I could tell she was beginning to find it difficult when she reached up and put her hand over her mouth for a moment, a sign she was holding back tears. She let her unruly hair fall back into her face and I heard her swallow.

"They'd do anything," she finished, "just to get you to cry or misbehave. Anything to punish you with those damned hobnailed boots."

"Is that why we don't go to church?"

She nodded. I pictured myself disemboweling ruffian nuns.

"And that's why we don't go to the Jersey Shore?"

She nodded. I pictured myself dismembering beach perverts.

I sat quietly for a minute while she stared into space and drew strength.

"Did you finish your homework?"

"No."

"Well, what are you doing sitting here talking to me when you haven't finished your homework?" She fitted a raggedy old purple headband over her forehead and pulled it back to solve her hair problem.

"I—"

"You know that the only way out of here is an education. Don't start getting lazy now, love. You have so much potential."

"I know," I answered, still listening to her echo. *Only way out. Only way out.*

She got up and turned on the kitchen light and ran some hot water into the sink for the dishes. "I'll see you later, love."

When I went back to my room (now my own room, for six whole months since Patricia moved out), I lay on my bed and sobbed softly to myself for my Uncle Willie. It seemed—even though I knew about how bad the world could be—that I still had no control over hormones and the adolescent urge to cry my eyes out over the oddest things.

But I wasn't just crying over an uncle I never knew. I was crying about everything a three-hundred-year-old brain would cry about. Like how annoying it was to be surrounded by spoiled, twentieth-century thirteen-year-old boys and girls all day, by twentieth-century grown-ups with no idea about what was really going on, who were caught up in *Dynasty* soap opera plots, in Reaganomics, in stuff that really didn't mean anything to anybody. I wanted to kill them, and felt simultaneously sorry for them. They were a galleon of starving sailors, and I wanted to sever each one of them in half for being so stupid.

But thirteen-year-old boys and dumb people and my long-dead, never-known Uncle Willie were not what the tears were really about. As I lay there, on the new pink bedspread we bought at Kmart the weekend before, I reached over my schoolbooks for a tissue and sobbed the hardest when I thought of what my mother had said to me when I left the kitchen: "Don't get lazy now, love. You have so much potential."

It was all about my potential. Since I became girl genius in first grade, I seemed to signify some sort of escape for her. She was so into education and my being smart that I knew there was no way to avoid college—which I already knew would be a complete waste of my time.

For the next five years, all I would hear would be questions about it. Where would I go? What would I study? Could I earn a scholarship? But I had more important things to take care of. I had three hundred years' worth of buried bones to dig up, a curse to break, and paradise to build with a man who would never come back from the dead.

But first I had to turn eighteen, graduate, and tell my mother that I wasn't going to college, and I guess I was crying for the night to come when it would be me who would make her sit at the darkened kitchen table and hopelessly mutter things into her bottle. I guess I was crying for the day Saffron Adams would ultimately switch roles—from girl genius with the hopes of a desperate family riding on her brain, to the biggest disappointment who ever lived within twenty miles of Hollow Ford, Pennsylvania.

# Dog Fact #1
### *All Puppies Are Anxious to Please*

Training your new puppy will be straightforward at first. Start with toilet training on newspaper, placing the pup on it when he first wakes and after meals. Remember to praise him when he uses the paper and scold him when he does not. Toilet training should not take too long, as puppies are anxious to please.

Simple commands, to go to his bed or sit, can be taught with relative success once your puppy knows what you expect from him. Dogs who have consistent, dedicated masters will always fare better than those who don't. A master who trains his pup for one week, then abandons training will see a significant drop in the dog's obedience. Confusion like this in the early stages is best avoided.

Remember that too much of either scolding or praising leads to a dog who is *too* anxious to please. A dog that needs his master more than he obeys orders is a challenge and often a menace.

I learned this the hard way at least fifty times. I won't bore you with the details. But I will say that you'd be surprised by how many people buy dogs for the wrong reasons. They seem to expect magic dogs, dogs that don't pee or bark, dogs that come trained and understand English.

Humans treat us like a box of chocolates half full of nibbled sweets. They claim they don't like the nougat, but they love the ones with the almonds; I love how pretty she is, but I can't stand the smell; I like the idea of a mutt to fetch the papers, but I'm too lazy to scoop up the minefield of shit in the backyard.

Dog Fact #1 is the most important fact to remember throughout the training of your puppy. No matter how much they frustrate you some days—peeing in the wrong place, barking at the wrong time, or not paying attention—puppies are *always* anxious to please, and to hear you say, "good dog." ❧

# .3.

# Junior's Habit

The next time I sat with my mother at the darkened kitchen table was almost three years later, after my brother Pat came home from seeing his Army recruiter. Pat was my favorite brother, I guess. He was good with his hands, helpful, and never macho. His recruiter had assured him that the Armed Forces exam would be easy, so he hadn't studied for it and, as a result, he'd failed.

I think the thing that hurt him most was the fact that my mother chose to sprinkle her sorrows with sips of whiskey rather than be a part of the conversation still going on in the living room. My father had always tried his best to deal with my brothers on his own, but he would often lose his head and say stupid things.

"But son, *anybody* could pass that test!" he was saying now. "I knew bigger morons in the war than you, boy, and they passed it."

"He said I can retake it next week," Pat argued. "It's no big deal."

"It *is* a big deal if you end up stuck in the jungle with a bunch of idiots! Don't wanna be held responsible for another man ending up dead, do you, son?"

That was the point where my mother left for the kitchen. I don't think it was in her Irish nature to let her sons be told they weren't good enough, but it wasn't in her Irish nature to disagree with my father, either. Besides, he was half stoned all the time on a high dose of Thorazine the doctor at the VA had given him. Arguing would be pointless.

Darren had done well in his first year of state college, and Patricia was training to be a nurse's aide at the local hospital. Once Pat left for the Army, if he finally got in, it would be just me and my awful brother Alfred Junior, who we called Junior. I was half hoping Pat wouldn't leave so I didn't have to be stuck with the little brat. Junior seemed immune to my father's strict influence, and he was totally spoiled by my mother.

We were in high school then. Pat was a senior, Junior was a junior, and I was a sophomore. I was finding high school to be pretty stress-free so far. I figured if I went through the motions, studied, stayed active, and donned black and red on Hollow Ford High School Spirit Day (Go Hawks!) that everyone would believe I was going to go off to college and do what they wanted me to do. My guidance counselor was sure I would earn a scholarship if I continued to work hard. With Pat deciding to enlist and Junior getting bad grades, it was easy to pretend (without having to do much) that I was a normal girl with a glorious and prosperous future. It was only when my mother wanted to drown her sorrows that I was disturbed from my studies. The night Pat failed the Army entrance exam was one such night.

"Are you hungry, love?" she asked, at my doorway.

I shook my head. "Just trying to study over the yelling."

"Why don't you take a break and come and have something to eat with your poor ole mother."

Down in the kitchen, she made me a sandwich and tea, poured a tiny drop of whiskey into her glass, and closed the door on the argument. We faced each other across the table.

"Poor Pat," I started. "I hope he can retake the test next week."

"He'll be fine. You'll see." She nodded. "What about you, love? How are you doing these days? We barely see you between school and your studies. Have you any boyfriends we should know about?"

I'd been so focused on avoiding adolescent bullshit at school that I hadn't even thought about boys. "Nope," I answered.

"Well, don't worry. Soon you'll have to beat them off with a stick."

When she said that, I looked down at my flat chest and skinny legs and doubted it.

"Are you sad again?" I asked, sipping from the hot cup.

"Sad? No! I'm thoughtful. Or thoughtless. Or, well something in between. Just thinking."

"About what?"

"About where you'll be in ten years. How proud you'll make us." She stared past me. "After this with Pat, and Al Junior's grades, we'll need you to keep us strong. I don't think your father can take any more of this sort of thing. Arguing with kids who have everything—just to get them to *use* it! How frustrating!"

"Pat will try his best next week, Mom, I'm positive."

"Well that's all well and good, but it's really Junior I worry about. He'll drive your father spare. But I shouldn't be telling you that, dear. I wanted to talk about you."

"About me?"

"I wanted to check in. School's all right?"

"Yeah, great."

"Do you know what you want to do yet?"

*Not really. Not really. Say not really.*

"Not really."

"Well, you must have *some* idea," she said, smiling.

"Nope. Still don't know."

"Remember when your Daddy was sick in the VA hospital and you said you wanted to be a doctor? Or the time we went to Gettysburg and you saw the filmstrip about the medics and nurses in the Civil War?"

"Yeah."

"You wanted to be a doctor then, too. Maybe it's a sign." She poured a little from her almost-empty whiskey bottle into the Waterford crystal glass she saved for these nights.

"I don't know. I really don't. I have a couple years to figure it out. Don't worry."

"Well, just so you know we're counting on you, love.

You'll be the first in our family to really *do* something with your life! With your father so out of it he can barely form a sentence, and your own mother too daft to write a bloody shopping list."

I flinched. My mother's partial illiteracy had been a family secret ever since I could remember. We all helped. If it was a form to fill in at the store for a raffle, we filled it in. If it was a check to write for the gas man, we would write out the amount while on a long errand to "find her checkbook" and give it to her to sign it. She never read us stories or helped with our homework, but busied herself with things around the house. I guess we felt her guilt and never mentioned it. After learning that she'd been more of a slave than a student at the school she was sent to in England, I hadn't questioned it so much. I figured it was something she would hide until she was dead.

"You don't seem as excited about all the opportunities as you should, Saffron. There's more to life than high school! Your future could save this family!"

"Well, you always said not to count my chickens, so I haven't," I said, and pictured myself knocking her off her chair with the butt of my musket. Knocking her out cold, so she would just shut up.

"But this is what you *should* be thinking about! I bet all the other students in your class could tell me what they might want to do in college. I mean, you must have had *some* thoughts about it by now. Maybe we distract you too much around here. Do you have everything you need?"

"Sure, Mom. I don't need any more. I just want to be

sure, that's all. I'll figure it out." I was sewing her lips shut with sail thread.

"I don't want to seem too upset when I tell you this, love," she whispered, "but you've *got* to succeed. You just *have* to. Your father can't keep up with everything in his state. I can't go getting a job after so many years being a housewife and raising you all. I need to know what you're planning soon, so I can dream of a day I won't worry like this, you know?" She drank the last of the whiskey in her glass.

"You'll be the first one to know," I answered, looking around the tattered kitchen to feel better about what she'd just said—to feel better about cutting her tongue out and feeding it to the circling sharks. "I think I'll get back to the books, then," I mumbled. I put my empty cup in the sink. She stayed seated in the dark, and I kissed her on top of her head on my way out because she looked like she needed it.

"You're a good girl," she said.

"Good night, Mom."

I walked past my brother and father in the living room. They had reached some sort of agreement, which made them able to sit silently watching a baseball game on TV together. When I returned to my room, I closed my books, packed them up for the next day, and sat at my window in the dark, watching cars drive by on the suburban road outside. The view was crammed with houses in rows, each with two cars in the driveway and a porch light on.

I had already tried several times to find a simple answer to my mother's question. She would never understand that I was born with enough knowledge to make her rich beyond her wildest dreams. She wouldn't understand it even if I told her. As far as I could see, there was no way to convince anyone that picking up at eighteen and moving to the Caribbean to search for old buried treasure was anything but insane.

The thing was, I couldn't go announcing that I wanted to be a doctor because, with my brains and my grades, there was a very real possibility that I could get a scholarship to some amazing medical school. Plus, it wouldn't be right to lie *that* much. I had learned to live a vague, fence-sitting lie whenever anybody approached me seriously about my future. A biology teacher offered me a summer job helping at the funeral home (for practice with cadavers, I guess) and I said no thanks. Susan, my best (and only) friend often daydreamed about college life and parties, and I would go along with her, discussing dorm rooms or dean's lists. It seemed no one but my mother wanted to hear the details, and she would just have to wait another year to find out what would really happen.

Pat left for boot camp that summer and Patricia became a certified nurse's aide. Darren was doing well on his business degree and Junior was doing well driving the rest of us crazy. He would fight over the stupidest things, like watching a certain TV program or getting in the shower first. I thought it was to make up for feeling stupid in school. He wasn't stupid, though, and that fall I found out what his problem really was.

It turned out he was into drugs and drinking and all the

stuff that spoiled boys get into when they're in high school. Some nights he would walk into the living room while I was studying and pick up my books and throw them at the wall. If I argued, he would chase me to my room and, when I locked the door, he would beat on it for ages. I'd never really trusted Junior, and this made me trust him less. One particular night right after New Year's, when he pushed me onto the couch and sat on top of my head, virtually suffocating me, I decided to care whether he became a total loser or not. I squirmed free and pinned him to the floor, my knee on his neck. In my head, I was slicing his optic nerve, squeezing the juice from his eye, like a slimy lemon, into his choking throat. He turned purple and, when I let him go, he left, slamming the back door behind him. And then I told my parents about what was going on.

I asked them to join me in the kitchen. My mother seemed delighted about something, and I hated to have to kill her good mood.

"I have some bad news," I announced. "And I don't want you to freak out."

They stiffened.

"Is this about your guidance counselor?"

"What?"

"She called us this week to talk about your future," my mother chirped.

"No. This isn't about that. We can talk about that later," I said as sternly as I could.

"So?" my father asked.

"It's Junior."

"What about him?" my mother interrupted.

I was nervous. I could feel that they weren't going to make this easy. My father sat on the edge of his chair just at the mention of Junior's name. My mother looked horrified and jumpy.

"He's on drugs," I said.

My father hit the table with a closed fist and then sat seething, while my mother tried her best to look surprised. After five seconds, he looked over at her. "You knew this, didn't you, Sadie?"

"I, uh . . ."

"You knew?" he asked again.

"I—uh—I found some pot in his room a few months ago. Flushed it down the toilet and told him that if I caught him again I'd tell you."

"Jesus, Sadie, why didn't you tell me then?"

"He's on more than pot now," I added. "I think he's trying everything."

"What is it with this kid? Why'd you let him get away with everything for so long?"

"I gave him one chance, that's all."

"One chance too many."

"Everybody deserves a chance," she said, looking toward the cabinet that held her glorious bottle.

He sighed and looked back at me. "Let's not argue while Saffron still has things to say. How'd you find this out?"

"Everyone knows. Plus, he's been acting weird. It's scaring me."

"Scaring you, love?"

"He's been pounding on my bedroom door so much lately that the hinges are starting to buckle."

"Alfred, you talk to him tonight and make sure he stays away from Saffron. She can't be bothered now that she knows what she wants to do with her future."

"I'll talk to him all right." My father nodded. Was he beating Junior with his M-16? Was he half drowning him in a marshy paddy field?

"I didn't want to get him in trouble. He's just getting worse."

"I'll take care of it, Saffron. Don't worry."

"Do you want a cuppa before you go upstairs?" my mother asked, already at the whiskey cabinet.

"Sure."

"We wanted to talk to you anyway, while Junior was out," she said.

"He'll be sorry he ever came home," my father muttered, his hand still tightly fisted. Was he making Junior play Russian roulette, like in *The Deer Hunter?*

"About what your guidance counselor said on the phone," my mother continued. "She said your grades are so good you could get a full scholarship, but you don't seem interested in applying for them. You know, dear, these things don't just walk up to you and bite you on the nose. You have to find them and apply. And you haven't taken one college handbook home with you, she said." My mother sighed. "She told us to be concerned that you haven't talked, at all, about any of it. I told her I already was. I mean, what does she think I am, some sort of eejit? I know it when my own daughter is lost."

"I'm not lost," I managed, stabbing her false self-confidence into her ear with a marlinspike. "I'm about as far from lost as you can imagine."

"Well?" my mother asked, sitting down with her glass, my tea, and a beer for my father.

They stared at me silently.

"I mean, maybe I won't go to college. Maybe I'd be better use to you in other ways."

Silence, then sighing.

*"Maybe you won't go to college?"* my mother asked her empty glass of whiskey, after staring at me wide-eyed for about twenty seconds.

"Yeah, maybe not. I do, uh, I do have a plan, though. I just can't tell you about it yet."

"A plan?" This was useless. She was as stupid as a ship full of whores.

My father stared at his beer. "Is this why you told us about Junior?"

I shook my head no. My mother stood up from her chair and leaned toward me over the table. She was shaking all over; her blue-white skin jiggled just on the surface of her angry muscles.

"If you think that having a son on drugs is bad, try having a son on drugs and the only hope of your family telling you she doesn't really like the idea of college, all on the same night!" she sputtered, tapping the Formica with her index finger. "Don't think that you can just make your own decisions about this! We worked our whole lives waiting for the day you would graduate and maybe—maybe start a family practice here. Or something."

"Maybe you should have let me decide for myself."

"Don't be smart with me."

"Don't be smart with your mother, Saffron."

"I'm just saying that maybe if you'd gone easier on me, maybe put on less pressure…" I felt bad for making it sound like her fault, and yet wanted to scalp her right there in her own kitchen, with her own blade.

"Well, you've decided nothing yet. And I promise you—you *will* succeed and that's final! You *will* go to college and that's final! I don't give a toss about what *you* think! You live in *my* feckin' house and you'll do as *I* feckin' say!" she yelled.

My father looked to her. "Is she the same age as Patricia was, when—"

She nodded.

"Oh," he answered, looking away.

"I know what you're talking about. You don't know enough to start diagnosing me here at the kitchen table. What do you know about any of that, anyway?"

"Don't put down your father."

"I'm not. It's true."

"Just go to your room and study!" my mother yelled. "Don't come down until tomorrow. We have enough to think about without you going mad as well."

I walked into the hall and closed the kitchen door. The minute I was alone, I regretted saying anything. But it seemed my guidance counselor (who I was now dismembering, phalange-by-phalange) already had the ball rolling. Maybe it was a good thing that I told them then. I was halfway through my junior year and in sixteen months, I would be eighteen. Free to go and pursue my old business, my old life, and get out of their house.

My father's assumption that I was acting on hormones incensed me, and made me feel a familiar trapped-with-the-ignorant feeling I'd felt my whole life. It seemed that the more I matured as a human, the more I wished to be back in a coat of canine fur. What was this but a fight for dominance? The baring of teeth and the protection of perceived property?

That night, when Junior came in, my father used so many obscenities that I thought my mother would secretly pray for weeks to get him forgiven. After a half hour of screaming and a search, they found two more bags of pot, a small vial of something white, and a tiny Ziploc bag of speed. My father dragged Junior to the bathroom and made him watch as he flushed it all down the toilet.

The next morning, Junior didn't bug me at the bathroom door like he usually did, and he didn't tell me I looked as skinny as a concentration camp victim like he usually did, and he didn't even look at me over breakfast. My father slept late and my mother said nothing all morning. Before I closed the door behind me on my way to the bus stop, she tapped me on the arm and handed me an ivory envelope. I shoved it into my backpack and forgot about it.

Once I got to my locker and was organizing my books for the day, I finally opened and read it. It was short, and in my brother's handwriting.

Saffron,

Below is the name of a doctor we would like you to see. I have made an appointment for this afternoon at 4:15, so you can make it there right after school. We feel you need to talk to someone about the confusion you are feeling at this time. We hope you are soon able to steer your ideas for the future back into reality.

Mum & Dad

There was the name and address of a local psychologist scrawled at the bottom. No wonder Junior had left me alone all morning. He was gloating. She'd had him write it to shame me, probably. A drug-addict loser having to write his smart little sister a letter about how she should get her shit together was exactly how my mother communicated.

I closed my locker door and spent the rest of the day nervous about the appointment. I'd lived a lifetime of half lies and dodgy explanations, but I doubted I could fool a professional no matter how hard I tried.

What struck me that day, as I sat through preoccupied class after preoccupied class, was the pure irony of it all. There I was, the rightful owner of what would amount to millions of dollars, and my parents were mentally withering away because of money worries. They wanted me to pursue a life as a doctor so much that they took a loan out to send me to a shrink, when, in fact, I could already help them if they would only let me.

# .4.

# Memories of Home—Paris 1659

Sitting just off the riverbank, bundled in every piece of clothing she owned, Emer Morrisey counted her money. She had two French coins, both nearly worthless—she could never afford a voyage back to Ireland. Although unsure what might await her there, she was certain it had to be better than begging the wintry streets of Paris. Ireland was home, no matter who ruled it now.

For eight years, before she was sent to Paris, Emer lived in the dismal rocky hills of Connacht—one hundred miles from her village—and never once thought there could be a worse place. But living rough in Paris had turned what she once felt was hell onto its back, wanting its belly scratched.

"Anything is better than being the bought wife of an

old man," she often told herself, but she often doubted herself too. It was 1659, and Emer was fifteen. After a long, cold year in France, she was unsure of nearly everything.

Her mother was the only one who made sure she didn't jump into the river and drown herself. On so many occasions since she had arrived in Paris, her mother had talked sense into her half-frozen ears, keeping her alive.

*You can't depend on men, Emer, your whole life. Sometimes you have to depend on yourself.*

Of course, her mother was dead now. Everyone was dead now. Ireland was dead, the king of England was dead, the dragon was dead, and as far as Emer was concerned she was dead, too, even though her mother wouldn't let her jump from the riverbank to make it official.

"Damn it anyway," she mumbled as she looked at her two worthless coins and buried them in a hidden pocket beneath her skirt. She got up, and began the walk to the small grotto that she'd lived in since running from the docks her first day in Paris.

"There's got to be something better than this," she said to herself, shivering.

Emer was considering another way out. Earlier that day, she'd heard from another Irish-speaking woman, a nun who fed beggars and nursed invalids, that a boat would soon leave for the islands. She'd said young women were traveling there to settle a bustling republic called Tortuga. It was already packed full of hard-working men from France and elsewhere in Europe, and the nun made it sound like Tortuga was a sort of husband market, where a woman would be able to choose a man she liked. To Emer, the nun's story sounded like a horrible trap for whoever was stupid or desperate enough to believe it. Yet she was feeling more stupid and desperate by the day.

Arriving at her small pile of rags and straw inside the grotto, Emer rearranged her layers of clothing and propped her bony body between two rocks to sleep. In her right hand, she grasped a small wide blade in case of unwanted visitors. In her left hand, she held a tiny carved crucifix in case of unwanted memories. She cried herself to sleep—as she had every night—imagining the long, stretching view of the patchwork valley that had once been her home.

"Emer!" her mother called. "Get down from there and find your brother! It's time to eat."

She often sat atop the tower of a small abandoned castle, looking in all directions. She pretended she was the soldier on watch, anticipating the attack of a rival clan or the dreaded English. Whenever she and her brother played war, he could barely contain himself when she chose the role of king.

"Emer, you can't be a king," he would taunt. "You're a girl. Girls don't become kings—or anything important."

"Shut up. We're only pretending, anyway."

"But if you're king, then what am I?"

"You can be king too," she would say. "We can both be kings."

"Can't you be a queen? Queens have just as much power. Why don't you be the queen?"

"Queens don't fight. Kings fight. I want to fight. Come on, Padraig, let's just play."

"Okay, but I get to be King of Munster and you can be king of anywhere else."

Padraig always won their make-believe battles. He was older, bigger, and stronger. He didn't know to let Emer win sometimes, but she didn't mind because she never wanted to pretend-win anything.

"Emer!" her mother cried again. "It's time to eat!" When she lost patience, her Gaelic was as harsh as a winter gale.

Emer raced down the spiraling stone steps, careful not to spoil her dirt drawings from previous days, and found her way to the wash bucket outside their small cottage next door. She wiped her wet hands on her wool skirt and appeared at the small oak table next to the fireplace.

"What were you doing up there all day?" her mother asked, half smiling and half frustrated.

"Oh, you know, the usual stuff."

"Did you see anything today?" Padraig asked, smirking.

"I saw the last two swallows fly south," she remarked. "And I saw Mr. Mullaly and Mrs. Mullaly in the field."

Her mother looked up from her cast-iron griddle. "The Mullalys?"

"Yep."

"What were they doing in the field?"

"Building something, I think. And hugging and kissing."

Padraig burst into laughter.

"Emer, you're not to spy on people from up there," her mother scolded. "That's none of your business. Besides, the Mullalys are our friends and neighbors. Why can't you do something more productive with your time?"

"What else is there to do? I can't go with Padraig and

Daddy to the field. I can't come with you because I get in the way. I like it up there. What if someone comes to take the valley? I'll see them first. I'll sound the alarm! I could save the whole lot of us!"

Her family looked at her, amazed at her fantasies. Often her mother would complain to her father about what was said within the child's earshot. At five years old, she understood things only adults should know, like the risks of living in free Ireland and how civil wars abroad might make them a target. She'd learned this and other things from a conversation between her father and her stern uncle Martin a month earlier, and since then spent most of her time in the lookout, just in case.

"Tomorrow you'll come with me," her mother decided. "We'll go see Mary and then we'll sort out some new shoes for you and your brother. Winter will come quickly this year."

"Won't I be in the way? You always say I'm in the way!" The last time Emer went with her mother to Mary's forge, she handled an unfinished short sword and cut her palm on the ragged blade.

"Just behave yourself. We won't be long at Miss Mary's, and if you just behave yourself you won't be in my way at all."

Emer began to panic. "But who will watch the valley?"

"I will," Padraig said, quite seriously.

"But what about Daddy? Doesn't he need you in the field?"

"He'll let me take your job for the day. Don't worry."

She looked at her mother to make sure he wasn't lying. "Is that okay?"

"Of course it is. Your brother has eyes just as good as yours."

She looked at him suspiciously. "You're sure?"

"Positive. I'll watch all day. I promise."

That night, after Emer had cuddled into bed with her warmer older brother, her parents spoke of the next day's projects.

The Mullalys were in charge of distributing weapons to various small outposts along the route through their territory, and Emer's parents were responsible for organizing those weapons. So far, they had hidden over a hundred different pieces in four different locations. Miss Mary had forged over thirty of them, pike heads mostly, but a few sturdy swords as well.

After a breakfast of porridge and a hen's egg, Emer and her mother walked a mile on the old forest path to Mary's forge. A small thatched cottage of two rooms greeted them, Mary hard at work above the bellows and sweating, her forearms as big as any man's after years of pounding shapes from lumps of metal.

"Emer!" she exclaimed. "How nice to see you, pet!" She stopped working and moved all sharp objects to the side.

"Hello, Miss Mary."

"Your mother tells me you've been busy in the tower watching the swallows all summer."

"They had five nests," Emer answered. "And three broods of babies this year."

"Three?"

"Yep. It was a long summer."

"A fine long summer!" Mary said, offering Emer a small

cup of brewed tea. She turned to Emer's mother. "And how is Mairead today?"

"Fine," Mairead answered, removing a sack from her back that was heavy with metal for Mary and a rolled piece of bullock hide for the cobbler.

Mary's house was suddenly too hot, and Emer took off her cape.

"Don't get too comfortable. We're on our way in a few minutes. Why don't you go outside and play while I finish some business with Mary?"

"But—"

"Just go outside and play and I'll be out in a minute."

Every time Emer played while her mother did business with Mary, she ended up with stings, bites, or bleeding pricks all over her body. She left the house and stood quietly outside the front door, in the only area that was clear of thorns or stingers, until a mix of boredom and curiosity overwhelmed her.

Slowly, she made her way round the chimney side of the house, creeping ever so closely to the thick limestone walls. By the time she reached the back window and could look in, she'd missed seeing what wares her mother had stuffed back into the large sack. She saw only a few lumps of bog iron and a pile of worn horseshoes lying on Mary's table next to some coins. In straining to see just how much money Mary had, Emer leaned directly into a large, vigorous nettle growing out of the wall and stung her forehead.

By the time she managed to inch all the way around the house again, sniveling and groaning, her forehead was swollen, bumpy, and red, and she was wailing.

"Did you meet a nettle again?" Mary asked, laughing a little.

Emer just nodded, crying in her mother's lap. Mary walked to the front door and ripped a weed from the path, ground it into a sappy green paste between her rough hands, and returned to smear it on Emer's wound. Emer flinched at first, but knew that if she allowed Mary to do her magic, the sting would disappear soon after. Her mother could do the same sort of trick with nettle stings.

Walking to the brog maker, Mairead thought quietly to herself and hummed a tune. Emer ran ahead and looked into fox tunnels in search of telltale fur, always returning to report what she'd found—not knowing how silly she looked with her sappy green forehead.

"Not a single hair in that one," she said. "That means that they don't live in there anymore."

"Mind yourself, Emer. Don't get too hot or your head will start to hurt again."

"It's fine, Mammy. I can't feel it at all anymore."

They continued down the small dirt lane and over the Carabine Bridge, a land bridge that acted as a trap for intruders. Emer took off down the nearby riverbank and touched the flowing water to her hand. She splashed some onto her face and washed off the paste that had dried there.

"Don't get wet now. We have a ways to go," Mairead yelled. "And don't wash that paste off."

"But it feels so nice."

"Emer, just do as I say."

She returned to her mother's side, smiling, and Mairead reached down to hold her hand.

That evening, after the cobbler had been visited and the dinner had been eaten, after her brother and father went to visit a friend, Emer sat down with her mother and pulled her needlework from a small sack. Ever since she could remember, her mother had taught her to embroider and sew. Even when they had so little money that they unraveled old bits of twill for thread, they sat and sewed for at least one hour every night. At her young age, Emer was very handy with a needle and could make simple designs on bits of scrap wool. Since she'd turned five, her favorite design was a Celtic cross, rounded at the top and wide at the bottom. She had begged every evening, the whole summer, for permission to embroider a big one on her own cape, but Mairead wouldn't allow it. That night was no different.

"Don't you want to improve your stitching before you try something so important?"

"No. I want to put one on my cape. It would be brilliant, wouldn't it? The other girls would be so envious."

Mairead imagined the gossip. "We just don't have the money for that much thread. You'll have to wait."

"But you gave Miss Mary a handful of coins today! Why couldn't you save some for me?" She began to cry, and her voice reached a high-pitched screech on the "me."

"You shouldn't be spying, Emer. I've told you that a thousand times."

"You're giving all our money to Miss Mary and you don't care about me!"

"That's not so. That money wasn't all ours, and Mary is a very important lady, making us these things. You should be less selfish, girl, and listen to me more often. Stop spying and sneaking around things you don't understand."

*"But I want to make a pretty cape!"* Emer screamed, losing all control. *"Why don't you love me anymore?"*

Mairead gathered all the sewing things and returned them to the sack. Emer tried twice to stop her, but had her hand slapped smartly. She rose with a yelp and raced out the door, up her stone stairway to the lookout. Upon her arrival, she found that none of her dirt drawings had been disturbed, and realized that her brother hadn't been there that day like he'd said he would be. She screamed again, and cried as hard as she could. People in the dusk-lit valley below shook their heads and pursed their lips with disappointment. Her father and brother heard her, too, a half mile away, and pretended they didn't as they continued to talk important business with their neighbors.

Before too long, Emer stopped sobbing. She just sat, peering into her starlit lap, and vowed two things: that she would never trust her brother again to take on her chore of watchman, and that she would one day stitch the finest embroidered cape the world would ever see.

# .5.

# A Monster Lurking

News traveled quickly to the valley. The Morriseys and their neighbors gathered in the cold to hear stories of Oliver Cromwell and his massive army from a worried young man on a horse. By Christmas just past, the man reported, Cromwell had not only taken Drogheda, Wexford, and Ross, but he'd landed a brutal siege on Waterford before retreating to rest his troops to the south. Emer and Padraig stayed out of sight, in their secret hiding place near an old well, and listened to the young man as he spoke of the massacres of people gathered in their churches for safety.

"He threw fire through the windows and stationed two men at each door to kill anyone who ran. No woman or child was spared, I tell you, not one! And that's not the least of it. His cannons have destroyed the best of our fort walls and his cavalry are faster than any Irish horse!"

"Whose side are you on?" someone asked.

"It's the truth," the young man argued. "I speak what I've seen with my own eyes, in Ross. His army breathes fire like a dragon! A monster that kills innocent babies! Have you readied your men and muskets? Have you found a place to hide your families, and readied your horses?"

"Now look here," Emer's father boomed, before anyone else could muster words. "I'm not readying my horses and I'm not going to hide. This is our valley and we'll have it that way until my body lies dead at the Carabine Bridge! How can you compare us to Ross or Wexford? We're not a walled town! We're not owned by any man nor shall we be! Let them come, and then come again, and meet with our pikes and our powder!"

The rest of the farmers cheered and yelped in assent. No, Oliver Cromwell wouldn't have their farms, their church, or their children.

"How do we know you're not one of them? If they killed every last beggar, then how did you escape?" Mr. Mullaly accused.

"A spy?" someone whispered. "A traitor?"

Emer's Uncle Martin added, "Maybe you're here to survey the next battlefield?"

The young man held his hand out and denied everything. "I came only to warn you of what's coming."

"Surely you are aware that we've known of this monster for months!"

"But did you know of his plans to take Kilkenny this spring?" The man looked at the gone-silent crowd. "He will surely pass through this valley!"

Emer looked at her brother. She could see his chest puffing out and his face twisting into a maze just like the other adults who had gathered. Suddenly, everyone in the valley looked twenty years older. She tapped on Padraig's leg in an attempt to whisper something to him, but when he wouldn't pay any attention to her, she quietly sneaked from their hiding place and scurried to watch from her panoramic outpost.

*I knew it. I knew they would come for us*, she thought as she climbed to her tower and sat on a large stone on the edge. *Now they can't say I'm just a simple girl who never does anything right. Now they can say I'm the one who sounded the alarm when Oliver came.*

She looked down at the meeting and the young man on his horse. The stranger showed the crowd several wounds on his chest and a large scar on his calf to prove that he was not a traitor or a spy. Then the meeting dissolved, and people began walking or riding back to their farms.

As her parents returned to their house, Emer heard footsteps behind her.

"I want to help you watch," Padraig said. "We should work in shifts."

"No. It's my lookout. Get your own."

"It was my lookout before it was your lookout."

"You get out of here. Daddy will need you in the field. I can do it myself."

"No, you can't."

"Yes, I can!" Emer screamed. "Now get out!"

"No one will believe you if you sound the alarm because you're just a stupid girl."

"Yes they will."

"No they won't, because you're stupid."

"I am not."

"Yes you are. All girls are."

"Stop saying that. And get out!" she yelled, pushing him.

He pushed her back. "Just share it with me," he said. "I promise I'll do a good job."

"Like all the other times you watched for me?"

"Yeah. Just like those times."

"Ha!" Emer yelled, pointing. "You never even came up here those times I asked you to! I know you didn't. You can't be trusted! Just go away!"

"It's my house and I'll do what I want! You get out! It's my house," he said, and pushed her again.

She turned around with uncontrollable rage and pushed him down onto the stone floor and kicked him. "You get out! Traitor! Spy! Get out!"

"What's going on up there?" her father yelled. "Emer, come down here!"

"I can't. I'm looking out for the dragon, Daddy!"

"Where's Padraig?" Mairead asked.

"Tell Emer to let me watch!"

"Get down here, Padraig, and leave your sister alone! We have work to do!"

"But, Da!"

"Get down here!"

Padraig gave Emer a quick hard pinch to her thigh and

she yelped in pain. Before she could retaliate, he was down the staircase, and she was alone again.

She made a point to look in every direction every minute, so that she rotated a fraction of an inch on each second. To keep track of her duties, she piled dirt onto the floor in organized mounds, and each time she looked one direction or another, she marked it on her pile of dirt, all the while humming the same tune her mother sang to keep the beat of her rotations.

After several hours of this, Mairead called up to her.

"What are you doing up there, Emer?"

"Just looking."

"Come and help me with the dinner, so. You've been up there long enough."

"What about the dragon?"

Mairead answered, "Just come down and wash yourself."

"Where's Padraig?"

"He's out with your father. Come down now."

"But I can't leave until Padraig relieves me."

"Of course you can. No one is coming tonight."

"How do you know?"

"I just do," Mairead answered, making sure to sound as annoyed as she was.

Emer couldn't bear to step down from her wrap-around view of the valley.

"Emer!"

She took one last look and barreled down the steps.

"Come when I call you, girl! No more of your stories about dragons."

"But he said that a dragon came to..." she forgot the name. "To... to other places."

"Who said?"

Emer stopped to think for a moment. "Padraig."

"He told you about a dragon?"

"Yes."

"What else did he tell you?"

"About Oliver and the horses that are faster than any Irish horse," she answered.

Mairead put her hand out. "Stop that talk. Your brother is in some trouble now, and I'd say you're happy."

"But what about the dragon?"

"There is no dragon. Your brother tells you lies to scare you, that's all."

"Well then, why did that man come on the horse today? Wasn't he the one who told you all about it?"

"That man was here to sell us dried fish. He comes every winter in case we haven't enough of our own food. I certainly will have a word with your brother when he gets back."

"I don't want to die. I don't want you to die. Or Daddy. Or Padraig. If the soldiers do come, can I hide in my secret place instead of in the church?"

Mairead stopped busying herself and sat down next to her daughter. Gently she asked, "Pet, why would you think we're going to die? Who told you that?"

Emer didn't answer.

"Emer? I told you what your brother said was a lie."

"Padraig wasn't lying, I know it."

"Yes, he was."

"And that man wasn't here to sell us fish, either."

Mairead looked at her little girl and began to cry a little, but said nothing.

"Mammy, I don't want to die."

With that, Mairead pulled Emer into her arms and rocked her as they hugged quietly. She said nothing until she found something other than "Oh, Emer" to say, which took over two minutes.

"I'm sorry. I know you can tell when I'm lying."

"So there is a dragon?"

"No. No. There is no dragon, but there could be some trouble, I guess. You know you're safe, don't you?"

"Yes."

"So please don't worry. Your father and I can take care of you and your brother no matter what happens upon us, I swear it."

Emer stopped crying and sat up on her mother's lap. "Can I be the lookout then?"

"Well…"

*"Please?"*

"When there's nothing else to do, yes. You can watch."

"What about Padraig? Will you tell him that I can?"

"Of course, Emer. You're the perfect choice for that anyway. He's too busy with your father."

"Good," she whimpered, and stayed curled in her mother's lap, nuzzling.

Certainly there was trouble to come. Situated halfway between two principal towns, one of which was Cromwell's present target, their small corner of the world would soon be crawling with soldiers, looters, and worse.

"Emer?"

"Yes?"

"Do you want to know what your name means?"

"What do you mean?"

"Well, I think you're old enough to know why your father and I named you Emer. We had good reasons, you know."

"Does Padraig know what his name means?"

"I think so."

"Then I should know what my name means too." She looked attentively at her mother.

"You've heard me speak of Cuchulain before, haven't you?"

"Yes."

"Well, Cuchulain was a great Irish hero. He was the son of a god and more beautiful than any man has ever been since. For fear he would steal the hearts of their wives and daughters, people searched Ireland for a suitable wife for him. But Cuchulain would have no one but the most beautiful. And that was Emer." Mairead raised her voice a little to capture Emer's fleeting attention.

"Wasn't Cuchulain a warrior? Didn't he fight in a war?"

"Yes. The War of the Brown Bull."

"Didn't he fight on a pole?"

"Yes, but that's not what I'm talking about."

"What sort of pole?"

"No mind what sort of pole. I'm getting to the bit where Emer joins the story."

"But how could he fight tied to a pole?"

"Well, actually he died on that pole. But that doesn't

matter because many years before the War of the Brown Bull, he met Emer."

"I knew he couldn't fight tied to a pole."

Mairead smiled. "So, it was known across the land that Emer possessed the six gifts of womanhood. With these traits and some untold others, she had her pick of a great many suitors. It seemed, though, that once Cuchulain had it in his mind to marry Emer, all the other suitors were too afraid to take her. And Emer, though she loved Cuchulain, refused to marry him until he proved, through his deeds, his honor. This made her father angry, because he didn't like Cuchulain. He tried many times to trick the warrior and sell Emer to various other suitors, but in the end, Cuchulain stormed her house and took her away to marry."

"So I was named after the wife of a hero?" Emer sounded disappointed.

"She was more than just a wife. She was a very good woman to have around for a feared, half-god hero like her husband. For if everyone feared him, how would they get things done? If no one dared cross him, where could they go without challenges and troubles to follow? You see, Emer had the gift of sweet speech and wisdom. She could raise her voice up high, and gain whatever they needed by simply asking. Her beauty was unsurpassable and ravishing. This was a great strength, as beauty can often cut through the hearts of the heartless. Most importantly, she was modest and chaste and—"

"What does that mean?"

"Chaste? It means she was pure and honest. Like you

tonight when I told you that lie. Like Emer, you made me tell you the truth."

"Oh."

"It was a combination of all these gifts, and the way Emer used them to get what she and Cuchulain needed, that made her a hero as well. And there was one other thing, which is very important. Emer was a master with a needle. With her skilled hands, she could sew most anything and decorate it with the finest of needlework. Like you, she had a talent for making plain things beautiful."

"But she didn't become king or anything, did she?"

"No. Of course not."

"And she didn't fight in battles?"

"I don't know. There is a part in the story where another woman falls in love with Cuchulain and Emer ventures out to kill her, but instead, after much talk and thought, they find a solution in which none of them need die. After that, she and Cuchulain were never meddled with again."

Emer sat and thought about the story. Was this some sort of lesson her mother was trying to teach her so she'd stop fighting with Padraig? Was she serious at all? "Does anyone else know about Emer?" she asked.

"The story of Cuchulain has lasted many centuries, pet. I'm sure many know when they look at you why you are also named Emer."

"Because I'm so beautiful?"

"Yes. And the rest."

"Will you and Daddy sell me off to some man like her father did?"

"No. But you have to understand that girls have a different

reason for living than boys do. Girls can have babies and can cook and sew and keep the stock and the yard and the house. Girls can do far more things than boys can. But it doesn't make us better than them, it just makes us a better pair."

"A better pair?"

"Like shoes." Mairead took the worn cowhide slipper from her foot. "If you wear one shoe, it wouldn't really work, would it?"

"No."

"Well, a man without a woman is like wearing one shoe."

"What about Miss Mary? She's a woman and she doesn't have a man."

"Her husband died a long time ago, Emer. She once had a perfect match like I do, and the rest of the mothers here do. The most important thing to remember is that Emer didn't allow her father to marry her off to a man she didn't love, and she didn't marry Cuchulain, either, until he proved his honor. She had a mind of her own and could wield it as sharply as any sword."

"So girls fight different than boys."

"That's right."

That night, when Emer closed her eyelids to sleep, she imagined her embroidered cape, just as she had every night since she'd vowed to stitch it. It was thick with flaxen threads woven into the most colorful design anyone had ever seen, and she was inside it, wielding her wisdom and beauty to fend off the thousand suitors lined up and down the valley wishing for her hand.

# .6.

# The Dragon's Breath—
# February 1650

Emer could hear loud cannons firing as she tried to sleep. Padraig shifted about beside her, sometimes jumping a bit when the noise echoed between the church and their small cottage next to the castle. They stayed silent for some time before Emer sat up and said, "That one sounded close."

"No, it didn't. They'd be a lot louder than that."

"Are you sure?"

Padraig swallowed. "Yes, I'm sure."

"I can't sleep, anyway. Do you want to play a game or something?"

"No. Try to sleep. We'll need our rest."

Emer lay back down, listening to the little man that her

brother had become. How did he grow so serious so fast? Only a few months before, he'd been chasing her around and teasing her like a proper ten-year-old. Now he said things like that. *We'll need our rest. Try to sleep.* It was as if the cannons miles away were pounding the childhood right out of him.

She waited a minute and then replied, "We'll need our rest for what?"

"Just try to sleep."

"What will we need it for?"

"Emer, just be quiet."

"But I'm scared."

He reached out and held her tiny hand. "Don't be scared. Nothing bad will happen to us."

"But Mammy and Daddy?"

"Emer, just go to sleep and think of something happy."

"Okay, Padraig. Good night."

Every time she pictured Oliver's soldiers, she thought horrible thoughts and heard terrible screams. Since the young man on the horse came, she'd had such bad dreams that Padraig often had to wake her and caress her back to sleep, repeating the same advice: *think of something happy.*

She curled up and thought of the happiest thing she could: what she would look like as a full-grown lady wearing her hand-embroidered cape.

The next morning, she woke to the same loud reports. They had been hearing them for over a week now, and for the past fortnight, twenty-four hours a day (even in the drenching rain), someone manned the tower, looking out.

All anyone saw from up there was smoke—lots of

smoke. In three directions. It rose in different colors—black, gray, and white—and sent a rank smell across the frosty valley, curling noses and making thoughts wander. Secretly, some were claiming that they could smell the burning flesh of animals, people, babies. Grown-ups walked with far-away looks, barely watching where they stepped.

So far, in each town that Cromwell took, he tried his very best to cleanse every Catholic—even the children. Some escaped death, and were moving west to a designated place for Catholics. Many had passed through their parish since Christmas, headed for the Shannon River and what lay beyond it, warning that no village would be spared.

It took a bit of life from everybody. Emer noticed that grown-ups never smiled anymore, her mother most of all. Most days she had to help Mairead in the yard with the stock. Several hens weren't well, and Emer minded them along with two orphaned ewe lambs. She was still allowed to look out from the tower, but it had proved less fun with adults around. She wasn't trusted to watch on her own anymore, and in a way, she didn't want to see what was coming. Every day, after one look at the smoke, she retreated down the staircase to her animals.

Her father was on duty at the Carabine Bridge a mile away, and when she climbed the tower that morning she waved to him and he waved back. He gave an additional hand signal to the man in the tower and went back to standing his watch. There were a few other men with him. They would hear far in advance if the soldiers were coming, because there also were men on horses posted on every road that led to their parish.

It was a special day. Though the usual Candlemas celebration was cancelled, Emer knew that her father would come home early and they would have a small celebration themselves, because it was also her birthday. She nursed her sick chickens and fed the lambs and returned to the empty house to see what else she could do to help her mother. Padraig's maturity had rubbed off in a way, and Emer felt a lot older than six, which was the age she would turn that day.

After tidying the fireplace and the dinner table, she set to work on her secret project. She pulled out her half-made emergency bag, a project she'd started to keep her worried mind busy. In her daydreams about the dragon coming, she always had this bag over her shoulder, filled with food to tide her over and an extra pair of stockings.

In ten short minutes, she finished the seam, tied a knot, and bit it with her teeth. Turning it right-side-out and smoothing it, she leaned back and squinted. "It's perfect," she said to herself, and pulled out a long, thick plait from her pocket. She began to sew it on as a strap, but heard someone coming and hid the whole lot under her thin tick mattress.

"Emer?" Mairead called.

"Yes?" Emer answered, smoothing the mattress back to its position on the bed frame.

"Where are you?"

"I'm here," she said, and walked into the kitchen.

"Happy birthday!" her mother said. "How does it feel to be six?"

"It feels old."

Mairead laughed. "It only gets worse, Emer, the older you get." She picked her daughter up and squeezed her. "Have you fed the lambs yet?"

"Aye."

"Well then, we're off to get your gift from Mrs. Tobin."

"Mrs. Tobin?" Emer wondered why a decrepit, gnarled-up lady like mean old Mrs. Tobin would have anything to do with her birthday.

"You'll see, Emer. Just get ready. I want you to wear your other dress, the longer one. Do you know where it is?"

Emer nodded.

"Good girl. Hurry now."

Emer was ready in a very short time, still wondering about her gift and not thinking about the lookout or Oliver and his dragon for the first time in weeks.

They walked past the church to the cross in the road and continued down toward the mill, where Mrs. Tobin lived with her son and his wife, Katherine. The day was damp and cold and Emer found it difficult to breathe through her nose without sniffling and snorting. It wasn't raining, which was a relief after three weeks of solid downpour, but it wasn't sunny either. A gray mist seemed to swallow the valley from the sky down, and Emer felt it touch her toes inside the thin leather. In the distance, the hedgerows were painted just dark enough to make out the taller trees that grew within them. There wasn't a bird in the sky, Emer noticed, not even a rook.

They met several men who were on their way to relieve other men on watch, like her father, who had been working since an hour before daybreak. The road had been filled with traffic of this sort every day since the cannons arrived—armed men heading this way or that way.

By the time they reached the old thatched mill house, Emer was tired.

"Come in, Mairead, come in," Katherine said from the door. Old Mrs. Tobin sat by the blazing fire, twisting her hands into each other, warming herself.

"And hello, Emer! Happy birthday!"

"Thank you, Mrs. Tobin."

"I'm afraid we can't stay too long. It looks like rain. Paudie will be needing some dinner soon, as well," Mairead said.

Old Mrs. Tobin gestured to Emer to sit at her side, while Katherine and Mairead stood and talked at the door.

"You know, I've kept my sewing things many years, hoping to grasp a needle again," the old woman said. Then she looked at Emer and laughed. "But we all know that God can only work miracles when he wants to, and these old hands of mine are far too tired. Your mother tells me you have great talent."

"I've been working on the cross for a year now, trying to get it perfect," Emer responded. "I want to put it on a cape, but we haven't any thread."

"Well, you'll have plenty of thread now," old Mrs. Tobin said, producing a timber box about the size of a brick.

Emer stood up, speechless.

"I've saved this old box a long time."

Emer opened it. Inside, there was every shade of dyed thread she could dream of, a dozen needles, and several spools of heavy thread, too. She threw herself into the old woman's arms and cried for a second, looked back at the box, and then ran into her mother's skirtfolds and cried some more.

"Emer, don't be rude. Tell Mrs. Tobin thank you," Mairead said, pushing her back toward the fire.

"I'm sorry," Emer managed. "Thank you."

The old woman smiled and patted Emer on the head. "That's all right. It was time for you to have it."

"Thank you so much, Kitty. It's very generous of you," Mairead said.

"We're all family now," she said. "We're all one family now, girl."

After a few brief words and several more thank-yous, Emer and her mother started back toward the top of the road. From there, they could see the lookout man on the tower, giving hand signals to whoever stood at the Carabine Bridge. Emer wondered if her father would be home when they got there, and if her mother would finally let her start embroidering the cape.

As she pondered this, Padraig and Uncle Martin approached on a horse. They stopped, and Martin leaned into Mairead's ear and whispered something. Padraig stared at Emer and tried to smile, but he knew too much to make it seem real.

"You can't go back now," Martin then said, loud enough for Emer to hear. "You best go back to Kitty's place and gather the children in the church." He rode off in the direction of the Tobins' house.

"But—Daddy!" Emer cried.

"Emer, be quiet a minute." Mairead stood still for a moment, watching Padraig disappear into the gray sky, and sighed. She crossed herself and muttered something beneath her breath.

Emer began to feel sick and sad again. Forgetting everything about her happy thoughts or her timber case of dyed thread, she began to cry. Her mother picked her up, brushing the hair from her face and speaking softly.

"We'll keep going and find Daddy. Just hold on tightly."

She began a slow jog with Emer trying to balance on her back, clinging to her neck, nearly choking her. As they neared the crossroads, they heard several explosions and musket fire. Emer felt a legion of horses pounding the earth, racing toward them. In her mind, she saw the dragon. She felt dizzy and blacked out.

She woke up in the back of the cluttered church, surrounded by familiar women and the rest of the village children.

"Mammy!" she shouted in a cranky voice.

"Emer! I hear it's your birthday," a woman said.

"Yes. Happy birthday! Don't get up," someone else added.

"Mammy!" she yelled again.

Mrs. Katherine Tobin appeared. She put her arm

around Emer and half hugged her. "You were dizzy. You need to rest, girl."

"Where's my Mammy?"

"She and your father have gone to the bridge with the others."

"Is Padraig here?" Emer asked, looking around for his familiar face.

No one answered. Emer jolted to her feet and put her hands on her hips. "I'm going to find my Mammy!"

Katherine pushed her down on the bench. "You need to lie down now."

Emer was sick of hearing about resting and lying down. She looked around to see how many doors were open, and who stood by them. After young Mrs. Tobin had left to mind her own children, Emer waited until nobody noticed her anymore. Ever so slowly, she moved off the edge of the wooden pew and crawled to the aisle, where she could blend in with the sixty other children. And before anyone knew she was missing, she was on the ground floor of the abandoned castle, calling for her mother.

"Mammy! Mammy!"

Emer hurried around the ground floor but found no one. She placed her box of thread and needles on the window ledge and climbed the staircase to the tower. The look-out was empty, and when Emer dared peek out, she saw that the dragon was winning. The Carabine Bridge had been blown, and around the scrambled dirt and mess lay dead horses and men.

On the edge of the scene, men with pikes stabbed horses and riders—most of them killed instantly by the long pikes and pistols Oliver's cavalry wielded. At least fifty Roundheads on horses were galloping toward the church at full speed. Emer tried to focus harder, past the dead bodies strewn across the road, to find her parents, but the crowd was moving too fast. There was too much to see.

She ran to each corner of the tower. To the west, there was no one. The farms and houses seemed empty. The smoke coming from the nearest eastern town, Callan, seemed the worst and the blackest. She turned back toward the blown bridge and watched the battle draw nearer— until a huge ball of fear worked up her spine, and she ran.

On her way down the stone staircase, she heard a noise downstairs and froze. She stayed quiet for a minute, and then heard the crackling of fire and the sound of horses. Then Emer continued down the steps, arriving at a massive fire flaming in the thatch roof of their cottage. The smoke was thick, but Emer managed to push through it. A bunch of burning thatch dropped from above and nearly hit her arm as it fell.

She squatted down under the smoke and surveyed the scene. The horsemen that had broken free at the bridge were riding from building to building, setting them alight and blocking the doors with whatever they could find. New horsemen raced up the road to the church, lashing at any villager willing to step in their way. Emer watched as one impaled an old farmer who tried to delay him. She pinched her eyes closed as he fell, but she'd seen the worst of it and fought hard not to cry.

She ran to their secret hiding place, where she and Padraig had agreed to meet in case of any emergencies. It was the same secret tunnel, under a hedgerow, where they'd first heard about the dragon. The old well had dried up before Emer was born and behind it, beneath the stones, was a den that she and Padraig had cleared out.

As she entered the tunnel, she checked to see that no one was coming for her. By this time, the soot and smoke had settled on her face and she looked like a coal-mine child, dirty but adorable in some sad way. Looking back, she watched the cottage spit flames from its windows and finally cried, leaving trails that showed the white of her skin. She saw the foot soldiers arrive on the knoll and saw the church begin to spit fire as well, each door shut firmly and guarded by soldiers. The screaming of her neighbors and friends turned into white noise crackling in her tiny ears. She watched a brown hen run through the scene, squawking and flapping its singed wings.

*I hope Padraig has landed safely away from here*, she thought to herself. Mrs. Morris, a distant relation to her father, ran from the church, on fire and screaming. One of the soldiers hit her on the head with the butt of his musket and then stabbed her with a bayonet. Jamie Mullaly, the Mullalys' young son, was knocked down by a horseman and trampled to death. Emer watched these and other things from her hiding place, each time pinching her eyes closed with her fingers before the moment of death, each time letting out a little yelp.

When Mairead appeared on the knoll with her long hair stuffed into a cap, wearing a pair of Paudie's trousers, Emer braced herself. A horseman approached and swung his pike. Mairead lashed out at him with hers. This went on for a few swings until Mairead ducked once, pulled a short knife from her boot, and stabbed the man's leg as he turned his horse around. Taking advantage of his confusion, she lanced her pike through his chest and pulled him from the horse.

"Mammy!" Emer whispered.

She wanted to run to her, but couldn't move. When she saw the next horseman approaching from behind Mairead's back, she closed her eyes again. She scarcely expected her mother to be alive when she opened them. But by this time, her mother had mounted the horse and armed herself with the dead soldier's pike. She and the horseman made several passes at each other, the soldier screaming unintelligible insults each time.

On their final pass, Oliver's man looked sure to win, nearly spearing Mairead in the chest. Instead, she caught the handle of his pike and pushed him back and off balance. He pulled unevenly on the reins, making his horse trip up on itself. In that brief moment, Mairead stabbed him in the neck with her pike. She dug her heels into the horse and galloped back toward the bridge.

Emer wished she were still on top of the castle so she could see where her mother was going. Mairead was riding the long way round, through the thick forest at the bottom of the knoll, and avoided the soldiers still on the road. She disappeared to the east.

A sound rose to the west—the sound of a hundred horses, Emer thought. She pivoted in her tunnel and peeked toward the crossroads. Over the edge of the hill rose twenty or so familiar horses, each with two men. Some of the men dismounted and ran behind the castle to the front of the burning church, looking for their families and leveling soldiers. The riders continued on, hoping to wipe out the hundred or so Cromwellian soldiers still fighting between the blown bridge and the knoll. Emer recognized her brother as he dismounted, and said her Uncle Martin's name aloud. Padraig looked directly at their secret hiding place, but didn't go to see if she was there. Instead, he stared up at the burning castle and the smoldering cottage beside it.

Emer watched as Padraig scanned the dead bodies for their parents, and then quietly hid himself behind the burning building. He looked again in her direction, but she was too scared to give him a signal or move. He rose and, picking up a stray pike, ran foolishly into a crowd of soldiers. Emer pinched her eyes shut and never saw him again.

It was cold in the tunnel. Emer felt hungry. It was only then, over an hour after she'd abandoned the castle, that she realized she'd left her gift from old Mrs. Tobin behind, and also the emergency bag she'd secretly stitched for a week and the food she was to fill it with when the time came. Just as Padraig had teased, she was too young and stupid to know how to survive on her own, and she cried about being hungry and dumb. She tried to think of what Padraig would say—and then realized that every one of her happy thoughts had just gone up in flames with everything else she ever knew.

# .7.

# The Invasion of Doctor Lambert

The psychologist my mother sent me to was a nice guy, I guess. He was about six foot three with a soft, rounded plump in the middle, and he wore a pair of round-framed glasses that he would occasionally push up with his middle finger.

My first visit was the slowest fifty minutes I ever lived through. I didn't want to say too much, so I let him ask the usual questions between bouts of silence.

"Why do you think you're here?"

"Because my mother is worried about me." Short and sweet—try not to show too much angst while already popping his fingernails off, one by one, with an awl.

"Why?"

"Because she wants me to be a doctor."

"And you don't want that?"

"No."

"What *do* you want to be?" he asked, realizing how condescending he sounded a second too late. "I mean, what are you interested in?"

"Lots of stuff."

"Like what?"

I talked about my favorite classes (history and advanced chemistry), but didn't name any one thing. Then I said, "I know what I want to do. I just want to do it, that's all. I don't want to talk about it for months and months before I do it."

"But you can't just go to college without planning," he said quite seriously. "You have to talk about it with someone."

"It's not college."

He smiled at me. He had trustworthy eyes, a brown sort of hazel with a twinkle. They nearly made me want to stop seeing myself whipping him with his own severed forearm. "Let's talk about school for a minute."

"What about it?"

"Your mother says you do very well."

"I do. It's easy."

"So, you're bored, then?"

"Yeah. You could say that." I looked around his disheveled office. "What's that?"

He turned around to see what I was looking at. "That's an eighteenth-century chest brought from Europe by my great grandfather."

"Are those brass?" Brass catches like on Emer's chest.

"I believe so. Have you seen one before?"

"In museums and stuff," I lied. "It's cool." I babbled for about ten minutes about my humanities class and our recent visit to Philadelphia to see the museums.

"Saffron?"

"Yes?"

"Why did you come here today?"

"What do you mean?"

"Well," he smiled, "you don't seem to want to be here."

"I don't."

"Because your mother sent you?"

"Well, do you think it's right that she just sent me here, without asking me first?"

"She's just trying to help," he explained. "She wants to make sure you utilize your potential."

"Do you know why?"

"What?"

"Did she tell you *why* she wants me to utilize my potential?"

He pushed his glasses up. "You know, you're not the first clever teenager I've met who's scared to go to college."

"Really?" I asked sarcastically.

"I think you're smart enough to know that if you just talk to me about what's on your mind, you'll be wasting less of your time, my time, and your parents' money."

"What's on my mind?"

"Yes."

"I couldn't tell you what's on my mind. You'd think I was nuts."

"You could try me," he said softly, raising his eyebrows.

"And what? You'd call my mother before the bus drops me at the corner and tell her all about it, right?"

He laughed. "I won't tell anyone. That's the rule."

"Sure. Rules. I still don't feel like telling you."

"Well what's the big secret? I mean, what is there to do instead of college that could be so awful?"

"I didn't say it was awful."

"Why are you hiding it, then?"

"You wouldn't believe me."

He sighed. "You could really try me, you know. I'm not on anybody's side."

"I can't tell you. I just can't. So, if that's the only thing we're going to talk about, then there's no point in us being here. I can't tell you, so ask something else."

He nodded his head and rocked in his chair, thinking.

"I *am* sorry," I said, feeling bad.

"No, it's okay. Why don't you tell me about your mother? You mentioned her earlier."

"I'm mad at her today, so I don't want to talk about her either."

"Are you mad at her for arranging this meeting?"

"That, and other things."

"Oh. But you don't want to talk about them."

"No."

"What else is going on in your life? Your mother mentioned something about your brother."

"Junior's on drugs."

"And what do you think about that?"

"I think what I always thought about Junior. He's a spoiled lazy brat and he'll end up a loser."

"Have you ever tried any?"

"Drugs?"

"Yeah."

"No," I lied. I had tried pot a few times with a stoner girl from my history class, and Susan.

"Why do you think your brother tried drugs?"

"I don't know."

"How did your parents react when they found out?"

"Normal stuff. They flushed his stash. And they sent me here."

He raised his eyebrows.

"They sent me here, and Junior is probably out smoking joints with his buddies right now."

"You think Junior should have come to see me?"

"If you had a choice, and two of your kids bugged you on the same day—one who's on drugs, the other who says she doesn't want to go to college; one who's been a discipline problem his whole life, the other who stays quiet, does her homework, and never acts out; one who gets awful grades and detention, the other who gets good grades—which one would you send to a shrink?"

"I would probably send the quiet one with good grades who says she doesn't want to go to college," he responded.

"Why?"

"Because maybe there's no saving the other one."

"Saving me? Saving me from what?"

"From bad decisions at a crucial time of your life. You do realize that you have opportunities other kids only dream of, don't you?"

"You don't know the half of it," I said, imagining an emerald nearly as big as Doctor Lambert's belly.

"Saffron, our time is up soon. Is this time good for you next week?"

"Do I have to?"

"It would be a good idea if we met a few times, at least. Maybe for the next month?"

"A month? Is that what she wants?"

"No. It's what I recommend. Once a week for four weeks."

"What do you think you'll find out in a month?"

"I guess whatever you're willing to tell me." He smiled.

I left the office and walked to the corner to catch the late bus home. As I stared at the busy people in their passing cars, I realized his questions had churned up everything I didn't want to look at.

My mother wanted to save me—from what? From bad decisions, from turning into a loser, from trying drugs—from what? All that was bullshit. My mother wasn't trying to save me from anything. She was saving herself. She was trying to utilize my potential so she could leech off me for the rest of her life. The shrink didn't know that yet, but right then I made a vow to tell him what sort of blackmail I'd been living with, ever since I'd been crowned the Adams genius at age six.

I would tell him about my mother's problems, her needs, her secrets. I would show him the letter on ivory paper in my brother's writing and tell him of her nights at the kitchen table with her whiskey bottle. If he wanted to find the root of my problem, he would find it in my mother's greedy lap. As for me? I would no longer be a towrope to her promised land, and I would no longer accompany her on her journeys down memory lane. After years of trying to be my friend, Sadie Adams would finally get from me what all needy mothers dread—a frightfully independent teenage daughter. If she wanted any part of being on *my* boat from now on, she'd better change her pathetic little song—because I saw myself keelhauling her for the rest of my life if she didn't.

# Dog Fact #2
*Never Lie in Your Master's Bed*

Puppies should learn independence from an early age. By giving your dog his own bed (territory), you are assuring that he knows his place. The howling ball of lonely fur when you turn off the lights for the night may be heartbreaking, but ignoring the cries will assure your dog's emotional maturation.

I lived for six years on a Wisconsin farm belonging to Francine Wilkes, a widowed homemaker who had borne no children during her forty-year marriage. It was the early 1950s and Fran had more than most of her neighbors did at that time, once Harold's life insurance payments came through. When she brought me home from a friend's farm, I was seven weeks old and already knew the secret of howls and whimpers. That night she put me in a box next to the large, black, wood-burning stove in her kitchen and kissed me good night. Before she put her right foot on the bottom stair, I howled. I heard her climb two more steps and I let out a cry-combination-coughing fit to seem pathetic. She stopped. One high-pitched sob later, she was mine. From that night on, I slept in Fran's lumpy feather bed, in the hollow where Harold had slept for forty years.

She fed me at the dining room table: freshly simmered ground meat (beef on Monday, Wednesday, Friday; chicken on Tuesday, Thursday, and Saturday; and on Sunday, a surprise) with cubes of white bread and milk for dessert. I got a warm, relaxing bath on Sundays followed by a two-hour grooming session and the usual evening routine. We would

·sit for hours by the open door of the stove and listen to radio programs. She loved the murder mysteries. I could feel her body tense up with suspense as I lay sprawled on her more-than-sturdy, corn-fed lap.

If I heard a noise at night I would wake and listen, but never get up to find out what was going on. Sometimes, if I found a good spot in an afternoon sunray, I wouldn't even bark at visitors (which, in looking back, I feel guilty for). Fran Wilkes treated me like a child of her own—I owed her at least a warning bark.

I outlived Francine by one short week. I could have stuck it out longer, but I saw no point. On the day the hearse took her from the house, the neighbors led me from the front porch a mile down the dirt road to their place, the farm I'd been born on. I was closed into a cold shed by myself and given a dish of kitchen scraps. For a minute I sat, expecting the woman of the house to return with at least one blanket, but to my disappointment she seemed to forget I was there. I howled for five nights straight. I scratched grooves into their front door and destroyed the back screen door. I chewed on water hoses and odd shoes, anything important. I cried from the porch as they ate their dinner and jumped on them when they came outside. If Francine were watching me that week, she would have been embarrassed. But like most humans, she would deny her role in my behavior. She wouldn't see that spoiling me was the worst thing she could have done to me—because not only did it wipe out any chance of me becoming a confident, independent, beneficial member of a family, but it caused me such feelings of loneliness and isolation that I died from going cold turkey without her.

Your puppy will try anything to get stuff he shouldn't have. Your job is to refrain from spoiling him. If you allow your dog to sleep in your bed, he will assume that he *belongs* there, and that's just plain wrong. 🐾

# .8.

# Junior's Discount Appliances

The next few weeks were awkward, to be sure. It took only one serious temper tantrum—complete with swearing, book throwing, and plenty of high-pitched screaming with my fingers in my ears—to scare the crap out of both of them. My father tiptoed around as if I were a card-carrying pantyliner, and my mother hovered between being especially nice to me or playing vacant. Junior had an incurable dose of senioritis, a disease which made him skip classes and drive around with his friends listening to Led Zeppelin and inhaling nitrous oxide from a whipped cream can. We rarely saw him.

On the nights I came from Doctor Lambert's office,

my mother wouldn't talk to me at all. The first night, she claimed a migraine and stayed in bed. After that, she just ignored me on Tuesday nights completely.

I spent part of my time reveling because I'd made her think twice about exploiting me, and part of my time feeling equally guilty, because I knew that it really wasn't all her fault. What else could she do with a kid who was born with a secret mission? The doctor only knew part of the story, and my mother knew even less. No one had a clue what was really wrong with me, and no one ever would.

I went to see Doctor Lambert for the last time in March. Our usual Tuesday meetings had lasted for two months, twice his recommended time, since I wanted to see just how far my parents would take their pursuit of my secret. And looking back, I think I liked talking to him about my problems at home. I hadn't been able to vent my frustrations in such detail for centuries.

Before Sadie and Alfred, there were other owners, other masters, and other canine parents, but none of them wanted me to go to college or expected much more than a growl at visitors and proper toilet training. Never had my past owners attempted to control me so much while choosing to remain losers. Sadie and Alfred were an exception. They were pushing me to achieve, and yet not doing a damn thing about their own situation. It seemed ridiculous.

Doctor Lambert got a glimpse at life with the Adamses—their habits, their secrets, their war stories, and, most importantly, their effect on me—and that was all. I never told him about my plans to dig up buried treasure or my vivid, violent daydreams. I never told him about the love I carried for a three-hundred-year-old dead man, either. During our last visit, he made me promise to tell my parents about my plans to travel for a year before college. That's what we decided to call it. We figured "travel for a year before college" sounded sane enough.

I knew at some point in the week that I would have to sit my parents down at the kitchen table and tell them the great news. It felt horrible to get their hopes up, but I figured their desperate hopes shouldn't be pinned on a teenage girl in the first place.

I arrived in the living room at eight. Both of them were staring at a rerun of *M\*A\*S\*H*. I asked if they had a minute to spare, and pointed to the kitchen. We went in and sat down. My mother put the kettle on the stovetop and my father walked to the fridge and pulled out a beer, never meeting my eyes. (Patricia once told me that he used to monitor when there were tampon wrappers in the bathroom trash can, to know when to look at us or not, on account of his phobia of menstruating women.)

"Doctor Lambert wanted me to share a few things with you," I announced.

My father shifted around and my mother mumbled, "Uh huh?"

"Well, he seemed to think that you thought I would be dropping out of school. I just want you to know that I'm not."

"That's a relief," my mother said.

"I can't believe you thought I'd drop out," I said, laughing.

"We can't figure you out at all these days, dear. We don't know what you'll do next."

"But aren't you being a little unfair? I mean, I haven't done anything differently. My last report card was the best this year."

"We're not being unfair. You said you didn't want to go to college. It scared us," she explained. "Right now, we have so much to deal with, with Junior, that having our shining star fall from the sky was enough to shock the hell out of us, love. That's all. You'll understand when you have children."

When she said that, I felt the ball of anger in my belly. First, she had me in college and running a local practice. Now, she had me having babies and obligingly understanding her warped view on life. I was only sixteen years old. Why was she making me imagine slicing her eyes out? Why was she forcing me to take my cutlass to the ligaments at the back of her knees?

"After I graduate next spring, I just want to travel for a year before college," I lied. "And then I'll come back and do everything we've always planned."

The two of them just stared at me with a depressed sort of disbelief on their faces. My mother was shaking her head slightly and my father took a long swig of his beer. I could imagine them yelling at Doctor Lambert the next day. Why hadn't he cured me? Why hadn't he changed my mind?

"Is something wrong? Doctor Lambert said you'd be happy to hear this. You don't seem it."

My mother said, "Well, it *is* a relief to hear you'll finish school."

"That's it?"

"What was the part about traveling and coming back? You're going to go away? Is that what you're saying?"

"That's part of the plan, yes."

"Where are you going?"

"I can't really say yet," I replied. "But if it doesn't work out, I'll fly right back here to Hollow Ford for a little while before I go off to college." I felt bad for lying.

"You can't say yet?" my father asked, annoyed, still looking past me at the cupboards. I loaded my musket with used tampons and fired into his throat. I doused a maxipad with gasoline, stuck his lips shut, and lit it.

"Not yet, no."

"Not yet? What the hell does that mean?"

"It's a year away anyway. Can't we leave it until then?"

My mother whined, "Well what will I tell the other parents when they ask me about where you're going to college?"

"Tell them I'm looking into going abroad for a year. That will shut them up."

"Abroad?" My mother's face nearly cracked with pain.

"Well, wherever. You can say Philadelphia—it just doesn't sound as exciting."

"Where would you get the money for that, anyway?" my mother whimpered. "Why are you ruining your life?"

"I'd get a job and save. Don't get upset."

My mother tried her very best to hold back tears while my father looked at the table and said, "Saffron, give your mother and me a few minutes."

I gave them a few minutes, which turned into a few hours. I sat watching whatever boring shows were on the television while they stayed in the kitchen with the door closed. I heard my mother's bottle come out and my father's beer cans snap open three more times before I went to bed.

The next day, my parents' attitude toward me took a new turn. They cut me off. First my father, who was frightened of blood and estrogen, and then my mother, who was afraid she would never see me again, like the rest of her scattered family. That conversation was the last time we talked about anything, ever.

Junior moved out in August, finally pushed by a fight he had with my father when he said the Army was for redneck losers, and he only came around when he needed something—usually money. My senior year in high school was, therefore, quiet. I took a part-time job at the local McDonald's to begin saving for my trip. By Christmas, I had over five hundred in cash saved in a book hidden in my bedroom. By New Year's, Junior had stolen it on one of his nighttime raids of our house, and I had to open a bank account and start all over again.

Throughout January 1990, things began to disappear from our house at an alarming rate. First, it was the television and VCR, and then the microwave. After that, it was the two space heaters and my hair dryer, my mother's small radio cassette player, and my father's barbecue grill. I soon noticed that certain pieces of furniture were missing as well, and the heat was turned down. On the first of February, the phone company disconnected our phone, and three times after that, I had to meet the gas man at the front door and lie for my father.

"My father called this morning from Argentina," I said to him once. "He said to tell you that when he gets back he'll pay you the full amount we owe. He got caught up down there. His mother is ill."

I think that winter was the hardest time in the history of my family. My father began taking pills of all descriptions, and no longer stuck to the ones he was prescribed. My mother claimed migraines and stayed in bed during the day. They never talked to each other. And as they came to the end of any money they had saved, my father clearly held my mother responsible, claiming any money ever given to Junior had led to this.

They never turned the gas off, and I remember thanking God because it was the coldest winter I'd ever lived through. Between the snow and sleet falling outside and the chilly reality engulfing our life—appliance by appliance—I found it hard to believe in anything but blind faith until spring came.

# .9.

# The Morning After— February 1650

Emer didn't sleep that night, as she lay curled in the cold den listening to the terrible noises of war around her. She could hear animals suffering, people screaming and crying, and wounded men moaning. Some of the injured were Oliver's and some were local men, but they didn't sound any different from each other.

By dawn, the village was silent but for the calls of hungry livestock and distant artillery. A cock crowed. Emer wanted to look for her mother or father, but no one was moving yet on the knoll, so she lay for over an hour watching a dying blue bottle fly instead. It spoke to her, pushing tiny, barely visible circles into the dirt.

Bzzz. Bzz. Bzz.

On its back and helpless, the fly went round and round while Emer could do nothing but watch and listen.

Bzzzz. Bzzz.

Bz. bzzz.

zzz.

She felt as helpless as she had when Padraig fell, but this time, she watched until there was no more life left. She didn't pinch her eyes shut.

bzzz. bzz.

zzz.

zz. z.

A man appeared on the road in a fancy uniform and chest armor, smiling. In the dull morning light, Emer could barely see him, but she saw his large teeth reflecting the rising sun.

The man walked confidently to the tall castle tower and looked up its high, blackened wall. He turned to a smaller man in a less-fancy uniform. "That will have to come down," he said. Then, the sound of a giddy child playing. Emer looked out and saw a wandering little boy, no older than three, giggling to himself, seemingly oblivious. The armored man ordered him killed without a second's thought. "Nits breed lice," he said, and then walked out of her view toward the remains of the church.

Emer heard footsteps, and turned to see a pair of boots blocking her tunnel. Her heart pounded as she held her breath and stayed quiet.

"Emer?" someone whispered. Her heart leapt at the sound of a familiar voice.

"Daddy?" she said.

The man crouched down and looked through the tunnel. It was her father's brother, Martin, the serious one.

"How did you know I was here?"

"Padraig told me yesterday in case we got separated."

"Padraig is dead."

"Yes."

"Mammy and Daddy?"

He shook his head. "I'm so sorry."

"You're not," she said, pouting. How could this be? How could everyone that mattered be dead?

He beckoned. "Come on."

"No."

"But before the soldiers wake up, we have to get out of here."

"Go away."

He reached his thick hand into the thorny tunnel and swiped for her, but couldn't reach. She feared him then, and flinched into her corner even tighter.

"We have to go now or else we'll never get out of here. Your parents had a plan."

"They're dead. Besides, their plan was to have me burnt up in the church with all the others."

Martin sat down, hiding behind the well wall. "We didn't know."

"The man on the horse told you, long ago. I heard him. That's why Padraig and I agreed to meet here. You didn't let him."

"We thought it was best."

"Go away. Leave me alone."

"Emer, you have to come now, or else I'll leave you here."

She thought about it. How did he know for sure if her mother was dead? How did he know anything? And what was he doing still alive? Every other man was dead.

"Why aren't you dirty?"

"I'm not asking you again, girl."

"You're sure Mammy's dead?"

"Yes."

"You saw her?"

"I saw her."

"Will you take me to her if I come out? I want to see her."

"Of course. You can see for yourself."

She crawled from the den and through the tunnel. Martin grabbed her hand and dragged her behind a hedgerow where no one could see them, then delivered a slap across her blackened face. "Don't you ever disobey me again. I'm your guardian now, and you'll do as I say."

"What about Mammy? I want to see her!"

"Don't be silly, girl." He hit her again, this time with his fist closed, and left a welt on her cheek.

Too shocked to answer, she followed along behind him and rubbed her face. They arrived at a small paddock with a horse. He mounted first and pulled Emer up by her right arm, nearly ripping it from her body.

"Ow!" she yelled.

He secured her in front of him, then kicked the horse and took off toward Cashel, where he had a small abandoned cottage already prepared. Her three cousins and Aunt Mary were waiting for them.

It took the whole day to get there, and when they arrived, Emer's bottom was sorer than it had ever been. She hadn't talked to Martin all day, not even when they stopped twice to eat and pee. He preferred it that way and said nothing. She relived that slap repeatedly, and she decided to hate Martin forever. Even when she arrived at a comfortable bed once in Cashel, she didn't utter a word. If it took silence until her dying breath, she vowed, she would make him understand that no man strikes a Morrisey woman.

As she fell asleep that night, it all seemed like a dream—the attack, the fires, the screaming, the killing, and the circling, suffering blue bottle fly—all in a far-away place where her parents were, where her brother was, where it was her birthday.

Cashel was already in the hands of the dragon. The walls and churches were in ruins, and each road was manned by soldiers in different uniforms. Emer felt owned there. She was sure no one was to be trusted. And she was old enough to know, when she caught Aunt Mary sewing the family's few gold rings and trinkets into the hems of different garments, that their future held more danger.

From Cashel, they traveled to north rural Limerick, where Irish people still lived in fear of attack. Emer felt the stares of villagers. She used to be like that, gawking at every empty survivor who passed through. They settled for some time on a farm there, and then moved on west before autumn. She'd discovered in those six months that Martin slapped his own children, and Mary too sometimes, whenever he was in foul humor or they said something he didn't like hearing. She said nothing to her cousins, but lost respect for them since they never tried to do anything about it.

"Your mother was a bad woman," her cousin said one day, a week before they left the farm.

"Are you just trying to get me to talk or do you really mean that?"

"That's what my father says. He says she was a bad woman who didn't teach you or Padraig any manners."

"She fought at the battle more than your father did. If I were you, I'd be ashamed that my father can only hit women and children but can't fight for the freedom of his country."

"What do you know? You're just a little girl."

"I saw the whole thing happen. Ask him."

Her cousin looked at her skeptically. "Your mother fought?"

"I saw her kill two soldiers and steal their horses."

"No you didn't."

"Yes I did. And I saw Padraig die."

"You did?"

"I went to the top of the castle and watched the battle at the bridge. But then they burnt it down."

"The bridge?"

"No, the castle, dummy."

"Oh."

"I miss Padraig," Emer said. "He was killed when he attacked the first soldier he saw. Uncle Martin sneaked away like a coward."

She got up and walked away. It was the first conversation she'd had in six months, and she felt like a traitor.

They came to the banks of the Shannon several days after they'd left the small Limerick farm in two sturdy traps. At O'Briensbridge, twenty English soldiers stood, letting the poor Irish pass once officials at the bridge entrance allowed them through. As they approached the long queue, Emer noticed that some people wore canvas shoes or none at all. Most were bundled in rags, begging for food. A man in front warned newcomers in Gaelic about the importance of producing papers. Two malnourished old women lay on the side of the muddy road, seemingly family-less, next to a makeshift grazing area for confiscated heifers and sheep. Emer couldn't help but look for Mairead, but all she saw were the war-stained faces of strangers, who couldn't do a thing to help her.

They waited three hours to get through, and eventually crossed the river into Connacht, the only territory left for the Irish. Her Uncle Martin smiled at the devilish men, and said something to them in English that allowed him to keep his horses and other belongings.

They reached an encampment after passing many rocky hills and valleys, where they settled in a tiny stick-and-stone structure and began their fight for survival. Many people died of starvation or disease during the winter. Food was scarce.

By Emer's tenth birthday, three years later, she was so skinny her ribs poked out and her eyes had deepened. Her Aunt Mary had tried everything to make her stronger, but nothing had worked. To add to that, she had stopped talking completely. Even Uncle Martin stopped slapping her, he was so disturbed by her silence.

In 1656, Emer turned twelve. Life was still the same silent, horrible, uphill battle every day, but one thing had changed. Around Christmas that winter, a new family came to live in the growing encampment. They came from Tipperary, and knew of the battles fought in her valley. Emer listened hard as they spoke one night, during a visit to the hut. A mention of the Mullalys, or the Morriseys, details from the battle at the Carabine Bridge. Complaints about what they'd lost and who they would never see again. The worst of their troubles, they said, were with Sean, their mute fourteen-year-old son.

They spoke of him as if he were a helpless child, even though Emer could see for herself that he was no boy anymore. She found it impossible not to stare at him. Seanie Carroll was a young man with a handsome face, a rare sight in the west, where even the youngest of Irish men were aged with work.

After the Carrolls left, Emer went to the bed and lay down to think. She thought of the castle and Padraig. She thought of her parents. She tried to remember things her mother had said, repeating them in her head to etch them there forever. She imagined Padraig telling her to find happy thoughts. Since the day Mrs. Tobin's gift was turned to ash by the dragon, Emer had been void of happy thoughts. But meeting Seanie Carroll changed that. That and the rest.

# . IO .

## Words of Two Voiceless Children

On Emer's thirteenth birthday, she woke up cold. Each birthday since the dragon came was harder and harder—the memories of her home place, and of a life with people who loved her, seemed a strange old lie. With Uncle Martin's family, there was no reason to speak, no reason to do anything other than what was asked: wash the clothes, fetch the water, do lessons and prayers with her youngest cousin, and help make meals. Aunt Mary was a warm woman, and outside the authority of Martin she treated Emer with a special regard, hoping the child might one day talk again.

"I see you've been walking with the Carroll boy," Aunt Mary said that morning.

Emer nodded a little.

"I'm glad to see you've made a friend, Emer, but you just can't go around with a boy and not know the dangers."

Emer continued to wash potatoes in a bucket of cold water.

"Boys have powers you don't know anything about. And soon you'll be too old to have a boy as a friend."

Emer said nothing.

"There'll be no more going off in the mornings to meet him at the spring well. You probably didn't know I knew about that, but I know all sorts of things."

Emer frowned. She and Seanie had spent a few mornings beside the well and the adjacent river, looking at each other. He still wouldn't talk, and Emer didn't know if he was the same sort of mute as she was. Could he not talk at all, or was he only hiding?

"Your Uncle Martin will find a fine boy for you in time. You see what a good lad he chose for our Grainne, didn't you?"

Emer thought of her cousin's husband. He was very like Martin, but Grainne seemed to like him. Emer found him brutish and simple.

"Besides, Sean Carroll is dumb. You can't go marrying a dumb man. Especially you! That would be absurd!"

Emer looked up at Mary, who was pretty much having a conversation with herself. Why was she going on about marriage? Why hadn't she said happy birthday? Surely thirteen wasn't the age to start talking about marriage.

"You do understand what I've told you?" Mary asked,

looking down at Emer. "Now that we've had this talk, you won't go off with him anymore, will you?"

Emer shook her head no.

"Good. You're a good girl after all."

After finishing her chores, Emer walked to the spring well for more water. She couldn't help but look around for Seanie. No other person in their village really understood the communication between them. Mrs. Carroll once spied from her door, watching the two teenagers walking silently, holding hands, making words with their fingers. Emer loved holding Seanie's hand. It was like holding Padraig's hand, or her father's. She would squeeze from time to time, knowing that Seanie wanted to say something but couldn't. His face would go a shade of frustrated pink. She would squeeze then, and Sean would smile a little and let go of whatever was troubling him. His first two months in the west had proved dismal, like everyone else's there. He had grown slimmer and slimmer, and she could begin to see the shapes of his skeleton through his pale skin.

What Emer hadn't noticed was that she was growing into a beautiful woman. Her legs were long and her cheekbones jutted out under her large blue eyes. Her hair, though thin and greasy, fell down her back in a plait, and wisps of it framed her freckled face. She was becoming the same woman who she used to dream would model her cape, the same woman she used to imagine walking around her home place with her mother. Womanhood was something she'd forgotten about since arriving in Connacht; her daydreams of awaiting suitors had disappeared. But Seanie Carroll changed that. From the first time they met, Emer was convinced he was the boy for her. She just *knew* it.

On her thirteenth birthday, Emer got no tidings, no affection, and no gift. Her uncle's family never mentioned how fast she was growing or how pretty she was. There were no Candlemas celebrations in Connacht, aside from a dismal mass for the Blessed Virgin.

She let the entire day pass without finding Seanie. When night fell, she went to the bed she shared with her cousins. It was there she received the most precious birthday gift of all. Her mother spoke.

*Emer, I miss you.*

"I miss you too, Mammy," Emer imagined herself saying.

*You are becoming so beautiful! I knew you would. You were a beautiful child, remember?*

"I remember."

*And clever! What mischief have you found in the west? Have you found a lookout? Is there a river to play in?*

Emer silently replied, "Uncle Martin doesn't let us play. He hates me. There's nothing here but work and death. No mischief. No fun."

*Emer, you know better than to have an attitude like that. A girl like you can make such dismal things beautiful. Don't you remember your power? Your name?*

"It means nothing here. No one has ever heard of us."

*But what of the story of Emer? Do you not remember that day I told you about her? About Cuchulain?*

"I remember," Emer answered. "But the six gifts mean nothing here, either. No beauty or sweet-talking can change this horror. In fact, I don't talk at all anymore."

*What about Seanie?*

Emer lay quiet for a second. "How do you know about Seanie?"

*No mind how I know. What about him? Don't you think you can find something to say to him?*

"Aunt Mary said I wasn't to see him again. That Martin has other plans for me than to marry a dumb boy."

*She did? He does?*

"Yes."

*Emer, think about the story of Cuchulain. Think about Emer's evil father. Stop sounding so beaten! You've only just become a young woman and it's your duty now to make sure you're happy.*

"Happy is a dream of the past."

*Happy is what you feel when you're with Seanie, if I'm not mistaken, Emer, and you can't go ignoring that, no matter how bad things are.*

"I'm not allowed to see him anymore."

*Neither was Emer allowed to marry Cuchulain. You'll find a way.*

Emer didn't answer.

*Have you stitched your great cape yet?*

"I haven't made one stitch since the fire burned all of our thread and buried the needles."

*Not one stitch? How do you expect to decorate your cape if you've had no practice? Promise me you'll find something to make pretty, Emer. It used to bring you so much joy. Maybe it will again.*

"I'll ask Aunt Mary tomorrow."

*Happy birthday*, Mairead said, in a voice now gone sad in Emer's head. *I miss you.*

"I miss you too, Mammy," Emer answered.

She propped herself up on an elbow. Was that my mind, she wondered, or really my mother? Why did she sound so disappointed? What does she think I'm capable of out here in this barren wasteland of rocks and wind? How does she know about Seanie? And if she can speak to me now, and know these things, then does it mean she is surely dead? Though she'd given up thinking her mother might still live, Emer took this confirmation with much sadness. She thought again of Cuchulain, and tried to remember the whole story as she fell to sleep.

The next morning, she approached her aunt's sewing basket. Trying to draw attention to herself, she rattled it and then placed it on her lap.

"Don't touch that, Emer. Those are my things."

Emer beckoned and Mary came to sit beside her.

"What are you trying to say? You want to learn?"

Emer opened the lid and pulled out a bunch of thread and a needle.

"Careful now, you need to know what you're doing. That thread is valuable and expensive. Oh. You've done this before?" she asked, watching Emer thread the needle on the first try.

"I'll give you a small scrap to practice on, if you want," Mary offered, pulling the basket from Emer's lap and digging to the bottom. "Try that one. And no more thread. You have to learn with one color. I don't want you wasting my thread on practice."

Emer made a few stitches and then made a few more. Mary watched, realizing that the child had done this before.

"Emer! You're very good, you know. I tried to teach Grainne how to embroider when she was younger and she hated it. Said it was boring, poor thing. Whatever they say about us grown-ups being sent out here to suffer, I think it's the children who've suffered most. My own child telling me that making pretty things was wasteful. Imagine!" she babbled, still watching Emer stitch. "Why didn't you show me this before now?"

Emer shrugged and continued pulling the needle in and out of the scrap of fabric. Soon her aunt could make out that Emer was making the cross.

"Mary, where's the damn girl now?" Martin yelled through the door. "The bloody trough is empty!"

"I'll send her now," Mary answered, taking the scrap from Emer's hand and hiding it in the basket. "Go and fetch the water."

Emer threw her a look, as if she were about to cry.

"I'll let you stitch when your chores are finished. Just do as I say."

She got up and secured the two buckets on her shoulders. Passing her uncle on the way out, she looked at the dirt and braced herself for a slap that didn't come.

When she arrived at the narrow river next to the spring, Seanie was there and he gave her their secret signal—two fingers raised in a wave. He smiled and she could feel herself melting. He was just so handsome! How could her uncle and aunt not want her to be happy? Her mother was right. The minute she saw him, she knew it. He *was* the one, and there *would* be a way.

He shuffled over to stand next to her and brushed his fingers across her hand. He helped her fill her buckets and lifted them onto her back. Emer returned to the house and filled the trough, but abandoned the buckets by the door and walked back to the well.

She and Seanie had a secret place, a shallow cave beyond the rocky hill. It wasn't a big spot, but it was private. Other kids knew of it, but there was a myth of a monster who lived there and how he ate children, so no one bothered.

They sat for a while, silent as usual, and held hands. Seanie looked out over the small valley, and Emer focused on the rock face beside her until she found the courage to do what her mother wanted.

"You're my best friend," she whispered. Seanie jumped a bit, startled.

He looked at her. She was mortified—now he would hate her for playing mute.

"You're the only boy I've ever liked, aside from Padraig, my brother. He's dead now."

He continued staring at her, not frowning or smiling, but just staring.

"My parents are dead, too. That's why I'm stuck with Martin and Mary. Mary told me yesterday that I wasn't to spend time with you anymore."

He smiled.

"She said that I can't marry some dumb boy."

"I'm not dumb."

They stared at each other, wide-eyed.

"I knew it!" she squealed. "I knew it!"

He looked serious. "I just don't have much to say. Well, I didn't."

"Me neither."

"Until I met you."

"What will we do? Will we tell them now that we can speak and that we're in love and that we'll marry in spite of what they say?"

Seanie laughed, and Emer felt stupid for saying such childish things.

"I'm sorry," she said. "I'm just scared because my uncle wants to marry me to whoever he chooses. I know you probably don't want to marry me."

"I do."

"You do?"

"I do."

"Well, what will we do, then?"

"We're too young now. No one would believe us, anyway. The people here are so busy with work, they don't believe in love anymore. That's what I think."

"I believe."

"Me too."

They sat in the cave for an hour holding hands and exchanging looks and a few words. Before they got up to leave, Emer leaned in and kissed him on the cheek. "I'm so glad you're not dumb like they said," she said.

"I'm glad, too."

As they walked back over the small hill, Emer felt like her mother. It was a small feeling, not yet filled with the confidence of a grown woman, but it made her feel happy and beautiful.

One morning two weeks later, while working on her small embroidered scrap, Emer spoke to her aunt.

"I think I'll need another scrap. This one is full up."

Mary stared.

"I've done my chores and my lessons. Can I have another bit of twill?"

"I can't believe it."

"No, really, come and look. If I stitch this piece any more, it will fall apart in my hands."

Mary sat beside her and hugged her. "I can't believe it. You've come out. You've come out! Martin!"

"Shh," Emer hissed. "Don't tell him. He'll only start hitting me again."

Mary hid her shame and went to the door. Martin was nowhere to be seen.

"What brought this on?"

"Things."

"What things? It was the embroidery, wasn't it?" Mary was already inventing a bragging story for her friends about how she'd cured a mute girl.

"Yes. And something else."

"What?"

"I can't say."

"Why not?"

"If I told you, you'd get very angry."

"Then you should tell me now and get it over with."

Emer thought about it. "Okay. It was my mother. She talked to me in my sleep."

Mary deflated. Mairead had always got in the way before—even dead she could win credit, while Mary was left with simple earthly work.

"She told me that I should find some thread and start to stitch again."

"Well, anyway," Mary interrupted. "How will we tell the rest of the family? Will we tell them tonight or will we let you surprise them?"

"I don't know."

"I can't wait to tell Mrs. Carroll. She'll think there's hope for poor Sean yet!"

Emer went back to her sewing, and Mary didn't know what else to say.

"Can I have another scrap today?"

"Certainly. You can have whatever you want today, Emer." She smiled and found a large square of wool twill in her dresser.

Emer set to work immediately, still working in only one color, to regain what she'd lost after seven years with no practice.

That night at the table, Emer asked for the salt. Her cousins were shocked and her uncle was angry. It was always that way with Martin. He could find a reason to be angry about anything, even if it was something that should have made him happy.

"Since when can she talk?" he asked Mary in a threatening tone.

"Since this morning."

"That's odd," he said, staring directly at Emer. "I heard that Sean Carroll spoke today as well. Does he have anything to do with it?"

Emer nodded.

Mary grabbed Emer's arm. "Tell me you haven't been seeing him since I asked you not to!"

"Only a few times," she lied.

Martin leaned toward his wife. "I told you, didn't I?"

"Oh Martin, they're children."

"He's no child," he boomed. "And you," he continued, pointing at Emer, "you should be smarter. I made a promise to your father to mind you, and mind you I will. Come to me after dinner."

That meant a lashing, and Emer knew it.

"Why are you punishing me for—"

"Don't get smart with me now, girl. You know damn well why. You put us through all these years of silence, all along able to talk? Do you know at all what we've done for you? How we worried?"

"Worried?" Emer yelled, figuring she'd get a slap anyway. *"You're* the reason I stopped talking! You and your lashings and slaps! Don't you remember the day you dragged me from the well into the hedge? Don't you remember what you did?"

"Stop that, Emer," Mary said, fearing she would hear things worse than she was prepared for.

"I will not!"

"You stop now or I'll—"

"Or what? You'll hit me and beat me and what? Kill me? I don't care. All these years you lied and blamed it on Cromwell's army, when all along you *knew!*"

Mary looked shocked. No one ever yelled at Martin.

He pushed himself from the table and walked with heavy steps to her, grabbed her by the arm, and pulled her from the chair. Before his hand made contact with her skin, she screamed.

"If you hit me, I'll run away and you'll never see me again!"

He slapped her face.

"I hate you!"

He punched her in the chest.

"It was all your fault! Now look at you!"

Her cousins watched in horror as their father leveled punch after punch at her abdomen and sides. Mary tried to stop him, and he lashed out and slapped her too.

"Don't think you have any control over me! I can do what I like!" he said, slapping her again—this time a swipe to her head, which pulled several hairs from her plait and splattered them across her face, now slightly bloodied from a bleeding nose.

"Yes! You *can* do what you like!" she said between blows. "Because you lived! Because you were too much of a coward to fight the English, so now you beat little children and your own wife!"

He stopped at that and held her tightly by the arms. He was close enough that his spit hit her in the face as he replied. "I fought hard in that battle, girl, and you'll spread no such lies about me!"

"Tell me," she answered, staring into his cold eyes. "Tell me—if you fought so hard, why are you alive? My father died at the Carabine Bridge! My mother fought until she fell! You're just a coward with clean hands, probably spared in a deal with Cromwell himself!"

By the time Emer finished her sentence, her uncle was

shaking her body so hard that her head was lashing from side to side. He punched her one last time, in the belly, and let her go. Mary picked her up and carried her to the bed.

She yelled two things before she fainted completely in Mary's arms. "Traitor! Bastard!"

# .II.

# Sold Like Meat

E mer lived one more year in the west with her aunt and uncle. From the night she'd called Martin a "traitor and bastard" she was kept in the house or in the yard, not allowed to do chores that would take her more than fifty feet from the front door. But she still saw Seanie during secret nighttime escapes. Her cousins gladly covered for her, in the knowlege that they would have more room in the bed for themselves.

Uncle Martin had arranged for her travel to France, where an important man was waiting to make her his bride. Emer listened to this plan, always knowing that things wouldn't come to that, always knowing she would end up with Seanie somehow.

At night, they would nuzzle in their small cave, sometimes caressing each other's damp skin, sometimes kissing for hours on end. Seanie was turning into a fine man. His hands had calluses and his muscles were more developed, although he was still skinny and underfed. Emer adored his strong arms, which were now growing a layer of manly hair and bulging with hard muscle.

She spent her days doing chores, basic English lessons that Martin still insisted on, and needlework. Her uncle hired her out to stitch other people's clothing, and used the money she earned to save for her future journey and to buy brew for himself. He told her once that he would miss her, but he only meant he'd miss the small change she could make for his nightly mug. He'd been getting lame over the years, slowly limping more and more until he needed a splint on his right leg and a walking stick to get anywhere. That year, he'd stopped hitting his family. Mary secretly thanked Emer once for facing up to him, as if she'd had something to do with his change of heart. In fact, Martin stopped hitting the family simply because he could no longer win a chase or balance long enough to strike.

Emer rose on her fourteenth birthday expecting the same old nothing. She'd spoken to her mother the night before, and vowed to follow her heart and run away with Seanie. But, to her surprise, when she woke up the family was waiting for her at the table by the fire, each wishing her a happy birthday. This couldn't be right. No one here had ever acknowledged her birthday before.

"How did you know?" she asked, still sleepy.

"How could we not know?" her cousin asked, now almost a grown man himself. "Since you arrived, Father hasn't stopped talking about the day he could get rid of you!"

"Peter, don't say such things! She's only out of bed."

"Get rid of me?"

"Now Emer, don't go getting upset. This is what happens to all girls your age. Don't be afraid."

"Afraid of what?" she asked, hearing something moving outside the door of the house.

"We'll miss you," Mary added.

"You don't make any sense," Emer said, looking around the table. "What's going on here?"

"I've packed your bag and put a special dress in there for you. You'll see it when you get there. Don't peek and ruin the surprise."

"Get where?" The door swung wide and collided with a small trunk. Everyone in the house jumped at the sound.

"Have you her things packed?" Martin barked from the doorway.

"In the case. It's all there."

Emer tried to run through the back door, but Mary stopped her. "Don't go being stupid now. You have a bright future in Paris."

"I'm not going to Paris," Emer began, just as her uncle entered. "I won't leave Ireland."

"Oh, you'll get to Paris. I'm going to make sure of it."

Emer looked at Mary, wide-eyed.

"He's going with you," Mary explained, still doubting his reasons.

Emer started to cry and ran again for the back door. Mary stopped her, but Emer pushed her to the side and ran to the well.

Seanie stood halfway between the field and the well, and by the time he saw her crying into her hands, Martin had sent his son Peter to drag Emer back to the house. She waved to him with two fingers and blew a kiss, and made a huge scene for the rest of the neighbors, screaming, "I love you, Seanie Carroll!" before she was shoved back into the dark house.

Outside the front door there was a horse and cart waiting to take them to the docks in Cork. Her packed case was on the back, alongside a few large jugs of the magic brew her uncle could no longer live without. Martin grabbed Emer roughly and pushed her up into the front of the cart. With a length of sturdy rope, he bound her feet and then tied her to the wooden frame.

As they trotted from the encampment, Emer cried, mostly. But then she saw a group of six or seven little girls playing by the side of the road, and yelled to them.

"Do you see this, girls? Do you see what you're worth? Look at me here, tied like a slab of meat to this cart! Remember me, girls! Remember me!"

Seanie came around that night and talked to Mary. He

couldn't hide the fact that he was heartbroken, and Mary tried not to look directly at him. *How many years?* she asked herself. *How many years have I let Martin ruin my life? And my children's!*

"My mother told me he tied her to the cart and took off like a man on fire for water," he said.

"She's exaggerating. You know Martin wouldn't do that."

"She saw him."

"Well, you know how Emer is."

"Yes, I do. I know how she is. She's in love with me, that's how she is."

*Why am I defending him?* Mary asked herself. "You're just a boy," she said.

"But I love her."

"Then you should be happy for her new life. She won't have to suffer like we do."

"Is that all you want for her?"

Mary looked at her raw hands. "It's enough."

They stared at each other. Seanie sighed.

"It won't be enough to make her stop loving me," he said. "And I promise you now, as I stand here, I will find her and bring her back where she belongs."

"Here, into this squalor? Why would you wish such a thing for a girl you love?"

"Because this is her home. Because we're the only family she has left!"

He made his way back to the well, then walked to their hillside cave, curled up in himself, and sobbed. For all his confident talking and promising, he felt paralyzed and helpless and doubted he would ever see Emer again. During the night, he gathered as many things as he could and started his journey east, toward the sea. Toward Paris.

A month passed before Martin returned on the cart. He arrived at midday and the first news he heard was the news of Seanie's disappearance. Mary told him as he ruminated over a mug of fresh brew.

"There's no way he'll find her now. She's chained to that boat until it reaches France, and she'll be met at the dock by her husband. He's just a stupid boy. He hasn't a clue about the real world."

"He went the same day you did. He could have followed you."

"The girl has no way of escaping. I'm sure of it."

Mary heard him say this and nearly choked. What sort of man was this? How many times would she listen as he went on like some sort of hero?

"It's a shame," she said.

"A shame we couldn't do it sooner!"

"Martin, stop acting as if she was any trouble. She wasn't."

"Shut up, woman."

"There were plenty of men here who were smitten with her. You could have at least not sold her off like a slave to a foreigner. The poor thing."

"Mary, did you hear me? I don't want to talk about it anymore."

She paced, her arms crossed, then turned to him. "You don't like talking about anything that has a bit of truth in it, do you? For years, I let you treat us all like nothing. Like nothing! But now? I won't have you telling me my business! You could never handle the truth, and it's caused you to do a great many stupid things in your time!"

"Woman, I'm warning you."

"Oh, do! And then what?" she crossed her arms again and cocked her head. "Will you tie me up like a common animal and send me off to Europe, too? Will you give me to your English *friends* to slave in the islands? What is it I should fear from you but a mouthful of hateful rubbish?"

He looked over at her and smiled an evil flash of teeth. "How about we go to bed?" he asked.

"What?"

"Oh, come on, Mary. I've been away a whole month and managed to keep my hands off the girl. The least you can do for me is that."

"Get out!" she screamed.

"This is my house."

She stood up and grabbed a broom. "Get out or I'll brush you out myself!"

"Shut up, woman, and let me alone. I should have known that leaving for a time would give you such satisfaction."

"I only wish you'd never come back!"

Mary walked out of the house and dragged her youngest daughter with her. She hoped that Martin would get up and look for solace in the tavern with his pals, but he didn't. He just went to bed and fell asleep, leaving Mary with little option for the afternoon.

# .12.

## The Passage of Once-Dumb Lovers

Seanie walked to the east coast of Ireland. In less than a month, he'd met with so many different authorities in uniforms that he was no longer afraid of what they might do to him. Once he reached the walled town of Drogheda, he made his way to the docks and started asking about passage to France.

It was nearly impossible for Seanie to find an Irish-speaking man on the dock willing to talk, but once he did, he clung to his arm and asked several questions in quick succession. The man answered back the best he could. He didn't know what boats were sailing where, only that he would be on one of them, working. When Seanie asked him who to talk to about a voyage to France, the man pointed to an Englishman who sat at the side of the quay, sipping tea from a china cup.

"I'm sorry," Seanie said, trying not to meet the Englishman's eye. "My English is poor. I have passage to Paris? My family awaits me."

"Paris, eh? What do they do?"

"They are farmers."

The man laughed. "There are no farms in Paris, I assure you!"

"Please sir. I would do anything to have Paris."

The man looked Seanie up and down. "Have you money boy? *Airgead?*"

Sean shook his head. "Work?"

"And you've worked on a ship before, then, have you?"

Sean shook his head again.

"I will see what I can do for you. Come back tomorrow." He waved Seanie away with his supple white hand.

Seanie walked that day with a hop in his step, thinking of Emer. He slept that night under a dock, nestled into sand, and dreamed until daybreak of kissing each one of her freckles.

Back on the dock, he found his Englishman again and approached him.

"You still want passage to Paris?" the man asked.

Seanie nodded.

"Well you're in luck, boy. That boat there"—he pointed to a huge, three-sailed boat—"is leaving today. Can you cook?"

Sean didn't understand, so he shrugged.

"You Irish boys prove useless in most things. I say, how did you survive at all?"

Seanie didn't answer.

"That one there, the *Fortune*. Can you read, boy? I guess not. It's that one there," he finished, pointing again.

"Thank you, sir. I can't thank you enough."

"Go on, before I change my mind."

Seanie walked to the gangway and climbed into the enormous ship. It rocked ever so slightly, throwing him off balance at first. He started slowly across the deck, eyeing each sail and its boom, avoiding the hundred ropes strung across it. When he looked up to the crow's nest he felt a bout of dizziness, so looked back at the deck.

"Who the hell are you?" a voice asked in Gaelic.

"Sean. Sean Carroll. I'm here to work on this voyage."

"Who says?"

"That man there," Seanie explained, pointing. "He said I could come aboard."

"Aye. Well, get to work, then son. They'll need you down in the store. We've got sixty more barrels to move down there, and then that whole pile of crates after that."

Sean found his way to the steps and descended into the earthy-smelling underbelly of the ship. There, he helped secure at least a hundred barrels and stacked more crates of food and provisions than he could count. It didn't occur to him that this was far too much food for a simple voyage to France. In fact, in his mix of fear and excitement, he didn't think about that or any other sensible thing until they were well on their way.

It was on his second night at sea when he discovered

that the *Fortune* wasn't aimed for France, or even toward the continent. The Gaelic-speaking man he'd met on his first day said something strange.

"You'll like seeing the sun, boy, after three months on this bloody ship. It's the sunshine that brings us all back, isn't it, lads?"

The Irish men grunted in assent.

"The sun? What do you mean?"

"The sun shines so hard down there that you'll barely be able to keep a shirt on your back! But don't you take it off, son, or you'll go the brightest shade of red a man has ever been! Ask O'Malley over there."

O'Malley answered with a laugh.

"I didn't know the sun shone so much more in Paris. I had always guessed it was the same as—"

"Paris?" the man asked. The rest of the crew let loose hearty peals of laughter.

"Isn't that where this boat is going?" Seanie asked, feeling his heart pound, half knowing the answer.

"No, boy. You have it all wrong. Is that what that English bastard told you?"

He nodded.

"Well, you can kiss your dreams of Paris goodbye, son. You're being sent to Barbados like the rest of us poor sods."

"Barbados? Where's that?"

"Down in the hottest part of the world, boy. Like hell on earth, I tell ya."

"We have to stop this boat! I must get to Paris! You don't understand!"

With that, the crew fell about laughing at him again.

Some even mocked his words, repeating them in girlish tones, howling and grabbing their bellies.

"There's no stopping the boat, and there's no chance you can swim to Paris, so don't think about trying," the man said. "Besides, what's so important about Paris anyway?"

"Nothing. I'm just—just—surprised." No matter how hard Seanie tried, he couldn't hold back the mighty sob inside his chest. He released it with an angry groan and buried his greasy head in his arm.

When the rest of the men fell asleep that night, Seanie was still awake, thinking of Emer. Had he just stupidly sealed their fate by believing the word of a lazy Englishman? He had wanted more than anything to save her from what she faced. He'd wanted to arrive in Paris and whisk her away before anyone saw them disappear. He'd spent a month on foot getting from Connacht to Drogheda, each night settling into sleep with one thing on his mind. Now it wouldn't be. Now he was stuck on a ship bound for hell on earth, and he couldn't save her from anything.

When her boat arrived in Paris, Emer was brought out on deck. Still bound at her rope-burned wrists, she winced every time she moved. But it was a relief to see the sun again. She'd been locked in a special room for over a week at that point, eating only once a day from a tray brought by the ship's cook. When she appeared on the gangway, two well-dressed men came to greet her. One was older and overly fat, the other was petite and quite young. She wished she could use her hands. She needed a wash and a new plait. She was sure she looked dreadful after a week in the moist, dark room.

"Emer Morrisey?" the older man asked politely, in Gaelic, his big mouth smiling so that his fat lips divided into two.

She nodded.

"You're more beautiful than your father promised! Let's get you out of that rope, yes?"

He looked back at his servant and snapped his fingers. The man produced a small, sharp knife and the older man used it to carefully cut the rope from Emer's wrists. She moved her hands in circles and stretched out her fingers, but felt more pain from the burns than she had felt when the rope was on.

"Do you recognize me?" he asked.

She shook her head no.

"Did your father not tell you what I looked like?"

Emer stood, confused. Surely this fat old man wasn't her fiancé. In all the bad images her mind had conjured up during the voyage, she had never thought of this.

"I'm the man that will soon be your husband, girl!"

She couldn't help but stare at him, dumbfounded.

"Oh, come on now, dear. You can smile with that pretty face, can't you?"

She made sure not to smile, and carefully looked around for an escape route.

"William, put her in the carriage. I have business to attend to." He turned to Emer. "Try and be a little happy, won't you? Tonight will be a very special night for you, love."

He grazed her face with his plump hand. "A very special night for you indeed!" He slapped her on the bottom and chuckled to himself.

She squirmed at the thought of it and followed the servant dutifully to the awaiting carriage. There, she was ushered to an ornate inner seat between two windows. On the right, she could see only the dock and several ships. She searched the ship for her presumed fiancé and found him talking to the captain very seriously. *Probably making sure the men on board didn't steal his precious virgin*, she thought. She wanted to vomit. When she looked to the left, she saw a more promising escape. Before her, a city larger than she had ever seen before sprawled from horizon to horizon.

The servant, William, sat patiently and watched her. "It's beautiful, isn't it?" he asked.

"Very big," she answered.

"I suppose, from what you're used to."

She nodded.

"If you don't mind me asking," he started, "why do you look so disappointed? I know what Connacht is like myself, and wouldn't fancy going back."

"I'm just tired," she answered, still watching the city. There was a crowd of people only a hundred yards away. Perhaps they were waiting for other passengers by the dock, or were there to board a ship. (Her mother spoke—*That way, Emer. That way.*)

"You'll be in a fine soft bed within the hour. You can rest then. We have an exceptional bath—I'm sure you'll feel right at home."

"I could use a bath."

"Did you find the voyage exciting?"

"I was bound and locked in a room with one meal a day, looking forward only to being the slave of a stranger. I'm sorry to sound so rude, but does that sound exciting to you?"

"I see. I see. Well, you'll need not worry about that sort of treatment here. Master is civilized, at least, and a jolly good man. I can promise you that. Ah!" he said, pointing. "Here he comes now."

She turned her head to the right and saw him approaching, two sailors behind him carrying the large case she brought as luggage. *Dear God, he is horrible*, she thought. *So fat that he might crush me, and so old! What sort of a joke is this?* She looked back at the crowd of people, and Paris. As William stepped down, to ready the carriage for his employer and open the door on the right, Emer pressed the door handle on the left and made her escape.

She ran, as fast as she could, toward the throng of people, not looking back for fear it would slow her down. A short chase ensued—she could hear the fat man yelling, and swearing in English at his servant.

"Run faster, you idiot! You'll lose her! *That's my fucking property!*"

Soon she heard nothing but the sounds of the crowd, the foreign giggles of women and children as they waited at the dock. She blended in, the same way she had in the church the day that Cromwell came, and then she hid herself in a pile of planks.

An hour later, she stepped out of the crowd—facing Paris as a free woman.

A year later, she had still found no happiness in France. That afternoon, though, she had finally done something about her situation. For weeks there had been signs posted, proving that what the Gaelic-speaking nun had said was true—each sign claimed that women like Emer would find happiness and husbands in a Caribbean republic called Tortuga. She had heard rumors from other women that it was a trick, promising only years of slavery in the hot sun. But after living for so long in the dark grotto in Paris, Emer figured she could do no worse.

The next morning she made the visit to town, brisk and careful, still afraid that the fat man and his servant might be looking for her. Emer signed a slip of paper and sighed. The man behind the desk smiled at her dumbly and thanked her in French.

She decided to block out anything her mother had to say until the voyage was preparing at dockside. No need to listen to Mairead now, she figured; no possible way to believe in an ideal world where the legendary Emer could actually *do* something about her desperate situation. When the day came to board the huge ship, she washed in the river and dressed in the only garments she owned. She braided her long, fair hair and let it hang down her back instead of hiding it beneath her cap. Leaving her blade under a bundle of unwanted rags, she said goodbye to her dismal life in Paris. She hid her crucifix in her pocket and walked slowly to the dock, thinking of Seanie. This voyage would surely sever any thread of hope that remained for them.

Her mother's voice finally broke through when she reached the queue for the deck. *Emer, trust yourself.*

Emer nodded.

She arrived on deck and found the small quarters she would share with thirty other women. Most looked like prostitutes and barmaids. Emer reminded herself that the men in Tortuga—pirates and murderers though they may be—needed women like any other man does. They needed love and hot meals, a home and a wife, the same as any man.

Emer didn't yet know what would really happen. She didn't yet know that these men had no idea she and her thirty young companions were even on their way—and that they weren't as welcome as the signs and posters had claimed. She didn't yet know that when she arrived, there would be no one man who would pick her out and love her, but the lust of one hundred men, prowling the night, with no notion of loving at all.

# .13.

# Modest Three Bedroom For Sale— Potential Abounds

The Adams family home went up for sale in late March of my senior year. It was a hard day. How many times had we heard our mother rejoice, "If anything ever goes wrong, at least we have this house"? I swear, whenever she said anything like that, I felt jinxed, and when the FOR SALE sign went up, I felt as if it was somehow her fault.

The house had come to them free of charge from my father's uncle, back when they'd moved to Hollow Ford from London just after my father came home from Vietnam. Stuck between two shag-carpet bi-levels with out-of-ground pools and the yellow glow of colonial-style bug lamps on new aluminum siding, our little sixty-year-old house looked dignified but run-down. It could barely compete.

But any money was better than no money, and my parents needed any money. In the time it took to find another place to live, some lucky family from Ohio agreed to pay my father $85,000 for our house. Over the next few weeks, I helped move the furniture we had left out into the yard, along with the rest of our redundant material clutter for a garage sale that earned us about two hundred bucks. It was hard to watch those things get sold, especially all by myself. Patricia would never have let her roller skates go, and Pat would have hated to watch his air rifle end up in the back of an old Ford station wagon.

We moved into a medium-sized trailer, with two tiny bedrooms and a kerosene heater in the living room. I don't know how much it cost or where the rest of the money had gone, but I think that, by that point, my parents had run up plenty of debt and probably used any extra profit from the house to pay things off.

The trailer park seemed like the land that time forgot. There was a pay phone fifty yards away from our place, under a streetlight, and the gravel roads had huge potholes that filled up when it rained. There were no kids, and most of the people who lived there were old enough to be my grandparents.

Junior didn't come around anymore after we moved. It could have been the two guard dogs the old Italians in the next trailer kept chained to their fence all night, or the fact that we had nothing left. Or maybe he'd overdosed and had fallen into a lake and died. With drug addicts, it's like that. You never really know.

By mid-April, school had become my main focus. Even though I hadn't tried, I started to become more popular because of my grades. It was nice. Up until then, I'd thought my senior year was going to be the same boring waiting game that my whole life had been, but I was actually having some fun.

First, Susan convinced me to join the Quiz Bowl team. Ms. Houseman put me in the starting line-up as the history expert, even though I couldn't make it to the after-school practices on account of my night shift at McDonald's. I made a few friends and had a good time traveling from school to school competing, even though we didn't always win.

Then, Susan dragged me to a few weekend baseball games because she had a crush on Jay, the second-base kid, and she wanted to show off the new car her parents had given her when she got her license. She even talked me into going to the spring dance, which was a complete waste of my time—though I did get to watch what normal high school students spent their time doing (mainly necking, drinking, smoking pot, and having sex in cars).

"You should go to the prom," Susan said one Sunday night, when she picked me up from work and drove me back to the trailer park.

I laughed.

"I'm serious. You should. You're going to be the valedictorian, right? So, you should go to the prom." She stopped at the red light opposite the gun store.

I stared at the samurai swords in the front window. "Yeah, okay. So who will I ask? Mr. Jones?" I giggled. Mr. Jones was my film and media teacher. "Mrs. Lindt?" She was the Home Ec teacher who always had lipstick on her teeth.

"You could ask someone from your smart club."

"Quiz Bowl."

"Sorry. *Quiz Bowl*. Is there anyone you like?"

What was I supposed to say? Of course there wasn't anyone I liked. Seanie Carroll was not on the Quiz Bowl team. Luckily, we were just pulling through the trailer park gates and I didn't have to answer.

"Damn! Can't they pave these roads? It's like you live in backwoods Arkansas or something."

"Yeah. I know. Watch out for the—"

She drove into the hole and swore. Trying not to feel the red-hot embarrassment I felt every time she drove me home, I looked out the window at the dark line of dirty singlewides. As we passed by them, I saw a young guy sitting on the steel steps of #20. He waved.

He was there again the next Saturday, and after I called Susan from the pay phone I decided to say hello. It was nice seeing a young face, acne-scarred or not, in the land of wrinkled retirees.

"Hey."

"Hey," I said. "I'm Saffron."

"I'm Sam."

I shook my head, but had no idea what to say next.

"You're on the Quiz Bowl team," he said.

"You go to Hollow Ford?"

"Only since January. I live with my grandparents now."

"Oh."

"And you work at McDonald's. I see you there all the time."

"Really? That's weird. I don't remember seeing you before."

Maybe that was a stupid thing to say. It made Sam look at his feet and shuffle. He reached up to his mouth and picked a small scab of dry skin near his lip.

"Are you going to Senior Skip Day?" he said.

I'd completely forgotten about Senior Skip Day. Susan told me I had to do it, but I knew I could get in trouble and so I hadn't made up my mind.

"I don't know. Are you?"

"I figure we're only seniors once."

"True." I looked at my watch. "Shit. I have to go."

"See you around."

"Yeah."

Twenty minutes later, as Susan rounded the dusty corner to pick me up, Sam was still sitting on the front steps of his grandparents' trailer. When I slid into the front seat in my God-awful polyester McDonald's uniform, she said, "Who's that guy?"

"Dunno."

Then he waved at me, smiling, and I flogged him for it.

"You don't know?" Susan raised her eyebrows.

"He's just some guy."

"Sure he is."

I reached for the volume knob, turned up the music, and waved to Sam as we drove by.

Nine hours later, Harry, my manager, dropped me off on the main road. As I walked back to our trailer, I saw Sam was still outside #20, building something.

When I got close enough, I saw that it was a plywood ramp.

And yet, I asked, "What's that?"

"It's a wheelchair ramp."

"Oh."

"My pop's coming home from the rehab hospital next week," he explained.

"Right."

"So, did you think about Skip Day?"

I shrugged and made a gesture like I had to get going. "I'll think about it some more," I said, and then walked slowly down the gravel road to our trailer—where I found my parents asleep on the couch with the heater set on *high*. I turned it down and opened one of the push-out windows to clear the burning kerosene smell. Then I peeked back toward #20, trying to ignore the small feeling of excitement gathering in my stomach.

# Dog Fact #3
## *Always Trust Your Nose*

One of the most important aspects of dog behavior is their need to scent their boundaries, defend marked territory, and locate approaching rivals—all of which is achieved through their amazing sense of smell. Dogs have about two hundred million olfactory receptors. Since humans only have five to ten million, they fail to understand why a dog may react to things his master cannot see. Most dog owners don't trust the hunches of a pet enough to change their plans and follow wherever the dog may lead (Lassie was a fictional exception, of course). Sometimes, though, you might want to pay more attention to your dog's bizarre olfactory behavior.

I learned this on the night of August 22, 1831. It started with the usual after-dinner walk to the tavern—man and his black Labrador retriever. My master was a bachelor named Tad Wheelan, whose family had lived in Southampton County, Virginia, since they'd gotten off the boat from Bristol in the New World fifty years before. He worked on a nearby plantation as a manager of exports. Tad was a subtle fellow, a Quaker and a quiet abolitionist; he never bragged, rarely swore, and always dipped his hat to passing ladies.

It was a hot night. An hour or so before Tad and I started our walk, Nat Turner (an over-enthusiastic lay preacher or a revolutionary, depending on who you talk to) and his slave rebels rioted and murdered every white person on their plantation, several miles away. Of course, neither of us knew this then, or we wouldn't have gone out. I'd had a definite whiff of danger before we left the front yard, but ignored it. I knew I smelled *something* bad, I just didn't know it was something *really* bad.

Sometimes when you're a man's best friend, you have to make tough decisions. You can't bark at any old thing that you sniff. You can't get your master out of bed in the middle of the night over a nesting rat or interrupt Christmas dinner because of a passing wagon. You have to choose your moments. But if the snout picks up the scent of spilled white blood, a Southern dog in 1831 would best use that moment wisely. I didn't.

By the time I identified that horrid smell of death, we'd gone too far. I nudged Tad's leg, stopped, and sat. He kept walking. I raced ahead and sat down in front of him and he laughed, thinking I was playing a game and hopped around me. I began walking home by myself, barking, but Tad continued to walk toward the tavern. By the time I caught up with him again, it was too late. Turner's rebels had started at us, a mangle of blades and clubs and a musket or two. Tad didn't move. I think he'd been daydreaming and was caught completely by surprise. The best I could do at that point was pretend to protect him, so I latched onto the nearest leg I could—and was promptly beaten to death still clinging to it.

Dogs trust their noses because it's their nature. In this instance, I should have trusted mine sooner. Humans don't trust anything—because that's their nature. Half of them have gut feelings they continually ignore. It's not their fault. Instinct rarely fits on the pages of a day planner, and even if it did, human beings would manage to complicate the hell out of it. 🐾

# .14.

# Fred Livingstone's Beach House—
# Billy's Bay, Jamaica, 1990

Fred Livingstone looked at his watch. It was five thirty and he still hadn't heard from his partner in Miami. He walked to his large teak desk, snatched the telephone from its cradle, and dialed. He waited through ten rings and hung up, then paced back and forth in front of his million-dollar Caribbean view and dialed again. This went on through sunset, and then into the evening until someone finally answered.

"Winston, what the hell are you still doing there? You said you'd call me at five," he gruffed.

He listened carefully, then raised his voice. "I don't care

who wants it! I gave you the fucking money, and now I want the fucking keys!"

Winston was Fred's live-in companion. At first, he was the gardener and pool boy. Then he moved in and started taking care of the place full time. Once he started doing housework and cooking, the relationship grew into a friendship and, eventually, both men agreed to become lovers for the sake of company—which is how Fred liked to describe it. *Company*.

"Get me that house and get your ass back here," Fred snapped. "Or else you'll be a beach bum again, eating from hotel garbage bins!"

After slamming the phone down, Fred stood by his window and bit his fingernails. A dog barked from deep inside the condominium and he realized he'd not fed Rusty, his large Doberman pinscher.

He arrived in his kitchen to Rusty jumping up and down like he was in some sort of circus act. Fred kicked him hard in the ribs. "Down, boy."

Rusty winced and cowered low to the ground, looking up with dumb, lovesick eyes. As Fred went to the cupboard to find dog food, Rusty jumped up again, planting both of his huge paws on Fred's back.

"Rusty, get down," Fred boomed, and punched the dog in the face.

Rusty knew the routine. Every day was like this. Even when Winston was around to feed him, Fred would always get a kick or a slap in somehow. Soon it would be Rusty's fifth birthday, and as far as he could remember, every day for five years Fred Livingstone had beaten him. Most times, Rusty pretended it was nothing and acted playful, but sometimes he felt fierce, like a dog his size should, and would growl a warning under his breath. Once he even had a dream that he'd swallowed Fred whole.

"Hello," Fred said into the phone while Rusty ate his dish of canned meat. "I was wondering if I could make a reservation for two … nine o'clock? Livingstone. Splendid, splendid. See you then."

He dashed to his bedroom and undressed, leaving the pile of clothing where it fell, and stepped into the shower. After a quick shave and his ritual application of athlete's foot cream, Fred stopped and peered into the mirror. No longer able to pass for fortysomething, he'd stopped dyeing his hair and working out. It left him looking like his father. Gone were the days he could flex a bicep in the mirror to feel better about himself—now he felt upbeat when the shower drain wasn't clogged with runaway hair or his skin wasn't blotchy. The best days were when he could avoid seeing his reflection completely.

He got dressed in a white linen suit, a short-sleeved, pink, button-down shirt, and a pair of loafers. He transferred a bulging wallet to his back pocket, combed his hair, and turned off the light behind him. After stopping at the marble bar in the foyer for a quick shot of bourbon, he looked down at Rusty, who was now standing at the front door. "If you shit on the carpet, I'll kill you."

# .15.

# Fred Livingstone's Dates

Fred Livingstone felt the stares of a dozen husbands as he walked to his private table. He felt them slice into his back, his sides, his groin. How many of them would be surprised to see him here with Sarah? Had they watched her walk the same route earlier and tried not to notice her? Would they envy him?

When he rounded the corner to find the table empty, he turned to the maître d' and barked an order.

"A bottle of your best red," he snapped, and sat down facing the dining room. He felt silly and stupid. A dozen husbands would snigger to themselves, knowing he was eating alone.

He looked at his watch, drank a glass of wine, then looked at it again. For half an hour, he looked and poured and drank and looked. At nine thirty, he ordered a second bottle. At ten, he ordered a small plate of salad. He ordered a third bottle at ten thirty.

"Surely she knew I was serious," he mumbled to himself. "Or did she stand me up on purpose? Fred Livingstone, you know how women are. Especially the married ones. One can never tell what they want. Roses? Jewelry? Too much expectation, not enough instinct, I say. Women always want too much anyway."

He thought like that for the rest of the night, his dark eyebrows burrowing deeper and deeper into a frown, making his usually attractive face seem ugly. When he was finished, he swaggered to the door, muttering. "I'll find her on the beach tomorrow. She's probably a little prick tease anyway. She'll soon find out who owns this town."

The Island Hotel Restaurant was empty but for the staff and two tables of tourists. Fred knew, somehow, that the dozen husbands would find out he'd been shafted, and he cast a suspicious eye on the remaining waiters and bartenders. He stumbled into the humid night air and drew a deep breath, coughing a little on the exhale and adjusting his waxed hair to the left. He called goodbye to the maître d' and walked down the dark gravel road to his condo, talking to himself.

"I'll see you tomorrow," he said, then raised his voice so she could hear him. "You'll see!"

Five minutes later, after much trouble finding the right key for his pink, bougainvillea-dressed condominium, Fred opened the door and was immediately jumped on by Rusty. His first reaction was to lash out with a kick in the dark, and he didn't know he was kicking the dog squarely in the bladder until he reached for the light switch. Rusty stood by helplessly as over four hours' worth of urine spilled out of him, uncontrolled. By the time the lights turned on, Fred was standing in a puddle of acrid pee that slowly crept up his trousers.

He bolted into action. Even though Rusty was a huge animal, Fred tackled him, squeezing the scruff of his neck until the dog squealed in pain. He then caught him by all four limbs and fashioned a mop out of him, making sure every part of Rusty's body was covered in his accident before he was through. He opened the door, tossed the dog out, and slurred, "Go and find another asshole to piss all over. And don't come back!"

This was the routine whenever Winston wasn't around to take care of the dog. And it would be all Winston's fault, Fred decided, as he showered to clear the scent of red wine, nervous sweat, and dog piss from his skin. He bagged his dirty linen trousers and threw them out the back window into the concrete alley. Before morning, some poor sod would find them and need them badly enough to scrub out the stains at the hem.

Thoughts piled up in Fred Livingstone's brain as he tried to relax in his king-size bed. His foul mood worsened just after midnight when Rusty didn't come back. Fred lay in bed, listening for the familiar scratching or the high-pitched whine the dog usually let out when he'd been bad and wanted to make up. The more he tried to listen for the dog, the drowsier he got, and finally he fell asleep.

At six, there was a scratch at the door. Fred groaned and rolled over. At seven, after a full hour of seething over being awake and hungover, he got up and stepped into the nearest pair of boxer shorts. He walked hurriedly down the long, sunlit corridor and opened the front door, expecting the usual sight of Rusty laid out in the morning sun. When the dog wasn't there, Fred felt angrier. He looked both ways and made a clicking sound between his teeth, but Rusty didn't come.

In the kitchen, while making a cup of instant coffee, he thought back to the night before and marveled at the pain in his head. He stirred sugar into his cup and walked to a wrought-iron, glass-topped table by his office window. Sitting down and scanning the beach for his runaway dog, Fred mourned the end of tourist season. The beach was nearly empty. Only a few weeks before, a group of college girls would jog by every morning at seven thirty, followed by equally attractive jogging college boys. Fred didn't know which he enjoyed more, but he missed them now that they were gone. In fact, he missed many things that were gone now, a thought which made him sigh and feel old again.

He thought back to Sarah. Had she said yes? She distinctly did. "She said nine o'clock tomorrow, I heard her," he mumbled to himself.

But the fact was, Fred hadn't really asked Sarah out to dinner, and he knew it. In his golden days on the island, thirty years earlier, he'd been a real gigolo. But once he started making proper money from his real estate dealings in the 1980s, things changed and women didn't matter anymore. Before he knew it, he was white and saggy from ten years at a desk, and shagging his personal assistant. The closest he got to beautiful women was through the lens of a hand-held telescope. Some days he would perch for hours in front of his huge window, peering at the topless European women, the round American girls, and even the flat-chested teenagers, all the while talking to them, muttering, inviting them to dinner, to a spin in his yacht, to Paris. Sometimes, when Winston wasn't around to cook him dinner, he would play out the role beyond his living room. He would make reservations for two and get stood up. He would sit for hours next to a packed picnic basket and small campfire on the beach, wondering where she was. This week it was Sarah, but there had been others.

He searched the beach all morning but couldn't see her. He even tried on some other women for size, but none of them fit like she did. The rest were ordinary, anyway, and he'd had plenty of ordinary women in his life already. His thoughts wandered back to a time in his past when no woman could resist him—a time when college girls were easy and date rape hadn't yet been invented—the time of his life. How many girls had he lured into his trap? Ten? Twenty? Fifty? He used to keep count. Had it ended at seventy-six? Seventy-six in four and a half years, not counting summers—or his year in love with Penny—averaged two and a half per month. "Only one every two weeks, Fred. You could have done better."

Life on the island had made up for that. So many tourist seasons had passed, each with dozens of conquests, that Fred could barely contain his elation at the thought of counting them all.

But they were all ordinary women, like the ones on the beach. Some firm and sexy, yes. Some young and pretty, yes. But ordinary. None of them better than any other and none of them elegant or graceful or interesting like Sarah.

By the time Rusty returned for more beatings, it was three thirty. Winston was due back at five, and Fred had wasted his day watching women he would never get close enough to touch from his second story floor-to-ceiling window. Rusty scratched at the rear entrance four or five times before Fred got up to let him in.

"Welcome home, asshole," he said as Rusty pranced past him, then slammed the door and followed the dog to the kitchen.

Rusty sat by the cupboard, obediently seeking food, as Fred jotted a quick note that read, *Your dog is an asshole,* and then continued on, leaving his dirty cups and dishes for Winston. He kicked off his boxer shorts in the hallway and went directly to the shower.

When he returned, Rusty was still sitting there, wincing a little with each excited breath. Fred looked at the clock in the kitchen and faced the dog. "He'll be home in an hour or two. You can wait, like I did all morning," he said, then walked back to his office and shut the door. He checked his messages and opened a large planning map before him.

On the days he wasted over the years, Fred took to making himself feel better by looking at how much he owned. He'd bought up eighty percent of the beachfront land on Billy's Bay, and now offered it at ridiculous prices to businessmen from Europe who didn't know any better. Most of it was completely covered in thick vegetation and sea grape groves.

He rolled the map back into a tight tube and sat in his Italian, pastel-yellow leather desk chair, which he spun to face the beach again. Rusty moved from the kitchen to the office door and rested his head on his paws. They both fell asleep, waiting for Winston.

A deep, sudden bark woke Fred from his slouched position in the chair. He bolted upright and wiped the slobber from his chin. Rusty had already gone to the door and bounced on Winston, who acted happy to see him and scratched him behind the ears. The dog bounded after Winston into the kitchen, where an extra-large portion of dog food was put before him. He set to work eating it.

Winston looked around at the mess one man could make in seventy-two hours. Fred had used every cup in the house, all of them still half full with sweet instant coffee gone cold. A pair of socks was thrown over a barstool, a wet towel grew musty in a ball on the floor. Mundane notes scrawled on scraps of paper lay everywhere: *Do laundry more often or buy me more boxers—Your dog is an asshole— Your mother called—I hate that painting in the hallway— Something in the trash can stinks.*

The office door opened and Fred emerged, looking indifferent.

"Some mess you make, mon," Winston laughed.

"Just give me the keys and shut up." Fred held his hand out.

"Ease up, Fred."

"Just give me the keys and get out," Fred barked.

Winston reached into his pocket and pulled out a ring with five keys on it. "Okay, Fred. There's the keys, right? If I go, who 'gwan clean all this up? And who 'gwan do all your shopping? Who—"

"Okay, I get the point. Just leave me alone." Fred walked back to the office and slammed the door.

He slapped the new key ring on the desk, fixed himself a bourbon on ice, and sat down to ponder. Winston began to clean the enormous condo, playing loud music wherever he went. Rusty had accidentally gotten locked between the glass door and the back door and no one heard him crying, so he finally had to squat and push right there on the terra-cotta tiled floor. What was worse was that he had to stay there and look at it, until someone found him and subsequently punished him; it was like spending the weeks before a murder trial in a cell with the festering dead body.

Fred found him. Winston's music had driven him out of the office to deal with the stereo, and then the smell of fresh dog shit drove him to the door where Rusty sat whimpering and looking sorry. Five minutes later, the dog was still trying to remove remnants of his own feces from his nostrils. It was drying in the fur behind his eyebrows, and he continually pressed his wide head into the sand to scrub it from himself. He ran to the sea and snorted salt water through his nose, and then took off toward the tree line.

In growth too dense for any human (unless armed with a sharp machete), Rusty and some other dogs from the neighborhood made tunnels and roamed them daily, sniffing and marking boundaries. Some of them had made a home of it, burrowing dens into the steady incline under screw pine roots and claiming chunks of territory. Rusty had a favorite spot too, and stayed there whenever he grew tired of Fred's beatings.

He found a sunny spot and groomed for ten minutes, then walked his rounds and stopped at a place between two tree trunks—a small space of only a yard or so. He positioned himself between the trunks, sat up tall, and took a huge breath of air. He exhaled, letting his bulky body fill the gap, and fell into a lazy, depressed snooze.

A few times, he shifted his weight and felt a poke in his rib cage from an object sticking out of the sand, then shifted again to avoid it like it was a loose spring in a mattress. After a few minutes of shifting, Rusty grew impatient with the sharp intrusion and got up. He backed away to sniff at whatever had poked him, and then leaned down to lick it.

Any human would have known that it was the corner edge of a shovel head. But to Rusty, it was simply a familiar metallic taste, one that reminded him of the Dumpster outside the Island Hotel Restaurant and the gatepost next to the pool.

# Dog Fact #4
## *Humping Inanimate Objects*

Adolescent dogs, when excited, often mount inanimate objects. This can embarrass owners, and is best controlled by doing something else and not thinking about it.

How many times have we heard a master exclaim, "That dog is simply shameless!" And indeed we are. Shameless and stupid at first. Do you think we *want* to be humping the furniture? Did you want to hump that awkward pimply sophomore in the back of your father's Buick? I doubt it, but you know, everybody has to start somewhere.

Dogs start with whatever is handy. The more there are other dogs around, the less your dog will feel the need to rub his most private parts against your leather sectional. I preferred a more malleable practice partner—a throw rug, a visitor's jacket, children's stuffed toys. That was when I lived in New Hope, Pennsylvania, in the 1960s with the bumper-sticker people. They had a collection that covered every square inch of their two cars and every interior wall of the small Victorian row house we lived in. Even my kennel in the backyard had adhesive slogans plastered all over it. They were fine people, though, aside from their undying need to get a message across.

Afraid I would get pregnant, the sticker freaks kept me locked inside a high chain-link fence and rarely walked me. I humped anything soft I could steal and hide in my house (mostly what I've already mentioned; lots of throw rugs, the rag-rug kind).

It's an instinctual, uncontrollable thing, very similar to

human puberty. There's no real joy in it, but we do it anyway because we have to. Our masters don't like witnessing it, because humans tend to have sexual hang-ups. To them, we seem *shameless and stupid*, which, if you really look at it, is just another way of saying *free and simple*.  ❧

Part
TWO

*It's not the size of the dog in the fight,*
*it's the size of the fight in the dog.*

MARK TWAIN

# .16.

## An Island of Desperate Men

When they landed in Tortuga, men flew up the ropes and stormed the boat, grabbing and groping any woman they could find. Emer hid beneath a bunk and shivered. In the melee, she heard women scream and slap, she heard men laugh hearty laughs and slap back. She escaped quietly, by way of the small ladder that led to the forecastle quarters.

After months below in the sweltering heat, Emer stood on deck and enjoyed the gentle breeze. She refastened her hair into a tight bun, exposing the back of her neck, and removed her overskirt, revealing a ragged sheer slip that kept the coarse wool from scratching her legs.

Emer listened carefully to what was going on beneath the deck. The crew had arrived, and forced manners onto any buccaneers who crossed the line. An ease swept through the ship, as the women thought about their past strife in Paris and realized that this Tortuga might not be so bad after all.

She headed back to her small bunk and retrieved her things—nothing but smelly garments that she had worn onto the boat, and her crucifix—and walked slowly toward the slatted plank that led to the shore. When all of the women were off the boat, some already holding hands with the first men they'd found, a black-haired Frenchman approached her. He was followed by a servant of some sort, who glared at her.

At first, the black-haired man spoke in French, but when he realized she couldn't understand him, he switched to a fluid English that Emer could nearly understand. She thought he said, "I have chosen you as the leader of these women."

What he'd really said was, "I am the leader of this village, and I have chosen you for myself." Smitten at first sight, the Frenchman watched her every move.

Emer smiled and replied, "I am honored."

It was only when he placed his rough hands on her breasts that she realized her grasp of the English language was rusty and inaccurate. She flinched and wiggled free, embarrassed. He grabbed her right wrist and placed his lips on her neck; she struggled to not cry or scream out.

Only a few paces from the dock, where the other women stood watching, she felt ashamed that she could not let him have his way. All during the journey from Paris, Emer had felt like a simple Irish girl compared to these women. Prostitutes had no trouble accepting advances. They had no scruples in the captain's cabin during the night, volunteering for duties she was still unfamiliar with. Emer felt stupid and naïve for all the nights she lay thinking about Seanie instead of reality.

The Frenchman knew, from the moment she flinched, that he'd done the impossible. He'd landed a virgin from a boat full of prostitues and beggar women. And it excited him and depressed him at the same time. He let go of Emer, allowing her to walk away from him, and quickly found a suitable older woman to drag to his hut.

Emer felt even worse shame after that, but soon remembered what her mother would say: *she was no man's prostitute*, no matter how out of place that notion seemed on the crazy island of Tortuga. And she was worthy of a good Irish man—or a good man, at least—and would settle for nothing less.

The next day, as she gathered fruit, Emer separated from the other women little by little until she disappeared into the thick vegetation to the north of the village. (Her mother whispered, *This way Emer, this way.*) She walked until the sun began to set, and then found shelter in a small, rocky cove.

"Another bloody cave," Emer said to herself, arranging a small pile of damp clothing on the flattest stone she could find. The last rays of sunlight gave her only enough time to get her bearings and make sure the tide wouldn't wash in while she slept, halfway between the beach and the forest.

*Why am I always finding myself here?* Emer asked herself. *Here, where there is no possible way out? In Paris, I ran from the fat man who owned me. Here, I run from all of them. Always running and ending up here! Damp caves or bunks below deck! Darkness!*

She looked at the flat rocks scattered on the sand, arranged by hundreds of tides. She thought back to the last time she felt free: the days atop the castle, fighting with Padraig, counting the swallows ... the days when her mother would smile and ruffle the top of her head and laugh out loud.

What was it Mairead had said about Emer, the legendary wife of Cuchulain? That she could talk her way out of anything? But what good was sweet speech when everyone spoke another language? When no man so far had been interested in talking?

She made a pillow out of the old wool cape that had made the journey from Connacht to Paris with her. She laid her head down and shifted a few times on the hard rock to get comfortable. Then, she reached into the small pocket of her skirt to retrieve the carved crucifix, clutched it, and prayed for safety.

The first intruder came at midnight. She heard a loud rustling of leaves, and then sniffing and snorting. Realizing it was just an animal, Emer lay still and listened for half an hour, then fell back into a half sleep where she was convinced she would hear whatever came next. But she didn't hear what came next—until he was in the cave standing above her.

Pausing only long enough to get her bearings and to

focus on the outline of the large man peering down at her, Emer rolled to the left and reached out for any object she could find. The man threw himself to his knees and grabbed her ankles roughly. She called out in pain and surprise. He jerked her toward him, saying something foreign, and then coughed and spat to his side and laughed. Emer found a solid rock and heaved herself up into a sitting position. The intruder jerked her again by her ankles and got a grip farther up her legs, just under her knees, nearly knocking her over onto her back. She jerked back and, with all her strength, brought the rock crashing down on his shoulder. He yelped in pain, letting go of her left leg to clutch his arm. She sat up straighter and aimed for his head.

Somehow, the leverage Emer attained from having her left leg curled under her, no matter how hard the intruder jerked on her right one, gave her the strength of an extra man. She pounded the rock into his head, again and again. He fell backward and to the side, his legs still folded under him, and didn't move at all.

Emer waited. He still didn't move. She waited for a few more minutes and, when he still didn't move, got up and fetched a smaller rock, one with a sharp edge that she could hold with one hand. Shaking and breathless, she dragged his heavy body from the cave. As she pulled the man by the shoulders, she heard the scraping of metal on rock and, investigating, found a short cutlass fastened to his belt. She removed it and parried with air, dancing back and forth. It was then the idea came to her.

Once she'd dragged the man to the sand, she put her ear to his lips and listened for breathing. There was none, so she undressed him. Back at her small makeshift bed, Emer groped around for the crucifix. Then she returned to the naked body, and, with the cross, said a few words in Gaelic above him for their combined sins.

Then Emer walked out to the surf. Starting with the man's blouse, she began to rinse out her new clothing, not knowing if there were bloodstains or holes in it that needed to be patched. She scrubbed the fabric together furiously, as if the sea could wash away what a dead man had seen and felt.

When Emer returned to the cave, she laid the clothing out to dry on the rocks and picked up the cutlass again. She felt its edge, and then tested its sharpness by clutching several strands of her long hair and pulling the cutlass through them, cutting the hair at chin length, away from herself. In a trance, she continued to do the same with the rest of her hair—clump by clump—until it was all relatively the same shape around her face, with an uneven boyish fringe at her forehead. She gathered up the pile of hair and walked it to the sea, throwing it as far away as she could and holding back tears.

*Sometimes, to defend your honor, you have to do awful things, Emer,* her mother said.

Emer sniffled. "I watched you kill two men, Mother, and I understand now."

*You should be proud you were able to defend yourself! Not ashamed!*

But no matter how Emer looked at it, she didn't feel comfortable with the murder. He hadn't been trying to kill her, and he wouldn't have. Did he really deserve to die for the sake of her honor? On an island of whores and desperate men?

Suddenly, she noticed a man walking toward her on the beach. She'd left the cutlass in the cave after cutting her hair, and now, making out the man's familiar frame, she ran back inside to find it. She hid in the corner nearest the beach, squatting, the cutlass perched between her thighs, and tried to slow her breathing.

He was speaking French, in teasing tones. She could hear from his voice that he was smiling. Then she heard him gasp as his toe met the dead, naked body of his comrade. She saw his silhouette lean down to inspect it.

"Are you in here, my little English girl?"

Emer watched his bushy dark hair flick around as he tried to adjust his eyes to the darkness within the cave.

His voice echoed. "Do not be afraid. You do not need to kill me too."

He sounded happy, as if he were playing a game with a child. And like a child, ten feet away, Emer suddenly didn't know what to do. She froze. Would she have to keep killing for the sake of this useless chastity? One man already lay dead because of this game. Need there be two?

Before she even felt him grab her, she was flat on her back on the rocks, her cutlass snatched, and he was pressing his full weight against her. He kissed her neck the same way as he'd done the day before, and breathed in the sweetness of her sweat.

The Frenchman reached down to Emer's breasts and this time she did not flinch—half for fear of a slap, or worse, and half because she was still frozen in her childish game of indecision. She didn't scream or squirm. She just lay still and let him touch her.

He yanked her slip up to her waist and she could feel his hard groin grinding against her thigh, now wet from seawater. Emer didn't know if she was feeling desire or repulsion, excitement or fear. He kissed her bosom and grabbed her tightly around the waist, almost crushing her ribs between his hands, before plunging himself.

She groaned in pain and pulled her hips from the hard stone to avoid injury as he thrust back and forth, panting, his head buried in her neck. Her hands moved to her sides to balance this whole event, trying to control the uncontrollable. Still frozen by her mixed emotions, Emer prayed that he would finish soon. She thought back to the nights she had lain in the boat, listening to the whores please the crewmen. How long had it taken them? Was time making any sense at all? How long has he been doing this?

And then he stopped. He hadn't finished, just stopped, and breathed slowly until he felt contained—then started at the beginning again, in her neck and breasts, taking his time as if he were her husband or a great lover. Emer didn't know what to do, and in a desperate attempt to end the terrible procedure, she opened her legs wider. The Frenchman seemed so invited by this that he began again, and continued for such a short time that Emer could barely believe it was over so quickly. He collapsed on top of her and breathed into her ear loudly. His left hand moved up her side and landed on her head, where he stroked her cropped hair and whispered something in French, and then repeated it in English: "I love you, woman," he said, and sighed. This English she did not confuse.

Emer's emotions spun back to Seanie. Every bit of heart she had left broke, and she cried. The Frenchman, still on top of her, flopped slightly to her right, and she let silent tears drop from the sides of her face into her ears. As he breathed, each tear blew cold. She shivered. Now she knew what was worse. Now she knew what was worse than all of the things she had been ashamed of in a day. It wasn't killing or running or hiding that was worse, and it wasn't the prudishness of her chastity or the innocence of her ideals. It was this. This right here.

A stranger who felt love in her, wrapped around her and inside her, who had taken from her the thing she had wished to be rid of only a day before—it felt worse than killing. It felt worse to endure such an animal act than it did to crush a man's skull. It felt worse because of Seanie, and because of her mother and because of her confusion. Now, she would never know what had just happened. She would always ask why. Why hadn't she fought, after killing another man only an hour before? Why hadn't she tried to escape and hide? Why hadn't she cared enough to do *something*?

# .17.

# My 20th-Century Boyfriend &
# Junior's Discount Medical Supply

Susan picked Sam and me up from school on Skip Day, and we went to the mall. Susan turned to go into Tower Records while Sam and I dug through bargain books on the tables set up outside the bookstore.

"Have fun, you two," she said, and I clenched my teeth. Ever since she started dating Jay, Susan had become one of *those* girls—an annoying, giddy, simple-minded baseball groupie. On several occasions, when she wouldn't shut up, I'd hung her from the yard arm and used her for target practice.

I spent a while in the travel section, looking at books about Jamaica and the Caribbean. I decided on one and bought it, then found Sam slumped on a bench next to the fake mall greenery.

"What's wrong?"

"Nothing," he said, but he said it all depressed-like.

"Come on." God, I wanted to kick him.

He looked up at me and said, "You know, the prom is in three weeks, and if I'm going to go I have to buy tickets now, and my pop said he could buy them for me if I wanted to take you, but I told him you probably already had a date, and now I feel like an idiot because I don't think you do, and I never asked. Do you?"

He was like a ship's dog.

"Do you?"

"Are you asking me to the prom?"

"Uh huh."

A week later, I found a great old beaded dress at the Goodwill in town and took it to Mrs. Lindt in the Home Ec wing, who helped me tailor it to make me look less flat chested. I tried to act excited, but really, the whole thing made me want to puke. To me, it seemed like just another opportunity for the rich kids to sit around and snigger at the rest of us.

And Sam was just complicating things.

He started acting all stupid around me, like we were a couple or something. He came to McDonald's every night and dropped by the trailer unannounced, which really pissed me off because it was hard enough living with my new-levels-of-loserdom parents without having to show them off to the neighbors.

By prom night, he'd worked himself up into a nervous wreck and his mood fluctuated between morose insecurity and babbling excitement. I began to hate him for it, so much so that, as I slipped into the dress, I half considered calling the whole night off. Before I could, he arrived at the trailer door with a boxed corsage and his hair combed and slicked down with some sort of shiny stuff.

I'd put on makeup, and this shocked him as much as his hair shocked me.

"Wow. You look great." The way he said it felt insulting—as if I'd never looked great before. Before I could answer, my mother was posing us next to the front window, inching Sam to the left or right to hide the peeling paper paneling.

"Hold that!" she said. "Saffron, smile, will you?"

I smiled.

"Sam, can you lean in toward Saffron a little? I can't fit you both in the frame."

She was backed up against the far wall of the living area, and I let her snap a few more shots before I suggested that we go.

Sam had left his pop's truck at #20, so we walked over there, and the old folks came out on the warm May night to watch us. There was something about how they looked at us that I tried to connect with. Though I felt as stupid as a sack of rat shit in my beaded dress, lacy shawl, and a wrist corsage, I felt a little bit of happiness for us, too.

But then, Sam opened his mouth.

"Uh, I'm not sure I can dance tonight. I think I sprained my ankle."

"You look fine to me," I said. "We don't have to dance if you don't want."

"Oh good."

What a pathetic lying jerk.

Sam's granny and pop took some pictures and then we got into the truck (Sam didn't open the door for me) and headed for the Jefferson Hotel. About a hundred yards from the trailer park entrance, I saw two guys walking down the road in hooded sweatshirts. As we passed, my eyes met with Junior's. I groaned.

"Do you know those guys?" he asked.

"No."

"So how come you made that noise?"

"I just did," I said.

"Did you used to date one of them?"

"No."

"Are you sure?"

I turned my head to look at him. He was clearly doubtful, upset, and, from the sounds of things, possessive. "Yes I'm sure. Though it's not any of your business."

"It *is* my business because you're *my* date."

And that was pretty much how the rest of the night went. When he found me having an innocent conversation with Mike from the Quiz Bowl team, he grabbed my arm so roughly it left a little red mark. When he saw me heading to the bathroom with Susan and two other girls, he asked, "Where do you think you're going?"

"To the bathroom."

"Just don't talk about me behind my back," he said. Susan looked at me and made a crazy face. I smirked. Wasn't this her idea to begin with?

Sam and I had one dance together, a slow number, and he grabbed my ass. Like, grabbed it so hard it hurt and I let out a little yelp. I walked off the dance floor, gathered my shawl and my purse, and waited for him to catch up.

"Why'd you do that?" he demanded.

"Let's just go home," I said. "I don't feel well."

"But, I—" He stopped when he saw my face. I must have looked three hundred years' worth of pissed off and ready to kill him. And I was.

He drove home emotionally. At first, he seemed sad and tried to get me to feel sorry for him, and then, when I didn't, he drove like an asshole. When we got back to the trailer park, he stopped at the entrance, put the truck in park, and pouted at me.

"I can walk from here," I said, reaching for the door handle.

"But I thought since we went out we could, um …"

I was already stuffing his eye sockets with salted limes, already carving his acne off, zit by zit, and feeding it to him. What more did he want? I made a move to open the door. He slammed the truck into drive and peeled forward on the gravel, aiming for every pothole there was. By the time we arrived in front of his granny and pop's place in a cloud of gray dust, I'd hit the truck's ceiling twice.

Before I'd regained my balance and straightened myself, he leaned in to kiss me. I recoiled a little, and then figured if this was prom night etiquette, and if it would get me out of ever doing anything remotely "normal" again, then I was willing to give him one stupid kiss. But then there was a knock on the truck's window and I saw Sam's granny standing outside, crying and gesturing toward the trailer.

"I'm so sorry," she said. "I didn't want to interrupt your special night, but Sam, I need your help."

Sam was out of the truck before she finished the sentence. She started telling him what happened. I was still in the truck and couldn't hear her. But I heard Sam say, "Who would steal a wheelchair?" and then I slowly turned the handle on the truck door and slipped out. I knew exactly who would steal a wheelchair.

"Two of them, in ski masks," Sam's pop said as I neared the front door.

"They pointed a gun at me!" his granny cried. "And they took all of our pills!"

I reached out and touched Sam's back, but he flinched. "Didn't anyone call the cops?" he said, and when they shrugged at him, still obviously in shock, Sam took off for the pay phone as if I wasn't standing there.

And then I realized that if Junior had been to Sam's place, then he'd have been to ours, too, and I worried about my parents. I walked (as fast as I could in two-inch heels) to our trailer and scanned a hundred mental images—Mom and Dad shot, sliced, hung, burnt, and beaten—but when I got through the door, I found them alert and watching *The Late Show*.

"Was Junior here tonight?"

My father stared at David Letterman. My mother said, "No."

"Are you sure?"

I looked around the room, trying to see the gaps Junior would usually leave. The toaster was there. The heater was there. The microwave.

"I've been here all night and I didn't see him," my mother said.

"Well, he robbed #20 tonight," I said. "And he stole Sam's grandfather's wheelchair."

My mother looked at me sideways. "How was your prom? Isn't it still early?"

"Mom! I just told you that Junior stole an old, handicapped man's wheelchair! Don't you care?" I stormed into my room to take the stupid dress off and get myself into a pair of jeans as fast as I could.

"How do you know he did it?" she asked. "I mean, it could be anyone, right?"

I walked into the bathroom to wipe off the stupid prom face I'd painted on, and then I saw it. The cigarette butt in the toilet.

"Did you hear me?" she yelled, aggressively. "Anyone could have done it!"

I poked my head around the faux wood accordion bathroom door. "Yeah. Sure. And so this is *anyone's* cigarette butt in the bathroom, then, is it?"

I heard some cars arrive and went outside. Two cop cruisers were parked outside #20 with their lights on. When I got there, Sam was sitting on the steps talking to himself. When he saw me, he scowled.

"Are they okay?"

"Yeah."

"Can I do anything to help?" I asked.

"Who would steal a wheelchair from two poor old people?"

I shook my head.

That's the thing with drug addicts. They steal wheelchairs and hearing aids and walkers and canes and seeing-eye dogs, and I'm sure if Junior needed a fix that he would reach right into every one of those trailer-park old people and grab their pacemakers. Sam didn't understand this, so he just looked at me and repeated the question.

"I mean, who would steal a wheelchair?"

# . 18 .

# My Great Escape

The police never found out it was Junior who stole Pop's chair on prom night, even though I found his cigarette butts outside three other robbed trailers and it was about the simplest puzzle there ever was.

After that night, Sam stopped dropping by to see me, which was a relief. The last thing I needed in my life was an overly possessive pseudo-boyfriend who couldn't take a hint. I was less than a month from high school graduation and the fulfillment of a lifelong plan. I started taking double shifts at McDonald's as the warmer nights approached. I had plenty to do without having to worry about a twentieth-century boy's fragile feelings. Ugh. The mere thought of it made me want to gouge my own eye out.

As the school year wound down, I tried to get myself in the mood for what lay ahead. I did my final senior research paper for AP English on King Philip's emerald—and concluded by blaming historians for misleading us into the belief that its whereabouts were a mystery. In the high times of privateering and piracy, we all knew where the emerald ended up. Well, at least I did, anyway.

I got my passport in the mail the same day I got my last report card. I'd aced finals and, as expected, I was crowned class valedictorian. I think my mother showed her pride by blinking twice after I told her.

All the other speakers at commencement had been awarded college scholarships and grants, and gave speeches about their glorious academic futures. I didn't want to speak but I had to, so I wrote a piece about how graduates should do what they want to do, and not let themselves be steered by anyone else's desires.

Parents probably didn't like what I had to say, but what did it matter? It got me as much applause as it got the others. It made my parents burst from their chairs and pound their pasty palms together, even though they probably hadn't heard a word I'd said. They were stoned out of their minds anyway, with new tablets my mother had gotten for her migraines. My father wore a wrinkled linen blazer with jeans and sandals, and a POW/MIA baseball cap. My mother didn't take off her sunglasses once.

I kept looking around for Junior. If he had any brains, he'd show up and try to take the cash out of all the cards I got that day, but he was nowhere to be found. Maybe he was in jail somewhere, maybe asleep in a crack house. Maybe uptown scoring more drugs.

My mother was still wearing her sunglasses when we got home from the ceremony.

"I don't want you drinking tonight, Saffron. I'm scared you'll be killed in a horrible accident or something," she said through my bedroom door. I sighed, sliced off a strip of her ear, and ate it like beef jerky.

"Don't worry. I'm only going to Susan's house and I'm sleeping over. I won't be on the road at all."

"What time will you be home?"

I walked past her and out the door. After all those years at the kitchen table, and all the years living through Junior's bullshit together, she hadn't the courage to tell me she was proud of me that day. So I refrained from answering her at all.

The next day, I arranged my flights from Susan's house. On Sunday night, I packed my few summer clothes and my father's collapsible army shovel into a drab duffel bag Pat had given me. Before Susan drove me to the bus station, I said goodbye to my parents.

"I'll call you once I get there," I told them.

My father searched for the missing remote control. My mother had a glassy-eyed stare. Neither of them made a sound. It was as if they were finally suffering from the years of imaginary torture I'd inflicted.

From the bus station, I traveled to Philadelphia, to spend one night and catch a plane the next morning. For two hours, as I struggled to fall asleep under the glow of a city night, I walked through my plan of action in my mind—each time throwing a different wrench in the works to see how I could solve unforeseeable problems. What if I get there and no one meets me at the airport? I'll find a taxi. What if I get to a town and there are no rooms available? I can stay with someone, I'm sure. What if I'm robbed or lose my money? That's why I bought traveler's checks. What if I can't find the bay?

That was the big one. What if I couldn't find the bay? Things would surely have changed since I'd seen the Jamaican coast in 1664. If an important town like Port Royal had sunken thirty meters under the sea, then what else would have changed in three hundred years?

In my mind's eye, I was confident I would recognize it somehow. Whenever I'd closed my eyes to sleep for the past three hundred years, I'd walked that sand in long, measured footsteps. But what if all my information was mixed up? I knew that no one had ever officially claimed Philip's emerald, but who knew? Maybe someone had already found it all and sold it, not knowing what it was. Then what? Back to Hollow Ford? On to medical school?

I got up four times to pee during the night. Each time, I was increasingly agitated about not sleeping. Finally, at four thirty, after listening to delivery trucks honk outside the supermarket across the street, I turned on the blinding fluorescent bathroom light, stared at my reflection, and decided to trust myself.

# .19.

## Fred Livingstone's Office

The only mirror in Fred Livingstone's office was behind a small bar in the corner. It often captured Fred's nose or chin in its beveled edge, causing a distorted reflection he couldn't help but stare at.

A week had passed since Winston brought back the new deeds from Miami. Fred knew he had to go to the bank to deposit them with the rest of his paperwork, but it seemed an eternity, forty minutes each way on the treacherous Jamaican country roads. Plus, there would be Winston, chatting and singing and generally being annoying.

"I can go tomorrow," he said, and propped his feet on his desk.

It was eleven o'clock and there was no one on the beach. He hadn't seen Sarah since the day she stood him up and enough time had passed, he figured, to know that she wasn't interested.

He closed his eyes and imagined her. "You look stunning," he said. "Beyond words you are beautiful, Sarah."

*Get to work, you flabby prick. Go to the bank.*

"Shut up! Sarah, excuse him. He is a rude, rude man. Where were we? Oh yes, you look stunning. That silk hangs so well on you. Versace? Oh yes, it was made for you, dear, made for you."

*You sound like a faggot, Fred.*

"I am not a faggot."

*You like men, Fred. You* are *a faggot.*

"Sarah, please, don't go. I can make him stop. Security! Sarah! Don't believe him!"

*Faggot.*

"You're the faggot," Fred said, pouting.

It was 11:05 and there was no one on the beach but Rusty, making paw prints in the wet sand and watching them disappear with the tide.

Winston knocked on the office door and called to him.

Fred didn't move from the chair, just laid his head back and feigned sleep. He heard the door open and then close again, gently. "You're the faggot," he whispered.

He got up and walked to his bedroom. He dressed in khaki shorts and a white dress shirt and put on a white pair of sport socks, but then peeled them off again and arrived back in the office ten minutes later in a pair of fungicide-dusted tartan slippers. It was 11:15 and no one was on the beach. It was June, for Christ's sake. Where was everyone?

Fred sat down at his desk, which was still covered in planning maps and property deeds, and wondered if 1990 would be the year the worst would finally happen. He had a plan for it, at least—he would sell the Florida land first, back to the Yank at a grotesque profit, and then move there himself. That way he wouldn't have to be in Billy's Bay when the stuffy Europeans showed up to view their holiday resort sites and found nothing but vegetation and an empty, rocky beach. He had nothing to worry about, really. They couldn't sue him. He would always have money.

*You won't if you keep giving it to that Jamaican poof,* he told himself.

"I pay him fairly."

*For what?*

"For working for me."

*Is that what you call it?*

"You're the faggot."

It was 11:30 and the beach was still empty. Fred picked up his telescope and scanned the surface of the sea. Far out, there were two enormous shipping vessels and to the west, there were the usual three or so glass-bottomed boats for snorkeling day trips from the tourist village two miles away. Closer still was the small fleet of local fishermen heading out to empty their pots, which they'd laid out at midnight the night before. And then she appeared.

She was blurred at first, before he had time to focus the telescope and catch up with her moving through the foreground. Immediately, he could sense that she was something special. She was walking fast, and his hand was too shaky to follow her, balanced only on the arm of his chair. He pushed himself up, rolled over to the glass table, and steadied his elbows. He could tell she was young; her small, firm breasts barely bounced at all. Her legs were as slim as any he'd ever seen. Her ass was exquisite, and she didn't let it fall from side to side like older women. She had no hips to swing as of yet.

"And too young to be married," he mumbled.

*And too young to ever notice you, you blubbery ponce.*

"You're the ponce."

*Why do you do this to yourself, man? You would never actually do anything with that little girl out there.*

"I've just been waiting for the right moment."

*Like your moment with Sarah last week? Like that moment?*

"She's a prick tease. I don't know how that husband of hers can stand it."

*You think so?*

"I know so."

*I've heard them screwing, Fred. They do screw.*

"You're just a pervert, then, listening to other people screw."

*And you're just a fat queer with a telescope.*

"You're the queer."

He held his hand out to silence the air and watched. She walked slower now, kicking the water with her delicate feet, letting the foam race up her white thighs and stream down again. Her fair, medium-length hair hung down her back in a wet lump and Fred could see that her skin was peeling in places.

"Would you like me to put some cream on your back?" he asked.

*Yes,* please! *I keep getting burned,* she answered pertly, handing him a bottle.

"I can do the backs of your legs too."

*I'm sure it all washed off from my swim this morning. Please, just get it everywhere.*

"Everywhere?"

She looked at him and blinked twice. *Yes, everywhere.*

Fred began applying tanning lotion to every part of her body. He lathered the inside of her legs, stopping just short of her flat crotch, and slowly worked toward her belly. His over-lubricated hands dipped under her coral pink bikini and around her breasts. Her nipples hardened, her breath grew heavy, her legs fell open. Fred reached down to his zipper. Then Rusty barked from the pool.

Fred's hard-on transformed itself into a frustrated fist. If only the office were soundproof. If only he had the energy to get up and beat the dog senseless. She was nearly at the end of his sight line, and he caught one last glimpse of her through his scope before the usual questions presented themselves. How long was she staying? Where is she staying? Where is she from? Is she here with her parents? A boyfriend? More girls?

He watched all day, but she never returned. Not during one o'clock *Oprah* (one bourbon) or two o'clock girl-on-girl flick (two bourbons) or four o'clock *McHale's Navy* (a beer and two more bourbons) or the five o'clock news, when Winston arrived home with two bags full of groceries and a new painting for the condo. Fred was remotely aware that he was home, and saw Rusty eating food from a bowl on the patio soon after, but he didn't get up from the chair. Instead, he fell into a pre-sleep, coral pink coma until night came, and then dragged himself to bed to have coral pink dreams.

As if the universe could read his mind, she was the first person he saw the next morning while he nursed his hangover after a cold shower at 7:15. She was wading, thigh-deep, in the sea. Fred reached for his telescope and sat back in the chair.

*You came*, she said.

"I would follow you anywhere," he answered, walking slowly into the warm, lapping water.

*Hey asshole, snap out of it.*

"Shut up! You'll ruin it!"

*You're ruining it.*

"I am not. I'm creating it. I'm making it happen."

*You're not. You'll never talk to her.*

"Shut up!"

*You shut up. You shut up and I'll shut up.*

She dried herself and walked east, slowly vanishing from Fred's view.

*Why don't you walk down to the beach like a normal person? Go and ask her to lunch. Go and do something!*

"I'm going out tomorrow. I can do it then."

*You won't do it.*

"I will."

*You're a fat queer who won't do it.*

"I am not and I will."

*Then go. Do it now. Go and catch up with her.*

Fred's heart raced. His temples pounded with decision. He looked down at himself and twirled his ankle around and admired his calf muscle. Why not ask her to lunch? Why not try doing something for *real?*

He stepped out onto the second-story sun deck and made his way toward the staircase that led to the beach. Just as he got to the banister, the coral-clad girl stepped back into view, making him jump a little. Rusty barked and ran down the beach gracefully. Fred watched, but couldn't move.

"Rusty!" he called. "Rusty!"

She looked up at him and squinted. He was sure she saw him, but she didn't wave. What was wrong with her? Why didn't she wave? She stopped to pet the dog and then continued walking, out of sight to the west. Rusty followed her for a hundred yards and then came trotting back to the house.

Still balancing at the top of the stairs, Fred Livingstone had lost his chance.

*You blew it, asshole.*

"I didn't blow it."

*You did. You didn't even wave.*

"I can wave next time."

When he could finally unhinge his left hand from the banister and forcefully unparalyze the hand that had never waved to beautiful bikini girl, Fred walked back into his office. Longing to feel better about himself, he began organizing his desk. He rolled up his maps and stacked folders. He separated out a small pile of things that had to go to the bank safe and gathered other things to put in his own.

He removed a large modern painting from the wall, opened his safe, and placed his new deeds in it. Moving back the way he came, he kicked a heap of dirty clothing to the top of the stairs where Winston would find them. It had been twenty-five minutes since he'd seen the girl in the coral bikini, and he still couldn't erase her from his mind.

"I *will* talk to her next time," he said, and no one answered back.

Fred turned on the TV just in time for the weather report. June in Billy's Bay is much like any other month—eighty-five and sunny. Sometimes the rainy season brought a bad storm or even an early hurricane, but most years it passed by unnoticed. So far that year the weather had been perfect, and Fred wondered again why the beach was so empty.

He heard Winston using the shower downstairs.

"It's about time I got out and did things. All this day-dreaming is getting me nowhere," he said, and there was no answer. So he moved his morning business to the sun deck to tan his toned calves and enjoy the scenery. After a half-hour nap in the sun, he heard Winston knocking.

"Come in!"

Winston moved slowly through the office and out the sliding door.

"You cleaned up, Fred!" he said.

"You know, I *can* do that sort of thing from time to time."

"You feeling all right now?"

Fred threw him a dirty look. "I never felt otherwise."

"You been cranky for three days now, Fred. I can tell these things." Winston smiled, and reached out to touch Fred's shoulder.

Fred flinched. "What do you want? I'm working!"

Winston just shook his head and stared.

"What do you WANT?" Fred boomed.

Winston spoke through a stifled grin. "I'm goin' to Black River today. You want to go to the bank?"

"No. Not today. I'll go tomorrow."

"You sure?"

Fred wiggled his hand in Winston's direction. "Whatever, whatever. Just leave me alone. I have work to do!"

"All right, mon, no prob*lem*."

"Sure, yeah."

Fred looked up at him from the handmade wooden lounge chair on the deck. Winston stood there smiling at him, goofily.

"What?"

"Just you, mon. I dunno."

"Well, go and figure it out somewhere else."

Winston laughed. "When'd you get so mean to yourself, Fred?"

"Just go away," Fred answered. And Winston left, still giggling to himself. Sometimes under his breath, he spoke like a Jamaican woman, like his own mother, in psalms and songs that Fred could not understand. On his way through the sliding doors he said, "Who feels it knows it, Lord," and yelped to himself as if that were a really funny thing to say. Fred heard him get in the car and drive away, still laughing. He ripped a large corner from one of his papers and wrote

*Stop saying that annoying rubbish* in block letters, and placed it neatly on top of Winston's folder.

And then she appeared again.

"God! What timing!" Fred marveled to himself.

When she was halfway across his beach, he stood and approached the stairway again. This time, when he knew she was looking his way, he waved. She squinted again, and covered her brow with her hand and waved back, but kept walking.

Rusty appeared and began to trot toward the sea, and Fred hurried down the steps to grab him.

"You'll stay!" he said to the dog, holding him forcefully by the scruff of his neck, every so often squeezing so hard that Rusty would squeak in pain. The girl looked back to the house and squinted again, but couldn't see Fred where he now stood with the dog. He waved, but she didn't wave back. He kicked the dog for that, and then watched as she vanished again behind the tree line to the left.

"Well, she *did* wave," he said.

*She wasn't waving at you, Fred.*

"Yes, she was. Of course she was."

*She probably couldn't really see you.*

"Oh, she saw me. She saw me yesterday. She came back today, didn't she?"

*Not for you.*

"What for, then?"

*She's just a tourist, Fred. You'll have to do more than wave at her to make something happen.*

"I will, I will. Next time."

*Sure, Fred, next time.*

Once an hour had passed, he peeled his eyes from the beach view and made a few calls. He had some selling to do if he was to cut his losses on the Billy's Bay property. Five hours and fifteen phone calls later, he was back on the sun deck scanning the pink horizon.

For over an hour, he gazed through his binoculars at three pelicans fishing. Then she came walking slowly into his view from the east, nearly a silhouette.

She stopped again, to adjust her short sundress, and then did something spectacular. Pulling the sundress over her head and leaving it on the sand, she walked slowly into the waves and continued walking until she was about chest-deep. There, she dropped down and floated face up, dove in and out of the sea like a dolphin and then stood up again, wet, glistening, and in water thigh-high. Her nipples jutted through the swimsuit and made Fred wince.

She walked so slowly toward the shore again that Fred was sure this was for him.

He reached for his zipper. "Jesus, where's the camera," he said, not caring about where it was.

*Fred, stop perving. She wouldn't ride you if you were the last man on this island.*

"She's looking right at me," he said.

*She's looking at the reflection of the setting sun on the glass in front of you, you fat fool.*

"She's not. She's taunting me," he answered, sighing.

Before he could argue with himself any more, he watched her slip the dress back over her body and walk away, squeezing the seawater from her hair. He was so distracted by this performance that he never heard Winston come home, and was genuinely surprised when Winston walked into the office.

An hour later, Fred sat on the edge of his bed applying foot cream.

"You have to go to Miami again tomorrow. You'll need to pack now, because I have you on the first flight in the morning."

"But—"

"But nothing—you work for me, don't you? Well then, you do as I say. Now get out of here. You're stinking up my bed."

# Dog Fact #5
## *Humping Among Friends*

Humans often credit their dogs with human emotion, logic, and forethought. They say things like, "I just don't know what Rover was *thinking* running out in front of a car like that!" Though he is man's best friend, it's important to remember that your dog is not the same as a human being.

Science can explain everything a pet owner might describe as doggie "emotion." It's a dog's nature, as it is most wild creatures', to return to a place if he's fed there and to be loyal to a person repeatedly feeding him. It's a dog's nature to fetch things that you've thrown, to repeat a trick if he gets a reward. The modern dog is much like a modern computer. You must train a dog to be your companion the way you have to install software before a computer will work. Some dogs are slower than others, running on an outdated or overbred motherboard, forgetting where they left their favorite toy only seconds before, walking into stationary objects. Some have countless gigabytes of memory, and can jump through hoops of fire and pee squatting over your toilet. But unlike our human idea of soul mates, your dog would be just as happy if someone other than you had picked them from the litter and trained them to do the same stuff.

I knew a pack of dogs once who gathered every night in their village green. I lived in Dublin, Ireland, in a growing suburb called Stillorgan. Most of the dogs there were well fed; we had a few strays from the traveler's camp up the road, and the odd fight when they tried to work our turf. I say our turf, but I wasn't part of the pack. I lived as a house pet—a rather attractive, fair-haired Chihuahua—and only saw the back garden for my occasional run.

Some trouble started one night when a group of lads were playing a game of five-a-side and Rico approached Spanky. Spanky was seventeen years old, barely roaming much anymore because of arthritis and asthma. Rico was a young scruffy thing, only two or three, and hadn't yet managed to hump anything but his master's kitchen chairs.

Spanky was half sitting, half lying on his side by a small ash tree when Rico began to toy with him. He leapt at him from the side and began roughhousing—a playful nip here and there, the odd growl. Spanky had trouble keeping his balance, and fell over. Rico hopped up and nipped at Spanky's neck, nudged him violently with his nose. And when Spanky finally managed to stand up again, about two minutes later, Rico mounted him from behind and began thrusting at him with what looked like an oversized skinned rabbit protruding from his underparts.

A few minutes later, the ten lads playing in the green heard a terrible yelping sound and went to investigate. When they arrived at the scene by the ash tree, they found the two dogs still stuck together, Spanky writhing in agony and Rico spinning, trying to pull himself free. One boy ran to his house and fetched a pitcher of cold water. The others tried to make Rico stop moving, but both dogs had threatened them with bared teeth, so no one actually did much but yell. A few laughed. When the boy returned with the water he aimed it at the dogs' rumps. They thrashed about with surprise until somehow Rico broke free and ran around the green, shaking himself dry, and disappeared. Spanky was soaked and began to shiver and vomit, so one of the lads took him home, where he died in his sleep later that night.

The next morning at seven thirty, the doorbell at Rico's house chimed. When his master answered the door, Spanky's owner barged right in and overpowered him, holding him by the arm, twisting it a little as he bellowed, "Your faggot dog raped my dog last night and fucking killed him!"

This is exactly what I'm talking about. Dogs don't have a "sexual orientation." They just do what feels right without having to overthink and label it like humans do.

You'd be surprised at the long list of animals who naturally exhibit homosexual behavior.[1] Rico wasn't the first dog to do that to another dog, and he wasn't the last. Unlike humans, he didn't have to fear being called a queer by the pack the next day either, although from that day forward, those dogs with writable drive space did lower their hindquarters when he approached. ❧

---

1. Cows, giraffes, rats, dolphins, cats, rams, goats, pigs, antelope, elephants, lions, porcupines, rabbits, female red deer, porpoises, mice, hamsters, burros, male mountain sheep, donkeys, hyenas, and male mountain gorillas, to name a few.

# .20.

# The Day the *Emerald* Changed Hands

As sunrise approached, Emer peeled herself from the rocks where the Frenchman slept and washed her body in the sea, twenty yards from the naked dead man on the beach. She stared at both men, ashamed.

She walked the five miles back to the small village with the Frenchman silently. Not even when she did understand his questions did she answer. If she was going to be a slave, then she would be a voiceless one—just like in Connacht.

For a fortnight the lovesick Frenchman kept Emer in his bed, busy, allowing her a walk once a day for fresh air. He asked her questions about Ireland and she would answer briefly, never saying more than a few words. He tried to teach her a few French phrases, but she refused. Twice he had to leave the village to do business, and left her in the care of his servant. At first, Emer feared the island man might hurt her too, but she soon noticed that he avoided all women and kept his attention firmly, even lovingly, on the Frenchman.

One day a supply ship came to the village dock, and while the men had a loud, all-night rum party, Emer crept on board in the Frenchman's clothes. She hid behind a crate of fruit and stayed quiet until the boat sailed again. The crew had been so hungover from their party with the buccaneers that they never even looked up on their return to the ship. When the Frenchman woke from a drunken sleep and couldn't find her anywhere, he went looking in the cave and around the shore for a day or two. He even borrowed search dogs from the governor, but couldn't find her.

A month later, the ship docked at a port south of Tortuga and Emer snuck off the boat. Still dressed in a successful sailor's clothes, she was propositioned by several ships at the dock as she made her way into the small village of Jamestown, an English settlement on the island of Barbados.

A week later, she sailed on a supply fluyte toward Martinique, acting as a general sailor and (happy for the meager pay) trying to stay as unnoticed as possible. But it only took three days on board for the other recruits to realize that Emer was no man. And only one day after that to realize that she was no ordinary woman, either.

As the day the *Emerald* changed hands began, a few men on board approached her and jokingly asked her to bare her chest. They opened their blouses and revealed their hairy chests, each boasting that theirs was the manliest, egging Emer to join in. She ignored them and ascended to the crow's nest, which seemed to her the safest place to be now that she'd been discovered. Then the fluyte's captain, a man of great height and kind nature named Richard Foley, was fetched from his quarters to eye a fast-approaching brig to the east.

"I know that ship," he said, squinting through the small telescope and saying its name in a whisper. "Ready the cannons, men. Come about!"

In the best male voice she could mimic, Emer shouted from the crow's nest, "Pirates, sir!"

"Descend and make yourself useful, sailor!" Foley ordered, turning to his first mate, who was tugging on his shirtsleeve.

"That's no sailor, sir. That's a woman."

"A woman?"

"Yes, sir."

Foley watched Emer descend the ropes. "Looks like a sailor to me," he said.

"She works, sir. Works hard, but she *is* a woman."

"You men! Go on! Load the muskets!" he shouted, then turned back to his mate. "Bring her to my quarters."

"Aye, sir."

Emer took her new orders with great sadness. As she made her way to Foley's quarters, the approaching ship grew near enough to be seen unassisted. The wind was strong and the crew was bringing the boat about, to face the pirates. Any minute, the fighting would begin.

"You wanted to see me, sir?"

He stood, ten muskets before him, packing each with powder and loading them with naked musket balls. "We have little time now. I hear you're a woman. Is that true?"

"I cannot deny that, sir. I am a woman."

"You'll stay here in my quarters until you hear that the fighting has stopped."

"Please, sir. I can—"

"Those are my orders."

"Sir, I—"

He piled the loaded muskets into his arms, barrels-up, and locked the door from the outside.

When the first cannon fired, Emer jumped a little. There were six cannons in total on the small fluyte, and each was manned by three gunners. Foley's crew was out of practice. The gunners got only one shot off before the ship was boarded.

She heard men running on deck; she heard men screaming, men dying, and men fighting. All of this while they still sailed with the strong easterly wind, while they were still tangled with the brig's ropes. No one screamed anything intelligible, as if fighting had its own language that all on board could understand. Emer heard more men board, more men die, and feared that the fluyte would be taken—and she would be taken—by pirates.

She looked around Foley's quarters and grabbed any weapon that looked back at her. Two small daggers fit perfectly into her boots, a sharp cutlass onto her belt. Before she left the cabin, she snatched a sturdy iron club and an unloaded pistol and put them in her pockets. She eyed the lock on the door and kicked it hard with the sole of her boot. It buckled. Two more kicks and it collapsed.

When she first poked her head above deck, she got sick. One of the men who'd bared his chest to her only that morning now lay dead, one arm missing, his eyes gouged out. Blood covered the deck, washing back and forth over other dead men and discarded weapons. She saw Foley standing atop two crates, fighting off as many as four men at a time. She surfaced and removed the iron club from her pocket, hitting the first pirate she could find with it. His head split open, and when he turned to face her she removed the cutlass from her belt and plunged it into his belly.

With no time to reflect, she moved on to her next victim, and then the next, making each one dead as if she had done it a thousand times before. Time twisted—into the same sort of shock-induced nothingness as when the Roundheads razed her valley or when the Frenchman had found her in the cave. She felt like an animal. She felt as big as the fires of hell, fueled by everything she'd ever suffered.

The brig began to free itself from them and Foley led the remaining crew to the ropes and ordered them to board. With a roar, Emer jumped from rope to rope until she found herself on board the pirate ship, surrounded by enemy sailors all with the Frenchman's face.

She'd lost her cutlass, and so she pulled a dagger from her boot and the pistol from her pocket. Her left hand brought the pistol butt down on the enemy's skull as her right hand stuck him forcefully with the blade. Only once did she find herself in trouble, her dagger still stuck in one man as another approached with an axe. Foley appeared and struck the man on the forehead with his cutlass. Emer grabbed the pirate's axe and continued to fight, killing close to ten men by herself, until the brig finally surrendered. Foley ordered his crew back to the ship. Emer walked slowly, feeling a bit dizzy over the dead. One man had a fine patch box on his belt and she squatted to retrieve it.

When she got back to their ship, the crew had already begun to toss the dead overboard and wash down the deck. The pirate brig bobbed dangerously close, and Emer wondered who would sail it. They had lost too many crew. There were barely enough sailors to take the fluyte to Martinique now, let alone sail the new ship behind it.

Foley had disappeared into his quarters, returning with a victory cask of quality rum and three unbloodied sailors. He ordered the men to disengage the fluyte from the brig and drop anchor. After passing a rum-filled ladle through the crew a few times, Foley asked the three men to stand on deck. He fetched a whip.

"These men are cowards," he said. "More than that, they hid while a *woman* fought for them!" The men looked surprised, and Emer tried to hide her face and blend in.

"What am I doing wasting food on your useless bellies?" he asked them.

Some of the crew looked around leeringly. Emer looked at her boots.

"You, woman!" Foley called, "Come here and tell us where you learned to fight so bravely!"

Emer continued to look at her boots. "Woman!" he ordered one last time, and Emer moved slowly through the remaining crew and took her place beside the captain. He handed her the cask of rum and she drank from it. Feeling sick from a mix of approaching drunkenness, embarrassment, fear, and exhaustion, Emer could do nothing but lean wearily on the nearest crate.

"I'll have her first!" a sailor called out. "I'll have her next!" another answered.

Foley banged his fist against the crate and began to scream at his crew. "Shut up, you idiots! She just saved our lives, she did! Have some bloody respect!"

"She didn't save *my* life, sir," someone answered.

"Right. Who said that? You. You in the back there. Come forward." A large man walked forward, still smiling. "Woman, kill him."

Emer still stared at the deck.

"Woman, do as I say."

"Captain, sir. With all due respect, we haven't enough men to sail these two ships to Martinique. I cannot kill crew we still need."

The Captain nodded his head, seeming to agree. Then he pulled a loaded pistol from his waist and shot the man where he stood. The crew fell silent and the three cowards went stiff.

He said to Emer, "You have good sense, but no honor." He turned to the cowards. "You three! Go clean that brig! I want it tip-top, sails and all, by tomorrow morning or you will all join him"—he motioned with his nose—"in Davy Jones's locker. Men! Lower the rowboats. You, you, and you—go with them and make sure they obey my orders.

You!" he barked at the first man who'd suggested having Emer. "Get up that mast. You've got watch tonight while the rest of us drink!"

That night, Captain Foley had to make a tough decision. He knew his ship was no place for Emer. Neither his loyal crew nor his new recruits would be able to resist her during the long journey from Martinique to the Spanish Main—the Spanish-owned coast of the new world of Central and South America. He half thought of leaving her at port, but knew what became of women stranded on small Caribbean islands. They were sold as slaves, worked as whores, or captured by pirates not unlike the shipful she had just helped destroy. There was only one option—to give her the brig and some loyal crew and let her make her own way.

For the next year, Emer sailed around in the *Emerald* looking for answers. Looking for an escape, or a home, or herself. Once, in Jamestown, she overheard two Irish men speaking of their home in a rocky place called Connacht.

"Well, at least it hasn't sunk into the sea," Emer thought, even though she half wished it had.

Her first mate, David, a young Welshman who knew the Caribbean's waters better than most, had been Foley's best officer and friend. It was David who Emer sent ashore to recruit men, and it was he who procured supplies and ammunition. He steered the *Emerald* into ports and familiarized Emer with the arts of navigation and map reading, secretly, by lamplight. As far as any of her crew knew, David was their captain—which was a fair assumption, because they never saw their mysterious leader. She often stayed below deck for days at a time, and only came out in the middle of the night, while they slept.

# .22.

# My Jamaica,
# 328 Years After I Last Saw It

From the moment I stepped off the plane in Montego Bay, my life became a sort of dream world. It was as if I split in two—my body down at the baggage collection area while my eyes watched from the door. My hand paying the taxi driver while my ears listened to the locals speaking patois.

I was frightened of the hordes of people gathered at the roadside, yelling to the taxi man. I was afraid of the erratic and dangerous drivers, the roads pockmarked with huge potholes. I grew so paranoid that I shivered with cold, even in the still, tropical air. Each time the taxi stopped, people approached—selling, begging, singing,

# .21.

# Praying for Wind

The crew are itching for a fight."

The sea had been quiet for nearly two weeks, and the *Emerald* was stuck in the molasses of light air. Not a passing seagull, no porpoises or sharks, just calm, still water and no breeze for fourteen days. Her crew was starving and Emer knew she had to do something about it, but she still hadn't figured out what. She prayed for the wind. She prayed for answers.

"I say, the crew are itching for a fight, *sir*," David said, sipping brandy from a small flask.

Emer continued patching two holes in her trousers and didn't answer.

"They grow bored with the little money they make shipping. Some speak of finding another captain, one who will fight against the Spanish."

"Do they threaten mutiny?" she asked, still concentrating on her sewing.

"The last two ships we met could have paid us all for our troubles."

"I'm no pirate, David. You know that."

"It sure is a waste."

"A waste?"

"A waste of talent," David answered, swigging the last of his brandy.

Emer looked up from her needle. "*This* is talent. How I make perfect stitches and hide them in the hem! How you were able to teach me so many useful things! Good English! Good navigation! *That* is talent!"

"But aren't you bored?"

Emer dismissed him to his quarters. She finished stitching her trousers and placed the needle and thread in a small sewing box and went to bed, thinking about what David had asked her.

Frankly, she *was* bored. She'd accomplished very little in the year she'd sailed the *Emerald*, and she could do worse than become a pirate of the Caribbean in 1661. Surely she could take on any ship and win. What did she have to lose? Seanie was already gone. Her family was already dead.

She called David back into her quarters.

He arrived, half dressed and quite drunk. "Yes, sir."

"You say the crew is bored?"

"Yes, sir."

"And not just because of the wind?"

"No, sir."

"So, what are they complaining about?"

"Well," David stuttered, "well, there are three sailors we recruited in Port Royal. They tell the others tales about Spanish treasure."

"Spanish treasure? What about it?"

"Well, they fancy getting their own ship one day and pirating the waters west of Havana, sir. They say working the *Emerald* will do nothing for their savings, not without taking more passing ships."

"Savings? Sailors with *savings*? I'd like to meet these sailors, David. Bring them to me tomorrow."

"Yes, sir."

"Savings. That's very amusing, don't you think?"

"Yes, sir. Amusing."

Emer opened her sewing box again. She sat up in her bunk and reached for something on the shelf above her. She unfolded the old woolen cape on her lap and inspected its ragged seams and hems. "No point in making something pretty if it's not perfect," she thought, and began fixing a raw edge with her needle.

But something inside her burned when she thought about Spanish treasure. She'd had enough of being poor and desperate. She was sick of rehemming the same old cape. *Maybe it's time I faced the facts*, she said to herself. *Maybe it's time I get what I deserve.*

smiling. Some stood back and glared at me through the window glass.

When I reached my hotel in Negril, a barb-wired compound guarded by men with walkie-talkies, a man showed me to my room. He seemed nice, but as my mouth asked him questions and my hand shook his, my eyes still perched somewhere else, fearing the worst of everything. No one seemed trustworthy. I locked my door and sat on the bed, listening to the squeaky ceiling fan above my head.

I even chickened out of going to dinner in the hotel restaurant and ordered room service. It was as if I had left Emer back in Hollow Ford, just when I needed her most.

I fell asleep early, feeling pathetic and stupid.

But I woke up determined.

After a breakfast of fruit and cocoa bread, I began my journey southeast, heaving my army duffel bag into a snorkeling boat I chartered to take me slowly to the next coastal town. That night, in an attempt to reclaim my courage, I went to a small live reggae show and danced a little. I met two girls there from Ohio who'd just graduated too, and even though we had nothing in common, I hung out with them for a few hours. Emer would have wanted to feed them their own giggly livers, but I still couldn't find her anywhere.

The next day as I ate my fruity breakfast, I looked at the other tourists eating their breakfasts. I imagined feeding the fat guy's eyeball to the skinny urbanite with the Brooklyn accent. I scalped my waitress and tacked her curly hair to the now one-eyed fat guy. If Emer would only show up, she'd think this stuff was hilarious. But she didn't.

When I found a crusty boatman and secured the next

leg of my journey, I imagined stealing the boat from him. I imagined holding his dreadlocked head under the water's surface. How he'd shake and quiver. How the sharks would eat him. Still, no Emer.

Later that day, when Billy's Bay appeared in front of me, I felt her stir in my ribs. I let the boatman pass and then asked him to turn around, so I could see the bay again.

"Can you take me there?" I asked, pointing to the empty beach.

He found the one route to shore between the jagged reefs and stopped the boat. I paid him and he nodded, then he steered the boat out again into the calm sea and headed back west.

I watched him disappear, and felt frozen. I had trusted my nose this far, and had no idea what to do next. I walked toward an arrow-shaped sign advertising a hostel and followed it, uphill on a path that cut through a thick grove of grape trees. When I arrived at the hostel, an adobe-type place built to withstand hurricanes and covered in blooming vines, I met the jovial owner, Hector, who showed me to his only spare room and talked loudly over cranked-up Bob Marley.

"Great view from the balcony," he said, pointing at the sliding doors. "Come down when you're hungry. We can cook up any time of day, mon." He took a loud hit from the enormous spliff in his hand and blew the sweet-smelling smoke from his nose.

"Thanks," I said, looking out to sea, still half frozen with doubt.

"I hope you don't mind good reggae, girl. We love our *roots* here, ya know."

"Yeah, that's fine, thanks," I managed.

When he closed the door, I locked it behind him and sat down on the bed. Every part of me wanted to burst into miserable tears, but instead I emptied my duffel bag on the quilted bedspread and looked at my stuff. I unfolded the army shovel and stared at myself in the mirror again, waiting to catch a glimpse of the woman who'd dragged me here—but all I saw was some skinny kid from Hollow Ford who was fooling herself.

# .23.

# The Bragging of
# Three Clever Sailors

Emer looked the three hungry recruits up and down. "So, you're saving for a ship of your own, then, are you?"

The three men were still adjusting to Emer's breasts—beneath her blouse, but visible for the first time in over a year. They looked over at David as if he had asked the question, but David kept his eyes fixed on his captain.

One man nodded. The other two still looked at David.

"Now, tell me about this 'savings.' I'm sure you lads have plenty of stories about it. Let's hear them."

"We haven't much, um, ma'am."

"Sir. I'm your captain. You call me sir."

"Sir."

"You haven't much compared to what? Compared to us? Compared to the Spanish?"

"We haven't much compared to the price of a ship, sir."

"David says you brag of a spot near Havana—a spot to cruise for Spanish?"

The three men looked at each other, dumbfounded.

"You know, Captain won't hesitate to kill you," David said.

One man piped up. "We followed a small fleet last September."

"West of Havana?" Emer asked.

"About seventy miles southwest, sir."

"And then what?"

"We just followed them. We were working a slave ship. We were on our way to Havana as well."

"A slave ship?"

"Yes, sir."

"Are you as cruel as all that? I don't think you are, somehow."

"We left that ship as soon as we got to Havana, sir. Slaving wasn't for us." The other two men shook their heads in agreement.

"So what of the Spanish fleet?"

"Well, uh, Michael here saw them unloading many crates of gold, sir, and gems."

She turned to Michael. "You saw these gems?"

He nodded.

"Did *you* see the gems?"

The talking man answered. "No, sir. I only knew from Michael about the gems. But I *did* see much gold, and many jeweled rings on the officer's fingers. I don't doubt the fleet is heavy with such things on its way back to Spain."

"How many were there?"

"About fifteen in all. Mostly galleons and frigates. I counted over thirty cannons on a typical galleon, twenty on the frigates."

"Twenty, eh? I'd say that slows them down a bit, carrying so much iron."

"They beat us to port anyway, sir, and we had but a ship of slaves with no guns at all."

Emer shivered. "Enough about slaves. Let's not mention them again."

"Yes, sir."

She sat still and thought for a minute. Fifteen ships, an average of twenty cannons each. That was three hundred guns in total. "Three hundred guns? What a fight that would be! And you think you could take them with a ship your savings can buy? Surely even idiots like you must have a better plan than that."

The man stayed silent and looked back at David.

"Stop looking at David! Your own mouth has put you here, understand! I would have no reason to ask you any of this had it not been for your jabbering."

"We hoped to recruit other ships and form a fleet, sir."

"Go on."

"We hoped to recruit pirates in Port Royal and Roatan. We hoped to get back to Tortuga and find willing buccaneers to join us. So many people here hate the Spanish. We think it will be easy to find them."

Emer tapped her lips with her fingers. "Seventy miles southwest of Havana, eh?"

"Aye, sir."

"And what would I see if I cruised there now?"

"The Spanish bring ships to Havana from Campeche all year long. That's the port a hundred miles southwest of Merida, on the Yucatan, sir." He stopped and looked at Emer, who nodded. "In Campeche we saw seven small fluytes loading with treasure."

"You did?"

"Yes, sir."

She looked each man up and down slowly, then handed them a few gold coins. "Say nothing 'til you hear more, lads."

The men looked at their money and shrugged. David walked with them to the ladder and returned to the doorway. Emer still paced the cabin, looking serious.

"After we get some more supplies, guns, and men, we will go to this Campeche and see what we can see."

"It was generous of you to pay the men for their reports, sir."

Emer laughed. "I didn't pay them for that. I paid them to stay loyal and to shut up. Hell, I didn't believe a word they said but for the slave ship. Tell me, why is it that men who work those infernal ships always look half dead afterward? Could you see it in their eyes, David?" David nodded. He'd seen it. "But the rest? All bullshit, I reckon. Just some story they heard from other sailors on a different ship."

Emer lay down on the small bunk and propped her head on several lumpy pillows. She pulled her cape from under the wooden frame and continued repairing the worn hems at its base. This was as good as a nap. It relaxed her and made her think of her mother.

Her plan to begin sinking Spanish ships southwest of Havana excited her and depressed her. Still lost without Seanie, she knew that gold would never fill the hole his absence had left in her. She had no need for fineries. No want for drink or whores. No knack for gambling. But why not try something new? And the sailor was right— the Spanish needed to be harnessed. They'd taken nearly all of the Caribbean for themselves, and did nothing but spoil the place and make slaves of its people. She would take on a private crusade to send King Philip a message. Finally, she might find a way to rid herself of the bad blood that coursed through her orphaned veins—and finally, she might wreak revenge on a dragon.

There was a knock just before daybreak.

"Captain, a ship to the south has spotted us," David said through the door. "And we've hit wind."

"Tell the men to stand ready," she answered. If for no other reason, she'd have to attack the coming ship for food or else her men would start dropping. Yet she felt fear and revenge deep in her empty belly.

After seventeen days stuck in the light air, the *Emerald* had picked up its pace. The approaching ship flew no flag, and Emer assumed it was the Frenchman. (Every ship that approached, since Emer left Tortuga, was the imaginary Frenchman.) The thought of him made her stomach turn and growl. But now she had a choice other than running.

David lined the gunners up and divided ammunition between them. He made sure the sailors knew which way to tack to get ahead of the wind and knew when to turn. And mostly, he made sure each recruit had a belly full of rum and a stark reminder: if we don't take this ship, we won't eat until we dock again.

Emer arrived as the port cannons fired. Surprisingly, the approaching ship did not fire back but continued heading toward the *Emerald*, on course to ram her. The crew turned the *Emerald* around and fired the starboard guns. Emer aimed a long-barreled musket and fired. She continued this until the boats met with a mighty crash, and then pulled the sharp cutlass from her waist and began to butcher.

Men piled onto the ship. At first, it looked like her crew would be badly outnumbered, but Emer soon realized that the men coming aboard knew little about fighting. Some didn't even have weapons. Emer injured three in her first strike, by holding her blade horizontally and spinning around, slashing an eye, two ears, and a neck. All three men fell to the deck and screamed for help.

Her men were having a similarly easy time in the brawl. Some even had enough time to stop and mutilate their adversary before moving on to the next one. Emer continued to drop one man after another, looking around when she could for their leader. What captain would send weak, untrained men into such a battle? For what reason? Emer feared she knew that reason. She feared that *she* was the reason. She could almost smell the French bastard where she stood.

The battle took less than an hour. David ordered the men onto the ship to fetch food and find its captain. Emer watched from the forecastle. When the men returned with no captain and no food, David looked to Emer for instructions. She rose and walked to the ropes, boarded the ship, and returned five minutes later with a crate.

The men stood on deck, still surrounded by dead and dying sailors, passing a bucket of rum around. "It's not without regret when I tell you there was no food on board," she said. The men noted Emer's voice and her tapered waistline. Had the three bragging sailors been telling the truth that morning? Was their captain really a woman?

"But I want you to take a good look at this," Emer said, kicking the crate out toward the men. "From now on, *this* will be our cargo! *This* will be our reward!"

When no men approached the crate, but instead stood gawking at her sweat-drenched figure, Emer bent down and opened it. David reached in with both hands and pulled an array of jewels and gold trinkets out. A string of pearls emptied onto the deck and rolled under the crew's feet, scattering. Then the men began to cheer, one by one. A sailor threw his hat in the air. Another hugged the man next to him. Another jumped up and down all by himself, feeling the rum sloshing round his very empty belly. They would be rich. They would be famous. They would be respected.

All of a sudden, there was a rush for the pearls. Nearly

every man was on his knees, snatching as many as he could. One man threw himself down on top of ten or more, searching with his one hand under him. Another stepped on hands that tried to reach out. Another punched a sailor for stealing what he claimed was his.

Emer stopped the melee by firing her pistol. She ordered the men to attention.

"Why are you squabbling over tiny pearls, men? Are you not savvy? We'll divide this cache as we would any other—each of us getting our share."

One man called out, "I want my share now!"

"Dewey has four, sir! He's not allowed four if I can't have one!"

Emer looked at her crew and saw children. So she did what any fair mother would do. She made the men return all the pearls, and then gave one to each crew member to keep for the night, to exchange later for his fair share. This arrangement seemed to make the crew happy, and allowed them to get back to work and move the ship closer to the Cayman Islands—where an imagined feast awaited them.

Emer walked to her quarters and met David, who had moved the crate there and emptied it onto her bunk. They marveled.

"A ship full of starving men, David. That's all they were."

"*Rich* starving men," he corrected her. He winked and walked from the room, still rolling a small pearl between his finger and thumb.

Emer was alone with her first pile of treasure. At first, she stared. Then, she laughed so hard she cried. Then, she bolted the door and undressed down to her knickers, rolled herself on top of the jewels, and fell into a rum-induced nap.

# .24.

# A Year of Many Treasures

Before docking the *Emerald* at the Caymans, Emer gathered her men on deck. "Any man who brags of booty will be left behind to find a new captain. Is that clear?" Most of the men nodded in agreement. She motioned to David and he began giving each man a handful of silver in exchange for their single pearl. "This is for tonight. Tomorrow you'll each receive your full share."

Once the crew was gone, Emer and David lifted the crate and headed toward the town's market. After finding a trader giving a fair price for their jewels, they returned to the ship to lighten their large load of coin. Emer had purchased a sack of fruit and two fully cooked fowl, and stayed on board to relieve the three starving men she'd left to guard the ship. Three hours later, David returned, allowing her to go on her own shopping trip.

After buying enough supplies for their scouting journey to Campeche on the Spanish Main, and directing the shipments to the dock, Emer found two small shops. The first was a clothier, a fine clothier who sold many great garments. She bought two cotton blouses, several sets of knickers, a pair of wide-legged trousers and a rather fancy hat. She looked over his selection of capes and chose two. Both black, one only inches longer than the other, they were perfectly plain and ready for embroidering. On an adjacent back street, Emer found a man who sold all types of thread and fabric. She bought two bunches of every color he offered, several packets of tint, a ground bark that would darken the shade of the thread, and three more needles.

On her way back to the boat, she stopped outside the tavern and listened to her men singing drunken songs, then headed back to the dock. David had tidied the ship and done inventory. They would be ready to go once they sold the captured brig and restocked their ammunition in the morning.

"Do you think the men will object to leaving tomorrow?" Emer asked.

David shrugged. "They'll do what we tell 'em. They're loyal."

"I'm afraid I don't trust any of them." Emer poured them both a mug of strong Cayman rum. "I reckon I only trust you."

"Well, that's a start."

They sat on deck together and watched the stars appear,

drinking for an hour until David leaned his head on Emer's shoulder and breathed loudly. "You know, we would make a good pair."

Emer laughed. "I think you'll need to go ashore for that, David."

"Admit it!" he said, rubbing his stubbly jaw. "We would!"

She looked at him. His eyes were bright blue, with long lashes, and he had lines round his mouth from smiling and the sun. His arms were strong and his hands were rough from a lifetime of hard work. He kept his dirty-blond hair tied in a tail down his back, and was usually clean-shaven. He was as handsome as Seanie—but he wasn't Seanie.

"Maybe in another time and place, but not here, friend. Here, we're comrades. That's all."

"You must crave a man after so long at sea! You aren't made of glass, are you?"

Emer stopped laughing and felt sad.

"Are you?" David pressed.

She sat up straight and tried to look serious. David noticed this and did the same, looking into her eyes and squinting drunkenly.

"I do crave a man, David. I crave one man. A man I probably won't see again," she said. "But I love him still."

David was silent.

"You think I'm daft, don't you?" Emer asked. "You think I'm stupid."

"No. I think it's sweet. It's sad, I reckon. You're a beautiful woman, you know, and it's sad that you wait for a man you'll never have."

"I might," Emer defended herself. "I might go back and

find him. That's what I'll do one day. He'll most likely be married by now, but—"

David interrupted. "Then why do you taunt yourself?"

"I can't help it. I just do." Emer folded her hands in her lap and looked at them. "Now, you tell me your story— then we'll decide which of us is worse off!"

David said, "I've never met a woman I've loved. I've never had a specific woman in mind. Just a quiet life, tending my land with a warm woman in my bed, is all."

"That's all? You never had one woman you dreamed of?"

"Not until I met you, no." David looked at her softly.

"Oh David, I can't be the warm woman in your bed! What would the men think?"

"The men wouldn't have to know."

"The men *would* know, and besides, I just told you that story. It wouldn't be fair. I would always be thinking of Seanie, and you would be fooling yourself."

"Who's fooling herself? You'd rather have an imaginary man than a real one? You should just face the facts, woman, and move on! This fellow. He's not here, is he?"

They worked to stand up and steady themselves.

"This is your only chance, sir, to have me," David slurred. "I'll never mention it again."

"See? You call me sir! What type of love affair would we have?" Emer giggled.

"No more impossible than your Irish boy coming to find you. You should forget him anyway, whether or not you choose to accept my offer. For your own good."

He made his way down the plank to the dock and walked in the direction of loud drunken sailors, leaving his last words echoing in Emer's ears.

Two months later, the *Emerald* docked in Campeche. Emer sent David to the shipwright to arrange repairs to the hull and a full careening, and gave strict orders to her crew to stay quiet and act like modest sailors—an order they had no trouble obeying once the whole lot of them became ill from a feast of bad shellfish. Most of the week was spent vomiting rather than drinking.

Emer found a small room in a tavern where she could watch Campeche's dock. The three recruits had been right. The town was busy each day with ships loading and unloading precious cargo collected from tribes of the new world beyond the Main. As she sat in a plush chair by her window, embroidering, she observed Campeche's people. African slaves were abundant, their white eyes and bare pink feet a contrast to the wealthy men in buckled shoes. These rich men lived in numbers here, larger numbers than Emer had ever seen.

Twice she watched as the governor of the town, a man of many rings and medals, came to the dock to inspect crates of pearls, gems, and gold. Something changed when she fixed her eyes on her first large sapphire. It was the size of a small apple and sparkled like nothing she'd seen before, making her squint through the lens of her scope. As she watched the governor cup it in his soft Spanish hands and imagined stealing it from him, she asked herself, "Why waste any more time coveting a long-lost Seanie Carroll when I could actually *have* things like this? If I have no option to be happy and good, then why not be as bad as I can be?"

When the ship was repaired, supplies were loaded and the crew was summoned from the small village. The *Emerald* set sail for Havana. They anchored about a hundred miles southwest and waited to rob ships traveling from the Spanish Main—which is exactly what she did for the next year.

A ship came every week, sometimes twice a week, toward Havana, the last stop before the long journey back to Europe. The ships were usually loaded with luxury items intended for King Philip, which Emer and her crew would pillage after a bloody battle. Deciding that reputation was paramount if she was eventually to become a feared and famous pirate, Emer began a quest to find her trademark. Some pirates etched their initials into the backs of victims, some liberated ears and tongues. Some disemboweled or hung or keelhauled, and she'd heard of a man who would feed his victims parts of their own sinew and flesh. Emer tried a few of these things, and eventually found that she enjoyed ripping an eye from the men she killed. Especially the men who'd glared at her body. It was a way to remind them to never underestimate a woman, she figured. One less eye to ogle with.

Over that year, they plundered nearly sixty ships and returned to port only when they needed supplies or crew. In the Caymans, she traded the *Emerald* for a 150-ton frigate christened the *Vera Cruz*. Twice they visited Port Royal and sampled its famous rum and wickedness. They were safest in Tortuga, though, where they cashed their booty in what had become a bustling, well-stocked pirate haven. Emer hated being there. It reminded her of Paris, her useless coins, and her worthless virginity. But after a year of ripping eyeballs out of Spanish officers, it was best to stay secure.

The captain's quarters on the *Vera Cruz* were spacious. Emer had room to twirl around in her capes, to practice her jousting, and to find new sexual positions with David—who, after their last year at sea, had convinced Emer that this was the most obvious solution to their problems. Emer figured it was either that or embroidery, and stitching could be tedious at times.

"You understand, David, that I cannot love you?" she asked.

"It's not love either of us is after, I reckon," he answered.

"I just want you warned, is all."

"Consider me warned," he said, though he'd been lying. How could he not love her? She was the most amazing woman he'd ever met, even if she was ten years his junior, as young as his youngest sister back home in Wales.

In that year at sea, plundering ships southwest of Havana, Emer made seven capes. Her first two were dedicated to her mother. They had Celtic crosses, two feet high, in green and red thread. Each cross was a maze of tiny, decorative knots, hundreds of thousands of them. But they were mere practice pieces, reminders of the days when a thin-haired five-year-old demanded things she couldn't have.

As Emer stitched these pieces, she practiced the art

of sea battle. Never too much double shot, or you'd sink the whole lot to the bottom. She taught her marines new strategies and shared her memories of Oliver's Roundheads to show how fast, loud action can stop the bravest of men in their tracks. As she sewed, she prepared for future misfortune by slipping gems into the lower hems. In her first cape, with the green cross, she included several tiny pearls from her very first take. In the second, she sewed her first cut stones, a dozen pink rubies.

Her next cape was Spanish colored—red, orange, peach, and lemon—with an image of a crimson dragon breathing fire. It didn't disturb her anymore, the sight of a dragon. They surrounded her on this hunting ground—Spanish dragons in each direction and her own, tied in knots, in the belly of her memory. She added opals and emeralds in the hems, sewing each jewel in place with a pair of minute red stitches.

Her fourth cape was an experiment: bright blue wildflowers intertwined with lightning bolts and skeletons, each bone a hundred stitches at least. She made this one as a penance. Sure, these were Spanish bastards who'd just killed, raped, and enslaved natives to pilfer their gold, but they were flesh and blood, too. No amount of praying would cleanse the shipful of sins she carried. To further clear her conscience, she didn't sew any booty into this cape, because it seemed insincere.

Her fifth and sixth capes were quite like the third: Spanish colors and fire-breathing beasts. But instead of confining the embroidered image to the back of the cape, Emer tried something new. She stitched right round the garment with licks of fire, covering three quarters of the wool with tiny specks of flashy thread and finishing the edges with blood-red knot work. She added extra knots after battles, one for each man she killed. These capes were longer than the others, extending past the knee with a mix of tassel work and fancy pleated edging. Emer had a difficult time choosing what to hide in them. Her treasure chests in the captain's quarters were stuffed. She finally decided on diamonds. And since she was growing more paranoid, she decided also to sew the precious gems into each seam along the main body of the garment as well as into the hems. This made these capes not only the most beautiful, but also the most valuable.

Emer took a break from stitching during the late summer of 1662, and began work on her seventh cape as autumn approached with its hard storms and lethal winds. This was another long cape, falling just below the knee. The evil design had come to her after a bloody sunset battle with a Spanish privateer. The top of the cape would resemble a sky at sunset, the rays jutting from a large red fireball. The bottom would picture a thousand dead men, legs and boots in the air. Tiny legs and boots specked with red stitches, protruding swords, and detached heads and eyeballs. Thousands of eyeballs. Another dragon breathing fire, white-hot specks of breath overpowering the sunrays, red drips of blood down its jaws.

She had scored a small sack full of blackberry-sized sapphires from her last plunder. She sewed these, along with the rest of her stash of diamonds, into every cranny of the cape's soft black lining.

Emer wore her frightful cape everywhere she went. By this time, she and her crew had become infamous. Just the sight of the *Vera Cruz* forced large vessels to surrender or tack quickly in the opposite direction, which ensured a chase. And yet no one seemed to be searching for them, the way other famous pirates were hounded and hunted by patrol boats and privateers. Emer became cocky, viewing the enemy as one big stupid man—unable to see her at all because she was a woman.

Twice, when a large Spanish fleet had passed them on its way to Havana, they disguised the *Vera Cruz* as an English patrol frigate. Emer called her officers to the deck and put on her best pirate voice.

"What does a pinnace offer us now, me lads? What fun be sacking surrendered ships? Is this not *our sea? Our turf?* Let us soon capture that fleet, says I! Let us finally get what we come for!"

The prosperity of the past year, and the ease of each battle the *Vera Cruz* fought, had made her lazy. She forgot about once being poor and hungry, and forgot about her lifetime of running—as if each jewel she robbed erased a same-sized portion of her memory. She stopped joining David in daily officers' chores and instead spent most of her time sleeping. Which was exactly how the Frenchman would find her, two weeks later.

# .25.

# Fred Livingstone's Head

After Winston revved up the old pickup truck and sped off to the airport, Fred Livingstone was alone again. He preferred it that way. Once accustomed to gala balls and posh parties, Fred could now barely make a trip to the bank in Black River without panicking.

He rose late the next morning—after eleven—still thinking about his perfect bikini girl. His head played tricks on him. In the shower, under the slow trickle the local water supply allowed, he closed his eyes and tried to see her, but saw other things instead. He saw Winston in a coral-colored thong, then naked on a coral-colored bed-spread. He opened his eyes and shook the image out of his head and tried again. This time it was Mother in a coral bikini, sitting on his bed crying. So Fred just opened his eyes and hummed until he was dried, dressed, and ready for the bank. He fetched the folders he needed from the safe and went to his office window.

He heard Rusty whining somewhere downstairs, but ignored him. He spun his chair to face away from the million-dollar view and closed his eyes again.

"Join me for lunch today," he started.

She smiled at him, then morphed into his mother. He opened his eyes, shook his head, then closed them again.

"How about one o'clock? The Island Hotel?"

*But you have to go to Black River, Fred. You have to get to the bank.*

Fred waved off the idea with his hand. "I can go to the bank tomorrow."

*You've put it off long enough, don't you think?* his mother said.

"Mum?"

*Yes? What?*

*Wow, Fred, you must have really lost it now.*

"Shut up."

*Can't see any women in your head but a dead one, eh?*

*Fredrick, what are you doing? Are you telling me to shut up?*

"Shut up! All of you!"

Fred opened his eyes, but his mother still spoke. *She's not* our *type. You won't find a Livingstone sort of woman in this bloody place, I told you.*

"I said shut up!" Fred screamed, and Rusty stopped

whining at the front door. "Well, if I have to go to the bank, I'd better have a drink first for my nerves."

*That's good, Fred. Don't think about that stupid girl anymore!*

He fixed a drink and sat down again, facing the beach.

*You have to do something about this, Fred. Something* must *be done.*

"I know."

*You have to do it* today. *You can't go banging that Jamaican anymore and thinking it's normal. It's not. There are cures for these things.*

*Oh yes!* his mother echoed, sitting naked in a coral Rolls Royce parked on the beach. *There are ways to get rid of such unspeakable thoughts.*

*You should go see a shrink.*

*Oh no!* his mother said. *No professionals necessary! Fredrick, just come to the club with me on Saturday and you'll have your pick of lovely, well-bred daughters. I promise you. They'll* be *dying* to meet you!

"Shut up! All of you! Shut up!"

After two more drinks, Fred felt numb enough to begin the journey to Black River. He gathered his things and went downstairs. When he opened the door, Rusty raced past him to pee on the nearest flowerpot. Fred tried to order the dog back inside, but Rusty was already in the vegetation so Fred closed the door and left. "Starve for all I care," he said.

He drove the single-lane road out of Billy's Bay slowly,

daydreaming about finding the bikini girl. As he drove past a row of cheap hostels, he scanned the porch railings for a glimpse of coral. He saw nothing but drying beach towels, so he drove on, muttering about finding the girl and teaching her manners. As he approached the large market town a half hour later, he felt pensive.

He found a parking space near the bank and gathered his things from the passenger's seat. Walking slowly, trying not to seem as paranoid as he was, Fred made his way to the bank while looking at the concrete beneath his feet. "She can't hide from me," he muttered. "I own this place."

He reached the double glass doors and slid through them into the air-conditioned foyer, quickly passing an armed guard on his way to the manager. "I'll teach her a lesson someone should have taught her years ago."

The next thing he knew he was falling backward, grasping all of his papers to his chest, trying to see what had just hit him. When he looked up from the polished granite floor, he saw a beautiful young tourist rubbing her forehead and scowling at him. The jolt had shifted her white T-shirt only slightly, but enough to reveal a small portion of the coral pink bikini strap hugging her shoulder.

# .26.

# How I Found Emer at the Bank

Hector, the owner of the hostel, let me eat from his kitchen and put it on a tab because he knew I was nearly out of cash. There were three others staying at the house, a guy from Australia (who I never saw due to his energetic sightseeing), and a couple from Berlin (who only spoke German and had an annoying habit of laughing too loudly).

That first night in Billy's Bay, I stayed in my room feeling sorry for myself while I unpacked. I put my shampoo in the shower, my toothpaste on the sink. I sorted through the now-wrinkled mix of clean and dirty clothing from my army bag and put the clean ones in the dresser in the room.

I pulled out my little purse and counted my traveler's checks. I made a small note of how many I had left on the envelope that held my return tickets. I unfolded and refolded my father's shovel a few times. I tried to feel excited, but I couldn't even leave the room. As I was attempting to fall asleep, the Germans laughed and laughed in the next room.

"Where are you?" I asked Emer, again.

She didn't answer, so I skinned them sloppily just to spite her.

The next morning, I took a walk up and down the beach. It was wider now than it used to be, fifty extra yards at low tide. The beach I remembered was rockier, and covered in thick vegetation. Now it stood in a mixed state of erosion. They'd removed many trees, and then piled tons of extra sand to cure what they'd caused. The few homes that scattered the coast were set back into the remaining trees. Some had walls around long, well-groomed gardens that led onto the beach, and some had no barriers at all but groves of sea grape trees.

I walked until I found the village Hector had told me about. It wasn't really a village—it was two tourist shops and a few beach-side food huts. In the short time I sat eating a plate of jerk chicken, three different women approached me aggressively, with their hands covered in aloe, commenting on my fair skin and my sunburn. Each time, I flinched and asked them to stop. It took me five minutes to explain to the last one that I didn't owe her twenty dollars. I tried to stuff hot chicken wings up her nose and shove a boiled eel down her throat, but it was just no fun without Emer.

I returned to Billy's Bay and spent the rest of day pacing the beach. It seemed simple. An even hundred paces from the rocky head on the western point led me to a grove of trees. Another hundred paces brought me past the trees to a glass mansion, half covered in blooming bougainvillea. My fortune lay between those two points—within those hundred yards—at the base of an incline.

As I walked, I tried to remember things that were long dead and gone with Emer Morrisey. I saw Seanie in my mind, lying dead on the beach, and my stomach tightened. I paced the length, one hundred fifty paces exactly, and searched the tree line before me. I would have to get closer to find what I was looking for.

I wasn't five minutes into my walk the next morning when a jumpy Doberman approached me and a man appeared on the deck of the glass house. When I first saw him I got an awful rush of adrenaline, the way I do when someone cuts in line or a Quiz Bowl match is about to start. And when he waved I felt threatened somehow, as if he were some sort of bad omen. The dog was great. I've always liked Dobermans (having lived as one twice, I have insight into their goofy, loving nature). It was the man who worried me—especially now that I'd paced enough to know that my treasure was somewhere near his house.

As I walked homeward along the beach that night, the

huge orange sun dipped lower and lower into the horizon. It was a moment I can't explain. Emer flickered inside me, and I longed for what she longed for. She ordered me to take a sunset swim, so I did, and it was like wrapping myself in a warm blanket of familiarity—even though I'd never once swum in an ocean as Saffron Adams.

Hector and I left for Black River early the next day. He dropped me in the center of the morning market and gave me two hours to check it out. I figured there was ample time to get to the bank and get a few things, so I pointed to a meeting place on the opposite side of the one-way road, and he sped off.

The market was loud and it smelled of day-old fruit and damp cardboard. There were busy Jamaicans moving tall stacks of pallets from stall to stall and women yelling at me from behind their goods, announcing the discount they would give and suggesting I try on their hats and jewelry. I continued toward the town center and crossed over a wide bridge. The river was crammed with boats carrying tourists, fishermen, and children, and the water had a thin layer of gas on the surface that shone like mother of pearl.

No sooner had I arrived at the bank and felt the relief of the air-conditioning than this old guy, rushing in the opposite door, walked right into me and nearly knocked me over.

He looked up at me from the floor. "My apologies," he said in an English accent. "I'm very sorry."

I bent over a little, covering my face, and rubbed the intense pain on my head where his chin had hit me. Then Emer Morrisey came alive and I got instant goose bumps.

He scrambled to get up. "Completely my fault," he said. "I wasn't looking where I was going."

I was still rubbing my head, which was starting to throb. "Okay."

I got in line and looked over at him periodically. He looked like somebody I knew. I figured I'd seen him in the village, or maybe I'd just seen him on the street and it hadn't registered.

It wasn't until we met again, less violently, on our way out, that I realized who he was.

"Do you need a lift back to Billy's Bay?" he asked.

"Huh?"

"Would you like a lift?" he said, annoyingly louder.

I squinted at him, confused.

He smiled and nodded, then stuck out his right hand. "We should start again. My name is Fred. Livingstone. We saw each other yesterday on the beach, remember?"

I squinted harder, until he did a lame reenactment of his wave. "Oh. Right. The glass place."

"And you are?"

"On vacation?" I said hesitantly.

He didn't like that. "Are you sure I can't give you a lift?"

"No thanks. I have one." I had an overwhelming urge to carve my initials into his back.

"How about dinner tonight?"

"No, thanks," I said. I wanted to rub salt into the *S*, into the *A*.

"Oh. Well. I'll see you later then," he stuttered, and left quickly.

My whole body felt cold and nervous, like it did when I saw Junior on the road on prom night. Did an old guy like that really want to take me to dinner? How did he recognize me after only seeing me from a hundred yards away?

And why did I feel like Emer was back now, twice as strong as she ever was, commanding me to kill him on the spot?

# DOG FACT #6
*Bad Habits*

Your dog is capable of doing some pretty awful stuff. It's up to you to maintain consistent affection, training, and discipline in order to prevent your dog from doing awful stuff. However, sometimes this is not enough. Some dogs are just born bad.

I've done it all. I've bitten letter carriers and chased cars and tractors and bicycles and tanks. I've worried more sheep than a shepherd can count. I've chewed on everything, from homework to framework to the family cat. I've even fought and killed my own.

Back in 1958, I was a pit bull terrier bred by an alcoholic ex-con who called himself "The Master." He was one of those in-and-out-of-prison guys who came to crave the systematic abuse he'd been a victim of his whole life.

When the Master brought me home to his rundown wood-shingled house, I was nine weeks old. He threw me into a filthy coop where the only other occupant was an aggressive Jack Russell who was always injured. A few times per week, the Jack was pulled from the cage and taken to the barn for an hour, and then deposited back in the cage, bleeding, missing lumps of skin and hair, and soaked with urine. Once he had healed and felt a little better he'd nip at me, and that made me mad. It made me mad enough that at two months old, I nipped back and took the little twerp's ear off.

The Master began "training" me then—starving me, beating me, chaining me, and teasing me. Twice he stood me on a concrete pad an inch deep in water and ran electricity through it, making me jump and howl. Sometimes he would shoot me with his BB gun all afternoon and then spray me with salt water. And other times, he would throw me, hungry, into a ring with a drugged rabbit or cat and I'd tear it to pieces.

One week when I was still a pup, I was brought to watch some older dogs fight at a neighbor's barn. The Master invited a bunch of his friends because they liked to drink beer, bet, and watch dogs kill each other. Before the real action started, they had a "warm up." It took two minutes for my sire, a two-year-old pit bull terrier champion, to kill my old cage mate, the Jack. They'd muzzled the Jack with a few strips of duct tape and he never had a chance. This was my destiny, the Master said. I was to follow in the footsteps of my father and make him lots and lots of money, which is exactly what happened.

I kept winning and winning, and he kept betting and betting, until I'd killed at least a hundred dogs. Some had their snouts tied shut or their teeth pulled out. Some were already so injured by the time they got to me that I couldn't figure out how they could call it a *fight*, but I fought anyway.

Fact was, I knew it was wrong. But once my canine-self got accustomed to life as a killer, I just couldn't stop. When they busted the Master two years later, they found me—crazy with rage—tied with a short tow chain, ribs showing, and they couldn't get near me without landing two tranquilizer darts in me first. Then, they put me to sleep on the spot.

Your dog doesn't have to be a killer to be dangerous. A

nip leads to a bite. And regrettably, biters are rarely cured. You need to be responsible for what your dog does, and this requires serious consideration. As hard as it is to face the act of euthanizing a pet, think about how much doggie prisons would cost. Aren't we feeding enough incurable scoundrels already? 🐾

# Part
# THREE

*What great things would you attempt*
*if you knew you could not fail?*

ROBERT H. SCHULLER

# .27.

# The Toll of Darkness and Light

As the *Vera Cruz* neared a port on the westernmost island of the Bahamas, Emer's crew didn't notice the three men standing on the dock with loaded pistols. The ship was in need of serious repair—her sails perforated by Spanish chain shot and her hull covered in thick sea growth that made her move too slowly through the calm water. The men worked to steer the ship in, secure it, and then reported to David that they had landed successfully.

David crept silently from the cabin, leaving Emer to catch up on rest she surely had missed the night before. When he approached the gangplank, the three men began to walk toward him. He could sense they were trouble.

"Who are you?" David asked.

"I'm the new governor here. This is my friend Mr. Thomson." The third man stood behind the other two, running his fingers through his thick black hair.

"What do ye want?" David asked.

"Are you the captain of this ship?"

David stared.

"Are you the captain of this ship?" the governor repeated.

The other two men began to walk toward David, and he held out his arms so they were unable to pass.

"We have serious business with your captain."

"Let me fetch him for you," David offered, but the men pushed past him and walked toward the ship.

Emer was dragged out of her cabin, up the ladder, and out to the deck. She'd managed to dress herself in a long-sleeved nightdress, and David was relieved.

As the two men pushed her down the plank, the governor leaned down toward Emer's ear. "What's your name, woman?" he whispered. Emer told him, feeling defeated. All that killing, and still nameless. Surely a man guilty of the same horrors would have his name in history books already.

The governor spoke loudly so that the entire crew could hear him. "Emer Morrisey, you are under arrest on this tenth day of March, 1663, for piracy and murder! You shall be tried, and then you will hang from our gallows where many other scoundrels have suffered the same fate. To these accusations how do you plead?"

Emer wrestled with the two men. One tied her hands behind her back with thick hemp rope while the other tried to keep her from jumping off the gangplank.

"Woman! How do you plead?"

The two men pushed her to the base of the plank and onto the dock. The governor asked again, "How do you plead?"

When she didn't answer, the man with the black bushy hair leaned toward her. He whispered something in her ear and she spat at him. He turned to the governor and said something, softly, and they started back toward the town, Emer stumbling behind, tugged by her bound hands. David followed, all the while looking at Emer's face and trying to gain some sort of idea, any idea, of what to do. She looked genuinely terrified, and said only one thing he could understand before the three men put her onto the back of a cart and took off.

She said, "French bastard!"

The small prison smelled like death—a mix of shit and sweat, gangrene, vomit and fear. Emer was locked in a cell by herself, the only light a reflection from above where one small window, too skinny for escape, graced the stone wall. She could hear nothing but the muffled sounds of the village outside and the few other prisoners moaning.

When David came to see the governor to plead for her freedom, at the risk of his own, he was sent away before he had a chance to speak.

"Do I look like a stupid man to you?" the governor asked. "I know who that *is* down there."

"But—"

David was ushered out by the Frenchman, who smiled

at him the whole way and spoke only when he reached the door. "She's mine," he said. "Forget about her."

Two days passed before anyone came to see Emer. She'd been given no food or water, and had lapsed into a determined trance. She sat cross-legged with her arms folded in her lap, refusing to lie down in the filth. She prayed a little, but knew that no matter how hard she prayed, the Frenchman would return and she would have to endure him. When she heard footsteps outside her cell door, she tensed and readied her body for what was about to happen.

But he only reached in and grabbed her by the hair, pulling until she finally regained enough balance in her numb legs to walk behind him. Before they came to the prison exit, the Frenchman pulled two wrist cuffs from his pocket, twirled them on his fingers, and fastened them tightly around her. He straightened her hair with his greasy hand and caressed her left cheek.

"We meet again, my little Irish girl. This time you will not run away, I assure you."

He walked her upstairs to the governor's small office and stood her in front of him. She shivered in her own sweat, looking pathetic, and felt a louse crawl in her hairline.

The governor was a slender man, too skinny (Connacht skinny in Emer's eyes), with a pointed face and large ears. He wore an excessive amount of jewelry for a man, and a ruffled blouse with an enormous collar.

"Do you admit, now, to the charge of murder, woman?" he asked, spreading his ringed fingers before him, tapping his fingertips. "Are you hungry enough?"

Emer thought about this for a few seconds and nodded her head. Hungry or not, she wasn't ashamed of murder anymore.

"Can you not speak?"

"She has little English," the Frenchman offered.

"Are you an ignorant, then?"

Emer stretched her shoulders and made a clinking sound with the cuffs.

The governor turned to the Frenchman, laughing. "Some good she'll do you as a wife, man! How will she know what you want for your dinner?"

Emer eyed two sweet pastries on the governor's desk. "Do you want these?" he asked her.

"When is my trial?" she asked.

The governor looked over to the Frenchman, raised his eyebrows, and shrugged.

"Two weeks," the Frenchman said.

"Two weeks," the governor said.

"Can I go back to my cell now?"

"I don't see why not," the governor answered, looking to the Frenchman for clues. "Would you like to take her back?"

He grabbed her roughly and walked her back to the prison below. When they reached the entrance, he left the cuffs on her and ran his hands over her body, stopping twice at her bosom and once at her bottom, where he squeezed her and left bruises. "God, you stink, woman," he said. "We'll have to wash you before you board my ship."

"I'll be swinging in two weeks," Emer said, "so you had best get your fill of me while I'm alive."

"Oh, you silly girl!" He unlocked her cuffs and kicked

her into the tiny cell and locked the door. "You still don't understand anything, do you?"

Emer sat in her cell for two weeks. Once a day they brought a bucket, a handful of dirty animal fat, and a small cup of sour water. She spent her time thinking about everything—the Frenchman, the governor, the prison, but mostly about David and her crew. Had they taken her share and gone back to the cruising ground?

What had the Frenchman meant when he'd called her a "silly girl"? She'd seen how the governor relied on him. She'd seen how the Frenchman seemed to be the one in charge. Would he steal her now and finally make her his slave? She thought about killing him.

Four weeks later, she'd seen no one but the guard who brought her food and water. Two months later, she took to sobbing at night, wondering what would become of her life. Four months after that, she made a plan to bribe the judge and governor. Six months passed, then eight months.

Ten months since her capture, and Emer still sat cross-legged in the small cell. She'd lost so much weight and energy that she could hardly do more than sleep. Her legs suffered from a lack of circulation and one of her toes had begun to rot. The stink was unbearable—a sort of inner stench, which she could taste in the back of her throat—and she wondered if she'd live long enough to hang at all.

One day she heard more than a single set of footsteps approaching her cell at feeding time, and two voices mumbling to each other. The Frenchman took one look at Emer, gasped, and turned to the prison keeper.

"What the hell have you *done* to her? You damned idiot! She's nearly dead!" He stormed back toward the stairway and up the steps. Emer could hear him cursing and yelling the whole way, saying things like, "She's no good to me now! How would you like it if I killed *your* woman?"

She sat very still and put her hands to her face. Bones jutted from every angle and her eyes blinked uncontrollably. Did she really look as bad as she felt? As bad as she smelled?

When the Frenchman returned, he carried two blankets. He unlocked the cell and helped Emer crawl out. Her limp leg dragged behind and embarrassed her, but he didn't seem to notice. She felt nothing in one foot below the ankle, and her muscles were so weak she couldn't move from exhaustion. The Frenchman wrapped the blankets around her and picked her up like a small child. Only then could Emer feel how weightless she'd grown. In the light of the stairway could she see her legs—skinnier than any in Connacht, not to mention a lot more discolored. Emer had gone green and yellow—not just on her feet but everywhere. Just a glimpse made her head flop down, and she went unconscious.

When she awoke in the governor's office, she was alone. Since she was too weak to escape, they hadn't handcuffed her or tied her to any furniture. On the desk, there was a plate of fruit and a large washing bowl of water. She heard quarrelling in the next room.

"You wanted her imprisoned. I did what you wanted."

"I didn't want her dead."

"If you wanted her healthy and strong, why didn't you take her with you?"

"You fool! You brainless idiot!"

"What did you expect from me? It's not my fault she was left for nearly a year!"

"You could have given her more to eat! You could have let her walk a bit."

"I have no say in what they feed the scum down there. And I most certainly took your orders seriously when you said not to let another man touch her. Did you think I could do that if I was parading her around the prison at the same time? You told me to keep her safe. I kept her safe. She's not dead. You can have her now. There's nothing so wrong with her that food can't cure."

Emer heard movement and a loud slap. "Not *dead?* You come with me. Come look at this ... this ... *thing!*" The door of the office swung open and the two men entered. The Frenchman pointed. "Look at *this*. This is *not* a woman! This is a ghost, Robert! You have given me a ghost for all my trouble! We had a deal—*this* was no part of that deal."

"I said I would make sure she was here when you returned. She *is* here, is she not?"

The Frenchman pulled a loaded pistol from his waist and pointed it at the governor's left leg. "I'll have that map back now, and those rings."

"Don't be ridiculous."

The Frenchman fired the pistol, and the governor fell onto his desk in agony. "The map," the Frenchman said, holding his left hand out, palm up.

The governor reached into his desk and grabbed a rolled map. He handed it to the Frenchman, and when he did, the Frenchman peeled the rings from his fingers. He picked Emer up and walked through the door, gently so she wouldn't hit her head.

When they were free of the stone building, the sun beat down on Emer's dying body and her head went limp. The Frenchman hurried to the dock, up the gangplank of his own frigate, the *Chester*, and screamed for the ship's doctor. His first mate, the man Emer had once thought was his servant, reached out to help steady his captain.

"Hurry! The woman is dying!" the Frenchman cried. Emer lost consciousness again, puzzled at the irony that surrounded her—puzzled about how she should feel about her rescue—puzzled about what would become of her if she lived.

# .28.

# Fred Livingstone's Bottom Drawer

Fred Livingstone inspected his chin in the rearview mirror.

"That bitch," he said, rubbing the red mark where he'd collided with the head of his beautiful bikini girl.

*You certainly made a mess of that, Fred.*

"Shut up."

*You looked like a creep.*

"Just shut up."

*You should watch where you're going, Fred. You never know who you'll bump into.*

"You think this is funny then, do you?"

*It is funny.*

"Just shut up," Fred answered, and he turned on the radio.

He drove home and parked the car in the garage, went quickly to the bar in his office, and inspected his chin again in the mirror. He fixed himself a large drink and sat down on the nearest barstool, resting his head in his hand.

"I blew it."

*No point in fretting, Fred. She'll be gone in a week or two. You'll find plenty more after that and forget she ever existed.*

"No. She has to pay. She has to pay for turning me down. No woman ever turns me down!" He gulped from the glass. "I'll take her out and get her drunk. She'll fall for me then. They always do."

*Fall over, you mean, right? Because of the drugs you put in her drink?*

"Oh, shut up, will you? You're always mocking me, and where are *your* good ideas? You never have anything *good* to say, do you?"

*I said something good this morning.*

"Oh, you did?"

*Yeah. You should see a shrink.*

Fred's voices were interrupted by a knock at the front door. He tried to see from the corner of his glass wall who it was, but the bougainvillea had outgrown its original position and now blocked his view, so he walked down the stairs and looked out the peephole in the door. There was no one there, so he returned to the office.

*I was right, you know. You* should *see a shrink.*

Before he could answer, the knock sounded again. He went back downstairs and looked through the peephole again. Still, no one was there. He unbolted the door and opened it roughly, but saw nothing. He walked out to the patio and looked both ways. No one was there.

*Hearing things, Fred?*

"Oh, shut up. You heard it too."

He walked back to the office and sat in his leather chair, swigging a sip of his bourbon and melted ice and swirling the crystal glass around.

"She can't turn me down! Not after turning me down in the bank!"

*She can and she will, Fred. You're wasting your time. She's a little girl. You're an old man.*

"I'm middle-aged."

*You're old. You're old and you're a queer.*

"I'm—" Before Fred could answer, the knock came again. He raced down the stairs, growling, and swung the door open only to find Rusty, out of breath and wagging his tail.

"Damn you! Fucking dog!" He brought the crystal glass down on the dog's head, shattering it. "You fucking asshole!" he spat, kicking Rusty in the ribs. The dog jumped back up with a yelp and moved away. Fred pursued him and grabbed out for his neck. Rusty avoided each grope, one after the other, until Fred gave up and went back inside. He returned to his office, fixed another glass of bourbon, and sat down in his yellow chair. When he leaned back and closed his eyes, he pictured the girl in her coral bikini, scolding him.

*You shouldn't hit your dog like that.*

"Let me make it up to you," he answered.

*Make it up to me?*

"Let me take you to dinner."

*She said you shouldn't hit the dog, Fred. She thinks you're an asshole.*

"Shut up and let her answer! You'll see!"

*I think you're an asshole.*

"What?"

She put a hand on her slender hip. *I said I think you're an asshole. You shouldn't hit your dog.*

*See? I told you! She thinks you're an asshole!*

"No, *you* think I'm an asshole."

*I do too*, she agreed.

"Well, fuck you both, then. I'll show you just how big of an asshole I can be."

*That's right, Fred. You show us.*

"This is *my* turf! This is *my* beach! This is *my* fucking dog and I can do what I like to it! Call me an asshole, will you? Call me a queer? I'll show you who's queer!"

*That's right, Fred. You show us who's queer.*

"Just shut up, will you!" Fred screamed, and then drank back his bourbon in one mouthful, swishing it through his cheeks and his teeth like mouthwash before swallowing it. It was four o'clock, so he turned on *McHale's Navy*, kicked off his slippers, leaned back into the chair, and promptly fell asleep.

At six o'clock, Fred woke to another knock at the door. Before he got up to answer it, he opened his bottom desk drawer to retrieve a can of pepper spray. His bottom drawer was full of that sort of stuff—a large rubber strap, a leather whip twisted into a perfect circle, a dart pistol, a pair of night vision goggles, two sets of handcuffs, two palm-sized cans of mace, and a boxed set of surgical scalpels. He put the pepper spray in his pocket and walked down the stairs. He readied his hand to catch Rusty by the neck this time, and jerked the door open quickly without using the peephole.

A young local woman with wide eyes jumped back. "Good evening, sir," she said. "I'm collecting for the Saint Elizabeth Literacy program. We help—"

"Illiterates?" Fred snapped before she could finish. He looked past her for the dog.

"Yes, sir. We teach people who missed out on an education."

Fred stepped out past her and looked both ways for Rusty. The woman retreated, frightened. He reached into his pocket, past the pepper spray, and pulled out an American ten-dollar bill. "Here. Now go away."

"Thank you, sir. Thank you very much," she repeated, and then hurried up the patio steps and back onto the road.

"Fucking illiterates." Fred walked out toward the pool and searched for the dog. As he walked back, he stepped on a piece of broken crystal still scattered on the doorstep and swore in pain.

"Goddamn that fucking dog!" he yelled, hopping and inspecting his foot at the same time. "Goddamn that fucking woman!" The local woman heard him from the road and walked faster.

When he returned to his desk, Fred opened the wound and picked the shard of glass out with a toothpick. He pulled an ice cube from his glass and placed it on the cut.

"That bitch doesn't know who she's fucking with!"

*She didn't break the glass, Fred. You did.*

"Now this will have to get ugly."

*Sure, Fred, ugly.*

"Stop fucking mocking me! I'm serious!"

*You certainly are, Fred. You certainly are.*

*Fredrick, stop with that swearing! I taught you better than that,* his mother scolded.

"Shut up, Mother."

*Don't you talk to me that way, young man!*

"I'll talk whatever way I want, you fucking old whore. You're dead. Why don't you just piss off?"

*Piss off?* She answered. *Why are you telling me to piss off? I'm on your side!*

Fred took the handcuffs from the desk and twirled them around on his index finger. "Will you all just *PISS OFF?*"

# .29.

# Loyalty a Million Fathoms Deep

E mer awoke to the sound of sailing. In the dim candle-light, she could make out only the nearest things: a basin of water and a cloth, a pair of wrist cuffs, a small, brown, corked bottle, and a bottle of rum. She reached out for the stool next to the bunk, but her arm flopped down to the planks beneath her instead.

She looked down at the shape of her body and tried to move her legs. Great pain rose from her right calf as she bent her knees and grabbed them, hugging them to her chest. She moved the blankets until her right foot appeared, swollen and discolored and wrapped with layers of white absorbent rags. Blood seeped through where her two toes used to be. She tried to wiggle the remaining ones, her big and middle, and her smallest, with no luck. They didn't move at all, not even when she tried her hardest.

Moving slowly, balancing as the *Chester* broke through fast waves, Emer reached for the rum and took a swig. She tried to remember where she was, what had happened, and whose care she was in. She drank two more swallows of rum before someone unlocked the door and opened it.

A man appeared, a short man wearing a round spectacle. He smiled when he saw she was awake and asked, "How do you feel?"

"What's wrong with my foot?"

"Your foot should be fine in a few weeks. Just a bit of gangrene is all."

Emer looked down. "It doesn't look fine."

"Trust me. I've been a doctor for twenty years and I know my business." He reached into the darkness beyond the candlelight. "Are you hungry?"

He brought the tray and placed it on the stool. Emer gagged at first, but then picked up a biscuit and brought it to her mouth.

"How long have we been at sea?"

"Four or five days. Only a few more to go, in this wind." He inspected her foot and applied some liquid from the brown medicine bottle.

"Where are we going?"

"You worry about resting and eating," he said, turning toward the door. "I'll tell Captain you're awake. He'll be quite pleased."

He locked the door behind him and Emer propped her

head with a feather pillow. She looked around for anything sharp, but there were nothing but blunt things. The best weapon she could find was the rum bottle. She worked to empty it, thinking she could hide it in her bed and strike when the Frenchman wasn't paying attention, then escape to the deck and kill everyone. She sat up and when her foot hit the floor, she cried out in agony, fell back into the bed, flushed, and passed out again.

When she woke up, her candle had gone out and she was in total darkness. The ship swung violently from side to side, causing items to shift and crash onto the floor. She held on to the sides of the bunk as the ship tacked one way and then the other, repeatedly. This was the movement of battle, for sure. Minutes later, she heard someone yelling orders and the gunners running above her from cannon to cannon. She felt the forecastle cannon fire and her heart thumped.

Emer wished she could stand up. She tried again, but couldn't get past the pain in her right foot. She lay down in the darkness and listened to the fight. Surely this must be the governor's best ship, sent to kill the Frenchman who had double-crossed him. Ironically, she found herself rooting for the crew of the *Chester*.

After an hour of gunfire, the boats met and there was fighting on deck. Emer smiled at the familiar language of battle the way she'd once smiled at the musical call of the returning swallows. She heard men fall to their deaths and men laughing aloud. She heard men skewering the dead, their blades sticking into the ceiling above her head. She heard men falling overboard, their bodies meeting the hull before they finally hit the sea. And then she heard two sets of footsteps approaching the dark cabin. Assuming her team had lost, she quickly lay flat and played dead.

"It's locked, sir," someone said.

"Kick it down."

There were several light kicks to the door.

"Harder!"

The door finally flew open, half of it snapping and landing on the floor next to the doorway.

"Sir, are you here?" David asked.

Emer sat up. "Over here." She reached out toward his voice.

"Come with us," he said. "Hurry."

"I can't hurry, David. I can't bloody walk."

The two men walked to her bunk and picked her up. She snatched the medicine bottle and shoved it in David's trouser pocket. When they got her upright, Emer faltered and felt dizzy. The men held her at the waist and the three of them moved through the doorway and up the steps to the sunlit deck. Emer closed her eyes and heard David gasp.

"Bring the doctor," she whispered to him. "The one with the spectacle."

David ordered his men to get the doctor. He carried Emer over the ropes and onto the *Vera Cruz*. The rest of the men continued to fight while they went below deck to her cabin. Everything was exactly as she'd left it almost a year before. Even her cape still hung on its hook.

When the doctor arrived, David left him in the cabin with Emer and one marine and went back above deck to finish the battle. He ordered the gunners to their places and the marines to untangle the ships and get aboard. When they did, the *Vera Cruz* sailed past the *Chester* twice, pouring endless double shot into her hull. The *Chester* began to take on water and sink as they tacked west.

When David returned to her cabin, Emer was lying in the bunk looking tired.

"What happened to her?" he asked the doctor.

"She is very lucky, you know. She could have lost her whole foot."

David said, "You'll stay with us until she's good as new, you will."

The doctor nodded. "We'll need some things."

"What things?"

"Medicine for her leg. Rum for her pain."

David looked at Emer. She smiled the best she could through her shame. "Now this," she thought. "A menace to my crew." He sat down beside her on the bunk, and took her weak head in his hands and kissed her.

"I have a surprise for you, Captain. A very big surprise."

"I've had my fill of surprises, David. Tell me."

"Well, if I told you, then it would scarcely be a surprise, now would it?"

"I order you!"

"Presently, sir. You can't order me. You can't even walk! You'll see soon enough what I have for you!"

She handed the small brown bottle to the doctor and allowed him to examine her foot and apply the dark liquid to the place where her toes used to be. He made her eat two biscuits and then left her to sleep.

Two weeks later, Emer was able to walk around her cabin with the aid of a crutch. Three weeks later, she could limp steadily without the crutch and began to turn the proper color. She walked circles in the cabin, and each day would make it through the entire ship's undercarriage twice. She ate one full meal a day, and had managed to keep down some dried meat. By the time the *Vera Cruz* reached its surprise destination, Emer was nearly healed. She would always limp, the doctor warned her, but it would become slight with time and practice.

David arrived one morning with a plate of fruit. "Today you get to see your surprise," he said, smiling.

She dressed in a pair of black trousers and a clean blouse. She attempted her boots, but one was still too small to fit on her swollen foot, so she left them behind. She fixed her battle cape around her shoulders and fastened the collar, now completely crimson with the knots of dead Spanish sailors.

As they neared the ladder to the deck, her men began to applaud and cheer. She looked up and saw that each had a small cup of rum in his hands.

"Close your eyes," David said. He led her to the starboard edge and then told her to open wide.

When she opened her eyes, Emer didn't know what she was looking at. At least fifteen ships surrounded them, mostly frigates like the *Vera Cruz*, but also several small brigs and a few enormous galleons as well. The crews on each of these ships cheered as noisily as her own, each holding up a cup of rum, toasting.

"What's this?" she asked.

"Twenty ships in all, sir. Good crews, competent officers, and four hundred guns or so."

Emer looked at the ships, and then looked back at David. "You did this?"

"We did." He motioned toward the crew. "The Spanish are due tomorrow or the next day. A fleet of about twenty, heavy with trade. We have two sloops tailing them, aye."

She looked at her crew, and then back at the fleet.

"You'd better say something, sir," David said, reaching down and squeezing her wrist.

She raised her cup and toasted her own crew first. "To the most loyal men alive! Verily! I owe you my life, I do." Then she refilled her cup, raised it again, and turned to the new fleet. And though she knew the men on board the other ships couldn't hear her, she said, "We'll take the Spaniards to the sea floor, or my blood!! Arg!" She let the rum trickle from the sides of her mouth and held her fist up. The men drank as if she'd always been their captain, and they held their fists up, too.

Men brought a basket of dried meat and a crate of fruit. Similar items were brought to the decks of the other ships, and the party began.

Emer leaned against the starboard rail, searching the decks and sails of her new fleet. She asked the men for a telescope and looked from ship to ship, inspecting her new men and her new guns. She recognized a frigate from Port Royal and waved, and its captain waved back.

Then, David gave a loud order. Simultaneously, all the ships raised a single flag to the top of their mast. It was Emer's flag—or so David had named it when he'd had women in Tortuga stitch them. It was black, with a red and orange dragon eating a one-eyed man whole. Twenty of these rose in the sea around Emer. She focused on them with her scope—and, in doing so, focused accidentally on a sailor keeping watch from his frigate's crow's nest.

From the side, the sailor looked familiar. And when he turned to face her, something hit her like a ton of double shot. She dropped the scope into the sea and grabbed the side of the boat with both hands. Her crew worried that she was relapsing, that the matching flags had been too much of a gesture.

But Emer wasn't overcome with embroidery.

She yelled for another telescope, and when a sailor delivered it, she carefully focused again on the man in the crow's nest three ships away. He waved a familiar wave—two fingers up, dancing from side to side—and she waved back, with two fingers, barely believing what was happening. David came to steady her as she began to quiver and sob hardy tears.

"What is it?" he asked.

Emer answered, "Lower a rowboat."

"What's the bother?" he asked again.

"Just lower the rowboat, aye, and get in it."

When they got to the deck above the boat, tears were still streaming down Emer's cheeks and into the sides of her wide, grinning mouth. David had never seen her so emotional. He asked, "Where am I going?"

"To meet that man, there," she pointed. He was still waving.

"Who is it?"

"Seanie Carroll," she answered, her voice shaky. "That's Seanie Carroll."

# DOG FACT #7
### *The Pack Is the Safest Place to Be*

Dogs have roamed the earth in packs for thousands of years. A pack works well for taking down big prey, which is what dogs originally did. During early domestication, the pack served to keep working dogs in order and obedient. These days, however, domesticated dogs have no need for big prey, rarely work, and no longer hunt anything more than a bowl of Alpo Chunky twice a day. But they still roam in packs if allowed. It's your job to make sure your dog steers clear of this dangerous habit.

It's also your job to do the responsible thing if you're left with a dog you thought you wanted but can't keep. Don't ever think that releasing a pet into the wild is a good idea. It's not. It's cruel and lazy—especially these days when there are so many shelters that can help you do the right thing. Stray dogs are not happy dogs. They can become a menace and can do serious damage and even kill.

Each year, in many cities and towns, packs of stray dogs take over neighborhoods and prowl the night. Sometimes the news airs a viewer's video, dark and shaky, with a dozen wagging tails barely visible. People are warned to stay indoors, to know where their children are. I find this funny, because humans all over the world are doing far worse things and aren't getting any airtime at all.

I learned a great lesson about human packs when I lived in Mexico (now Arizona) as a gray wolf from 1865 to 1877. I lived with the Apaches, and I was happy. They, however, were not so happy. Having had decades of hassle from the

Mexicans, losing many of their relatives and children and now facing new soldiers from America, the Apaches didn't have much going for them, luck-wise. They eventually, like all the native tribes in North America, lost their luck, their land, and many of their lives to the new invaders. I was killed by a man named Nelson Miles, who shot me in an attempt to make Geronimo surrender—but it didn't work. Geronimo didn't surrender until 1886, nearly ten years later. My gray wolf descendants were shot dead too, but only because they got in the way and seemed scary as they roamed in large packs across the plains.

Expecting modern dogs to stop roaming in packs is pointless. It is as pointless as the Apaches trying to get their land back. Pack mentality is built into every dog, the same as "finders keepers" is built into every imperialist. (One hundred and thirty years later, I find it amusing that if I ask modern Americans about genocide in Native American history they are outraged, and say I haven't heard of the *great* consolations provided. They speak about spacious reservations, government handouts, and casinos. Hundreds of *fabulous casinos*. As if Native Americans are the world's *luckiest* people.)

The truth is, humans roam in more fearsome packs than dogs ever have. All over the world, this very minute, human packs (armies, political parties, PTA parents, corporate bodies, country club socialites, and high school cliques) are operating to recruit new members and eliminate outsiders because of one thing—security. It's safer in the pack. Everyone knows that. 🐾

# .30.

## Hector's Roots

"Dat man is crazy, ya know," Hector said when I told him about Fred Livingstone.

"Yeah. I figured."

"I mean it. Stay way from him, girl. He's trouble."

Hector drove so fast, and played his roots so loud, that my stomach turned. Though I trusted him, I couldn't look out the front windshield, so I kept my eyes firmly planted on the road signs we passed.

When we got back to the hostel, I rushed through the small lunch Hector's cook had made us so I could get back to searching the beach. I hoped to find a different way into Fred's sea grape grove, and finding it while he was still in Black River would save me a lot of trouble.

Stupidly, before I left, I called the trailer park in Hollow Ford to let them know I was okay. For some reason, when Junior answered the phone I wasn't the least bit surprised.

"I got your room," he began.

"Good for you, Junior. Is Mom there?"

"No."

"Where is she?"

"Asleep."

"Asleep?" I sliced off the top of his head, like a machete through a coconut.

"Yep," he answered, half talking to someone else standing next to him.

"Will you tell them that I called?" With the pointed tip of my boot, I kicked his brains into his skull until they were mush.

"Sure," he said, still talking to someone else.

"Okay. See you in a few weeks," I said.

"Well, you can't live here," he replied. "I put all your stuff in the Goodwill bin."

I knew that meant he'd sold it, so I didn't say anything.

"I had to do *something* with it, didn't I?"

"Sure, Junior," I said, and hung up.

A feeling of sadness poured over me. Had he thrown out my yearbooks? My pictures? I thought of favorite sweaters and my two pairs of handmade mittens. My black Doc Martens boots. My books. My small collection of worthless but sentimental jewelry. My report cards. My beaded prom dress.

I was sad, but surprised that I didn't care more. Those

things had meant a lot once, but something had changed. I had changed. I wasn't just some skinny kid from Hollow Ford anymore. I was about to begin a new life as a new person. Before I wasted one more minute thinking about Junior, I took off for the beach, determined to find what I was looking for.

At about two thirty, I passed the glass house and continued for fifty steps. To my right was the sea grape grove, fenced on the road side. I looked around, noting a landmark that I would be able to see from the road—a perfectly fan-shaped shrub—and continued to the end of the grove. There, I crouched down and crawled past the undergrowth.

I wasn't ten steps in when the Doberman appeared. I heard him, first, crunching crisp leaves under his heavy feet, then saw his slow, tired body fifty feet away. It was obvious from a distance that something was wrong with him. I didn't see the blood until he came closer. It had matted most of his facial hair into brown clumps.

"Oh no. What happened, boy?"

He came to me, whimpering a bit under his breath. I inspected the wound in a sunbeam and found a small shard of glass lodged in the top of his head where the blood trickled. I picked it out and tried to press the cut together and apply pressure, but the dog couldn't stand still with the pain. I walked slowly toward the sea, and he followed lazily after a few seconds. I walked into the shallow water and scooped up a handful of salt water, placing it gently on his head and hoping he wouldn't freak out too much. I was very aware whose house I was fifty yards away from, whose dog this was. I washed the cut and gently scrubbed out the blood in his coat. He didn't flinch once.

When I returned to the grove and crawled my way through the growth toward my perfectly fan-shaped land-mark, the Doberman loyally followed.

I patted his back. "Good boy."

As I squatted and paced fifty steps from the roadside fence, he trotted behind me and counted along. When I stopped and began moving dead leaves from the ground with my hands, he circled me and watched, curious about what I was looking for.

I looked at him, face to face, and smiled. "Where is it?"

He cocked his head, nudged me, and led me through the trees toward the glass house. As we got closer and closer, I started to doubt that the dog knew what he was doing, and I slowed down. I certainly had no intention of another audience with creepy Fred Livingstone that day, or ever again.

The dog stopped about twenty feet from the edge of the tree line and sat down, panting and looking at me. I crept toward him, and when I got there, he stood up and nosed an area of worn, compacted sand. He whimpered again.

The dog knew what he was doing.

He knew there was something special under that spot.

He nosed a protruding root and scratched it with his paw. He did the same thing with another root. Then, as if he was frustrated with me for being so stupid, he wedged himself into the worn area and lay down in it.

"Is this your bed?" I asked.

He whined and shifted himself around, trying to get comfortable, and then stood up again. He nosed what looked like another root—but when I felt its sharp edge, I knew it was something else.

I sat down in the sand to get a closer look. As I pulled it back and forth, stealing it from the grip of three hundred-year-old sand, I recognized what it was. I'd completely forgotten about the shovel Emer buried that night long ago, and could hardly believe my own luck.

I'd envisioned days of stealthily searching through the small forest, sweating, swearing, frustrated, and tired. I'd accepted the fact of a second trip already, and had prepared myself for a third, if necessary. I'd thought of every scenario except this one—finding my buried treasure in one short week. Suddenly, Junior Adams was slotted right into place next to all the other assholes I'd ever met. So what if he'd thrown out all my things? So what if he'd moved in with my parents and probably stole all their stuff and treated them like crap? What could *I* do about it? I didn't have the time to slice a hundred shallow cuts into his lips and make him suck limes. I was too busy to make him swallow oiled musket balls. I had more important things to think about now, and a lot to do.

To celebrate my good luck, I walked to the village and ate my first plate of green, very dodgy-looking curried goat. I washed it back with two Red Stripes, which gave me the tipsy courage I needed to make my final plan.

I would dig.

Tonight.

When I arrived at the hostel, Hector was still sitting on his porch, listening to his roots and playing dominoes with his cook.

"Saffron, girl!" he said. "You want a game of domino?"

"No thanks. I'm beat."

"Come on! Sit here! Take it teasy!"

I walked into the kitchen and got a bottle of water from the fridge. When I passed by the phone I thought about Junior again, and my parents. What a pathetic bunch of losers. "Not me," I thought. "Not me."

As scared as I was about the task ahead, I was more scared of what I already knew. There was no way in hell I was going back to Hollow Ford, Pennsylvania, to live like a loser. There was no way in hell I was going to let them drag me down with them.

# .31.

# Fred Livingstone's Blood

Fred's foot would not stop bleeding, no matter how much ice he piled onto it. He tried wrapping it up tightly with paper towels and masking tape, but his blood took only five minutes to soak through, leaving him worried that he might have to go to a hospital. He wrapped it tighter and tighter until, on the third attempt, the blood stayed where it belonged, away from his yellow Italian leather. He leaned back and switched on the television, propping his bloody, taped foot on his desk next to the pair of steel handcuffs.

*You should go to a hospital, Fred.*

"It's fine."

*It could get infected.*

"It's fine. Stop nagging," Fred said. He shifted in his chair and turned up the volume on the television.

*I think you killed the dog, Fred.*

He swatted the idea with his free hand. "He's fine."

*I think he's dead.*

"Well, think what you want. He's fine," Fred answered. He pulled his foot nearer and looked for blood. He inspected his toes and scratched between them, releasing dry flakes of his skin and fungus onto his hand. He brought his fingers to his nose and sniffed them.

*Fredrick! I've told you to keep those tennis shoes out of the house! Why must I ask you again?*

"Oh Mother, stop nagging."

*I'll stop nagging when you get up and move those wretched things out of my house! Honestly! How can you live this way?*

"It's just athlete's foot, Mother."

*I don't care what it is! Just get them out!*

Fred pushed his chair back and got up. He limped to his bedroom and into his en suite bathroom and sat down on the toilet. His foot looked terrible in the bright light. Blood had dried and left brown stains everywhere—between his toes, around his heel, even under his toenails. He ran some water in the Jacuzzi and unwrapped his foot. The last layers of paper towels stuck fast to the wound and Fred had trouble pulling them free, so he pulled off what he could and let the warm water dissolve the rest. His foot wasn't in the bath a minute before it began to bleed again. He started to worry as the water turned red, and made a quick effort to rub the brown stains from the rest of his foot with his fingers. He grabbed the nearest towel and washcloth and dried himself, inspected the wound for any signs of infection, and then pressed the washcloth into it. He reached for the magic cream and unscrewed the lid from the tube. Starting with the space between his callused big toe and the next, longer toe, Fred rubbed the cream in, as he'd done ten thousand times before.

He hopped to his office chair and collapsed into it, all the while holding the washcloth to his wound. He wrapped more paper towels around the whole lot and applied masking tape, propped his foot up, and turned up the volume on the television.

*Why don't you find a good porno?*

"Stop telling me what to do."

*You never minded before, Fred.*

"I don't have to listen to you."

Fred ignored himself and took a light nap, but startled himself awake ten minutes later.

*She's telling people about you, Fred!*

"Rumors," Fred replied, half awake.

*She's telling them about your dog. About how you killed your dog.*

"I didn't kill him. He'll be back later."

*He's dead, Fred. You killed him.*

Fred sat up in the chair and poured another glass of bourbon. He reached in the ice bucket and retrieved two ice cubes and placed them under the washcloth on his foot, then put two more in his glass. He changed channels until he found some light pornography and turned the volume down.

*Now that's more like it. Ooo. Look at* her, *Fred! What an ass! I bet you could bounce a squash ball off that ass!*

"I bet you could."

*I bet you could bury your face in there and never come out.*
Fred didn't answer.

*I bet it's like honey down there, Fred. What do you think?*
Fred ignored him.

*God, Fred. You are* such *a faggot!*

The guys at Princeton were always calling Fred a faggot. Back then, when he ran with the frat pack as its only exchange student, it didn't bother him. It was just something to say. Those were the days when the voices were barely audible and the visions were barely visible. They'd all joined the pack the same way (one hundred blows to the ass with a paddle, two from each brother) and they would all leave the pack the same way—as hungover grown-ups with an education that might get them somewhere.

Fred was voted "Most Likely to Direct Porn" at the senior bonfire, a prediction that, at the time, he'd half hoped would come true.

The phone on Fred's desk rang, and he knew it was Winston.

"Hello, Winston. Fine, fine. How did things go with you?"

Fred drank back the rest of his bourbon and listened. Winston hated the noise and action of Miami and never failed to moan about it. "You'll be home tomorrow, old boy," Fred assured him. "Try to think about something else. No. I can't promise you that, Winston. You know I can't run this business on my own. We'll talk about it when you get here, okay?" He eyed his throbbing foot in the flickering pornographic light. "Okay, me too. Right, Winston. Good night." He placed the phone in its rest and sat back again.

*Why did you say that? You don't love him!*

"Shut up. He's lonely. It just came out."

*It came out because you* do *love him, Fred, don't you?*

"I do not."

*You do. Admit it. You love him. It's okay. It's nothing to be ashamed about.*

"I don't. I just said it because—" Fred paused. He didn't know why he'd said it.

*He'll be really pissed off about you killing the dog, you know.*

"I didn't kill the dog."

*He'll see the glass on the patio.*

"I'll clean it up in the morning."

*To hide the evidence of you killing the dog?*

"He's not dead."

*Prove it.*

Fred got up from his chair and limped down the stairs and to the side door of the condo. He opened the door and called the dog. Rusty didn't appear. He waited a few minutes, trying to focus in the darkness, looking for any movement, and then went into Winston's kitchen and fetched a tin of food. He brought it back to the door and opened it slowly, making sure the dog would hear the familiar sound of the can's lid popping. But the dog didn't bounce out from anywhere. Fred left the tin of food by the door and went back upstairs.

*I told you. The dog is dead.*

"Well, you're wrong. You're wrong about a lot of things."

*What things?*

"Everything."

*Like what, Fred? What am I wrong about?*

Fred turned the office television off with the remote and limped to his bedroom.

*Tell me! What am I wrong about?*

"That girl, for one. You said she was too young, and she's not. You're always saying I'm a queer, and I'm not. You're wrong all the time!"

*Not about the dog.*

"Whatever. Just shut up and let me sleep, will you?"

Fred slept soundly and didn't worry about Rusty once. When he woke up the next morning at five, he'd even forgotten about his injury until he saw a huge stain in the bed where his foot had been—a wide circle of brown dried blood. He examined the carpet and saw that he'd bled there too, and left footprints to and from the bathroom during the night. "God damn it!" he said, propping himself up and pulling his sopping foot onto his other leg.

Fred stripped the bed of its creamy cotton sheets. He tried to remember the trick his mother taught him. Was it cold water or hot water? Baking soda or lemon juice? He dropped the sheet at the bedroom door and removed the now-brown washcloth from his foot. The bleeding had pretty much stopped, but the wound had become a swollen, gaping hole overnight and Fred worried, again, that it might be infected. He searched the bathroom for something strong and found Listerine. Before he poured it over his foot, he took a long swig from the bottle.

"GOD DAMN IT!" Fred screamed as his foot recoiled from the shock. *If it stings this badly, it must be working,* he thought as he fought back tears.

# .32.

# Lost Lovers Found

While David went to fetch Seanie, Emer went to her cabin and tidied herself. She brushed her hair and applied a dot of perfume oil to her neck, her armpits, and her knickers. She worried.

"What if he hates me as this murderous woman?" she asked herself, and then tried to remember the girl she was when they last saw each other. A simple girl. An orphan girl. An owned girl. She felt better once she rationalized things—surely Seanie had some bad history under his belt by now, too. Perhaps worse than killing many men and plundering Spanish ships.

David was having trouble thinking about the plan to sink the Spanish fleet. He was too busy rowing between large boats to retrieve Seanie Carroll from the *Virginia* and feeling replaced. He tried not to feel too sorry for himself, but it wasn't working. Even though he knew that Emer never returned his feelings, he loved her more than he'd ever thought he could love a woman. Now he would have to give her up—after all his efforts to impress her! After all his work to assemble the fleet! How unlucky could he get?

Things got worse once Seanie climbed into the rowboat. David grunted and smirked—the closest to a welcoming smile he could manage—and Seanie looked pained and impatient. The two rowed violently back to the *Vera Cruz*, not a word between them.

David reluctantly showed him to Emer's cabin and knocked. Emer called out for them to come in. She got up from her bed and hugged Seanie tightly, then held him at arm's length and looked at him, then hugged him again. Seanie grinned and laughed loudly, shook his head in disbelief, and blinked back tears.

"Seanie, this is David, my first mate and best friend. David, this is Seanie Carroll, the man I once told you about." The two men shook hands and nodded to each other. David left as soon as he could.

Seanie sat in the armchair next to Emer's bunk and stared at her in the lamplight, smiling. She found herself crying, and then embracing him again, weak and sad as much as relieved and happy. She'd left her cape hanging on its hook and tried not to seem like the monster she'd become, tried to seem like a Connacht woman, or like someone who might have just thrown grain to the hens or washed the clothes in the river.

"How in the world did you land here?" she asked in slow Gaelic.

Seanie laughed. "I was meant to be looking for you," he said. "In Paris."

"You were in Paris?"

"Well, no. The boat never went to Paris. I wanted to find you and bring you home, Emer. As it was, the boat I found was going to Barbados. I had very little English," he explained. Every time he looked at her, he shook his head and sighed. He held her right hand in his left and squeezed it with each sigh. "I worked three years on the plantations there before I finally got work as a marine on board a supply fluyte."

Emer thought of all the marines she'd killed on board supply fluytes. Eyeballs of such men stared at her from her embroidered cape. "That's dangerous work," she said.

"Not half as dangerous as being a feared legend of the sea, I'd say." He motioned toward her foot.

Emer didn't want to tell him about her missing toes. "Oh. I guess I have a long story too."

Seanie had stared at her long enough. He'd watched her face make familiar expressions in the yellow glow as her eyes sparkled at him. Something told him to kiss her, then, and he did. It was a long kiss. It was a mature kiss—how parents kiss, how grandparents kiss. He moved onto the bed and twisted to face her, and held her so tightly she was uncomfortable. Uncomfortable, but didn't care—just as she didn't care all those nights in the Connacht cave, when her arm went numb beneath her from lying on his chest.

They lay down to face each other. Seanie propped his head up and Emer cuddled into her pillow. "And what's your long story, then? How did my sweet Irish girl turn into a frightful pirate?"

Emer smiled. "I'm not that damned, am I?"

"It's not so bad, to be feared out here."

"Well, it is if you're just a nice Irish girl like me." She giggled. "Oh, I don't know! Where do I begin, Seanie? Paris? The horrible man who my uncle sold me to? I never had the chance to see him twice, I ran so fast. After a year begging the city streets in snow, I took the boat to Tortuga. They needed women to breed."

She shifted uncomfortably and looked away from Seanie's stare. "No different from Paris, really," she added. "I ran so fast, and then ended up here. And now it's the bloody Spanish. Have you heard the stories of how they torture the natives? What they do to their slaves? Worse than anything *we've* seen, and how can that be? I tell you, it will be quite a day when I sink the whole bloody fleet to the bottom of the sea! Quite a day!"

Seanie kissed her again, for her enthusiasm. He remembered the day she first spoke to him, how excited she was and how her eyes beamed with the same zeal. Funny how things change, he thought. Funny how the same childish eyes could be so brutal, those eyes that once burned with marriage dreams—funny how now, although they pictured something completely different, those eyes somehow seemed just as sweet.

Emer remembered her foot and pointed. "That, I got in prison. It's only because I've spent the last year in a dark cell that I look so like a ghost. I lost two toes. Just gone. Now

I've only three there and a limp for life. I'm lucky I didn't die, though, or so the doctor tells me."

"I really can't believe it's you," Seanie said.

She smiled and caressed his bare arm. "It's really me. God, I missed you, Seanie Carroll. I never thought I'd see you again." Tears welled. "And now we're about to make history! The biggest robbery on the high sea!" Emer reached over him for the rum bottle and took a swig, then passed it to him.

"And what do you think they'll have on board?" Seanie asked.

She stopped to think and then shrugged. "I don't rightly know, but I expect it will be worth it anyway! So far, the Spanish have given me some rare and wonderful things, so I have high expectations." She reached under her bunk and slid her chest out to where she could open it. She pulled out a black pearl. "You know, these are more precious than diamonds."

Seanie rolled it between his thumb and fingers. She had always been so clever and headstrong. He was glad she'd landed here and not in a place where none of it would matter, like as the owned wife of any man. He even half wondered if his own intentions had been reasonable. His faraway dreams of marriage and children seemed more like a prison than paradise for her now.

When he didn't speak for a while, Emer turned to him. "Are you all right, Seanie?"

"It's the biggest thing that's ever happened to me, it is. I never once thought that joining a fleet of pirates would actually bring me to you! Can you believe I half considered leaving the ship before we came out here? Because of my silly Irish morals?"

Emer's silly Irish morals were hidden somewhere dark alongside her mother, so she tried not to think about them. "Well, we're here now. We'd better get used to it," she said. "I should warn you that I'm never letting you out of my sight again, long as I live!"

"Ha!" Seanie laughed. "Well, I should warn you of the same! Even if you tire of me!"

He grabbed her and squeezed her tightly, tickling her and kissing her face repeatedly. She laughed and thrashed until he stopped tickling. They kissed again and again, as if they had suddenly become a couple who were celebrating a fortieth wedding anniversary. It seemed as natural to them as breathing, this loving each other—and they gasped for air as if they'd been under deep water for six long years, frantically trying to resurface.

# .33.

# Dreams Come True

As Emer lay in her bunk with Seanie, she heard her crew having their party and realized she was being utterly selfish staying below deck. She wanted to find David and say something to him, so he would know she was sorry. She knew that he loved her. He hadn't been hiding it.

She and Seanie got up and he helped her with her cape, commenting on the outstanding embroidery work. He wondered how she would fight these Spanish marines with only one foot, and made a comment about minding her during the upcoming battle. When they got to the deck the party was in full swing, men falling about laughing, a few fighting, a few singing jolly songs. Emer held Seanie's hand, and this was widely noticed.

David was standing alone at the stern of the *Vera Cruz*. He seemed stranded there, stuck inside a web of ropes. Emer left Seanie with the singing men and went to him.

"Spanish ships twenty miles away, sir. Saw them with my own eyes, I did."

"David, you're drunk!"

"Aren't you, sir?"

Emer nodded. "I have to talk to you."

"With respect, sir. Save your words."

"I know it's not fair. But you always knew this might happen."

He looked at her and smirked. "I never knew a man could come back from the dead! No, sir! I never knew that!"

They stood, silently looking out at the horizon as they had a thousand times before.

"David?"

"What?"

"I'm sorry."

He softened. "I only wish things could be different."

"I know."

"If you don't mind, sir, I suppose I'll be finding other work when we're through."

"After all your work to make this fleet? You can't!"

"I can settle down and find my place. I suppose you'll be doing the same thing." She didn't answer. David looked out to sea. "I'd say we'll be pounding them before morning, with this wind! It's our lucky day!"

Emer tried again to meet David's eyes, but he dropped a wall between them. She backed off and acted professional. She even said "Carry on" when she walked away.

The men were drinking at an awesome pace. The baskets of food were empty and Emer watched as they danced and sang, knowing that these strangers were willing to die for her—a thing more noble than she could imagine.

By the time Emer's fleet surrounded the Spanish that afternoon, the same men were quiet and ready. Their twenty ships crept toward the enemy on all sides, tacking briskly to make time. The Spanish could see them, of course, and their only chance to save themselves was to outrun them. As Emer's ships moved close enough to fire their cannons, the Spanish ordered as many tons of cargo overboard as they could. Shirtless men appeared on the decks, throwing crate after crate of Caribbean sugar and rum into the sea. But no amount of shed weight could help them now.

Chain shot ripped through the Spanish sails, three or four tons at a time from all directions. One of Emer's fleet had already collided with a slow Spanish frigate, causing a backup on the eastern side of the battle.

"Fire!" David screamed.

"Men! Ready your muskets!" Emer joined in, positioning herself directly between Seanie and another man, propped to balance with one foot.

She grabbed a gun and began aiming for the crew of the nearest ship, a great galleon that shone with gold paint. She fired, reloaded, and fired again, and when the cannons finally ripped through enough sail to stop the fleet from gaining any more sea, she dropped her musket and turned to David. She ordered a switch to grapeshot—a cheap mix of everything imaginable: nails, chips of iron, even small rocks and broken glass—to flatten the Spanish crews. Any man on deck would suffer, and Emer wanted her enemy to suffer a long time before she boarded and put her men's lives at risk. Seanie continued to shoot with a long musket, aiming for the men who were yelling orders.

The hours passed quickly. Her fleet split the Spanish into four smaller groups, picking off the weakest first. Emer led her fleet round and round the Spanish ships, knocking down at least half their crews with her grapeshot. Ship by ship, her marines boarded, cut down the Spanish sailors, and pillaged. When the marines returned, she switched to plain round or double shot and plunged the plundered ships into the sea. One Spanish frigate on the west side had already sunk. Two others had moved in to rescue stranded crew and were being singled out for boarding. Each of her four groups did this—board, kill, pillage, sink—until, by sunset, nearly half the Spanish fleet was sunk. Toward the east, Emer noticed two galleons separating from the melee.

"Those two, David. Take me to them." David ordered the crew of the *Vera Cruz* to make it so. Two other frigates followed.

Emer readied her cutlass and pistol and gave Seanie her long-handled axe. As they approached, one of the Spanish ships fired its three port cannons, and Emer ducked. A single ball of burning iron landed on deck with a dull thud, only cracking the planks beneath it. She watched it roll toward the mast and then roll back again, burning a groove into the wood in its path. A sailor fetched a small keg of seawater and tossed it over the ball, creating a sort of steamy mirage of the battle. Still balanced between the two men, Emer ordered her crew to board the shining galleon just as the red shine of Caribbean dusk touched the waves.

Her crew piled onto the ship two by two and began taking down every man they met. Emer and Seanie climbed aboard with the last batch of her marines.

But when they landed safely on the galleon's deck, she realized that swordplay was impossible with only one good foot. Walking had been easy, yes, but this was not walking. She tried to jump from one plank to another, flinching in pain from her two missing toes. She managed to skewer a Spanish sailor or two, and clubbed one across the face to knock him out, but she couldn't swashbuckle like she used to. She stayed alert and defended herself in the dark, mostly helping Seanie and the other marines. A hack here, a slap there, a few clunks and swift punch in the balls, until— eighty-four dead men later—the ship was hers.

As the sun rose, Emer helped search the galleon even though she was in pure agony from the right knee down. David saw her limping up the final steps to the deck and put his arm around her waist. *Where is this Seanie fellow now?* he asked himself, half hoping Seanie was floating dead in the sea. His face was covered in blood, a deep cut had been slashed into his scalp, and he wore a strip of cloth around his head to stanch the bleeding.

"Easy now, Captain. You need to get that foot up, you do."

"It's done, David! We did it!"

"Aye, sir, we did." He smiled. "'Tis a glorious day to be alive."

Seanie arrived then, much to David's disappointment, and helped balance Emer on the ropes. She smiled and squeezed David's hand. "You deserve the captain's share of this. I had little to do with our success."

"I'm sure the officer's share will be more than enough," he answered soberly. "You fought well under the circumstances."

"I mean what I say, friend. You'll have my share and that's the end of it." Emer took a deep breath as they lifted her onto the deck. She slipped her aching body over the edge, landed on her good foot, and hopped toward the forecastle landing with David still holding her under her arms.

"Will I help you down, then, sir?"

"No, we should be all right from here, thank you," Seanie said, knowing for sure, right then, that something had been going on between the two of them.

They arrived at the bed in her room, and Seanie made Emer sit down and hold her boot out to him. He gently shimmied it off and removed the thick bandages that were now soaked with blood. "I'm going to fetch the doctor." He walked out of the cabin.

When neither Seanie nor the doctor returned, Emer reached for a bottle of rum and gulped. What a day this had been. She'd finally punished the Spanish, and yet she didn't care what jewels the searching men found or what gold she'd just stolen. All she thought about was Seanie and the questions that surrounded him. What would they do now? Where would they go? Would they go back to Ireland? Was she able to become a proper Irish woman again?

Seanie returned. "David wanted me to tell you that

the fleet is splitting now. He reckons we'll all meet in Port Royal over the next week, if that's all right by you."

She nodded, and the doctor arrived. He washed her foot with salts and warm water. He located the bleeding wound and treated it. "That could be septic, Captain. You'd want to rest awhile now and stay still."

"I see no reason to go anywhere today anyway," Emer replied. "Come and check on me tomorrow."

Seanie locked the door behind him and sat down on the bed. He made sure Emer was comfortable and fixed her a tray of food. They had a bed picnic, snuggled safe beneath the warmth of blankets, and giggled a lot. When they were finished eating, neither took a minute to say much before they undressed and disappeared into each other's skin for the first time. It was as easy as performing an underwater somersault for Emer, and made her stomach feel similar butterflies. As the sun set on the day Emer Morrisey finally sunk the Spanish fleet to the bottom of the sea, she and Seanie made love eight times. Once for each of her remaining toes.

As the *Vera Cruz* sailed southwest toward Port Royal, her crew took turns drinking and dreaming aloud.

"I reckon I'll settle down. Buy some pigs. My pa kept pigs," one said.

"A ship of my own! Arr!" another replied. "And a fine wench in my bed!"

Only two other ships from their fleet were still visible.

The rest had gone in different directions after moving the bulk of Spanish plunder into the hull of the *Vera Cruz*.

Emer woke up quietly and turned to face Seanie. She stared at his sleeping face and tucked him in tightly with her blanket. She rose, testing her foot, then put on her trousers and limped out the door through the men's quarters. She produced a large key from her pocket. Once inside the cargo hold, Emer locked the door and lit the lamp that hung next to it. The room sparkled.

"Spanish fools," she thought, shaking her head. She leaned down over two open boxes and touched a few shimmering things, then found a crate to sit comfortably on. She pulled out her dagger.

The first four boxes she opened were filled with standard gold doubloons, more than she'd ever seen before, but somehow they didn't excite her. She leaned toward one of the locked chests and dragged it forcefully over the planks. Try as she might, she couldn't get the chest open, so she moved to the next one and tried it, concentrating on two loose hinge pins. When it opened, Emer felt a lick of surprise to see nothing but black fabric staring back at her. She dug her hands in beneath it and found three tied sacks.

Getting up, she moved to the door for the lamp, brought it to the pile of crates, and placed it on a hook above her head. Then she picked up one of the sacks and untied the knot at the opening. Polished gems poured out of the bag like fast water onto the black fabric. Most were red or burgundy—rubies, a few garnets or amethysts, some small and round, others as big as her big toe, or bigger. Emer soon found that the sacks of gems were divided by color. The second one held mostly emeralds, jade, and malachite, and the last one mostly opals and a few sapphires. She searched the bottom of the chest and found similar black fabric, but no more treasure.

She went through a few more crates of gold doubloons and one filled solely with gold seal rings, cast in different designs. She tried on a few of them, admired her hand held flat in front of her, then took them off and put them back in the crate.

Emer went back to work on the locked chests. Surely this was where her real riches would be, so she dug into their hinges with great determination.

When she opened the nearest one and removed the top layer of fabric, Emer saw that it was filled to the very top with jewelry. Gemstone rings in gold settings, elaborate necklaces strung with precious rubies and diamonds, various-sized jewel-encrusted crosses, and a single sapphire pendant necklace so big Emer could barely figure who was meant to wear it. It seemed it would look best on an animal the size of a horse rather than a human, and a vision ran through her mind of a rich Spanish man whose carriage horses wore jewelry.

She pulled the huge pendant over her head and moved over to the next chest, which was filled with native artifacts. What sort of culture had made these frightening figurines? Two were the size of a forearm, solid gold creatures with two heads. One little figure had only one head but a long rolled tongue and searing eyes. Beneath them were four matching solid gold daggers, with smoothed emeralds set in the handles, and below them was a heavy surprise for

King Philip's birthday—which Emer unwrapped quickly. Then she sat staring at it in the lamplight as if she'd just unearthed a spaceship.

This emerald was twenty times the size of any gem she had ever seen, brighter and clearer than cut glass. But it wasn't its size or luster that Emer marveled at most. It was its color. Only once in her life had she seen this shade of green before—and as she peered into the emerald, it showed her an image of her early home, her little verdant valley by the river. She wrapped it again, gently, and put it into an empty crate.

The next chest was full of a mish-mash of things—snuffboxes, more Incan and Aztec trinkets, a few prize pistols, and a small sack of carved jade pendants. The last chest held forty perfect black pearls, larger than musket balls. Emer returned to the chest that held the figurines and removed them. She found the four matching daggers and removed them, too, adding these things to the crate with the emerald.

The crate was now full, so Emer reached for a second, smaller one and emptied its sparkling contents onto the floor. She had little interest in mixed gems or pistols, so decided to pick out a few beautiful pieces of jewelry—the four-string rose-sapphire-and-ruby necklace, two large jade rings, several crosses, an enameled snuffbox, a handful of larger gemstones. She removed the sapphire horse necklace from around her neck and put it, with the jewelry, into a sack, which she tied and placed in her second crate.

Emer looked around for anything else she might want, adding the small sack of red gemstones to her collection.

She placed lids on her boxes and stood up. After putting the lamp back on its hook by the door, she extinguished its flame and left the cargo hold. She carried the two crates to her room—where Seanie sat eating a grapefruit—and then returned to lock the cargo hold door. Three marines were standing there now, peering in, their jaws hanging open in amazement.

"You could buy a lot of pigs with that, Whitaker, I reckon. A lot of bloody pigs."

"I reckon I could buy all the pigs in the world with that much loot, aye."

"Stand aside men," Emer said, key in hand, hurrying. The men stood in drunken attention. Emer locked the door.

"There's plenty there to go around, lads. You'll have your share by the time we get to port."

"Whitaker reckons he could buy all the pigs in the world with that, sir. What do you think?"

"I suppose he could," she said. "Or at least all the pigs he could want, no doubt."

Whitaker saluted. "Aye, sir."

When Emer returned to the room, she kissed Seanie and peeled a grapefruit. "Good morning." When he looked at her as if to ask where she'd been, she answered, "I had a look at the Spanish booty." She motioned for him to get the crates. "Go on. But save that one for last," she said, pointing to the large crate. Seanie lifted the lid from the other and pulled out the sack. He weighed it in his hands and looked puzzled.

"Open it," Emer said. Seanie peeked inside. "Oh come

on! Open it up! Have a good look! These are as much yours as they are mine!" He dumped everything onto the bed and shook his head with disbelief.

"Now," Emer said, "let me show you what's in the other one."

She took out the figurines and the daggers, adding them to the pile of jewelry on the bed, then sat up and reached for the emerald, asking Seanie to close his eyes. When she had freed the stone from the cloth, she gave the signal. Seanie fell forward several inches with awe.

Emer held the emerald up in the lamp light, where it shimmered and glistened them both back to Ireland. Seanie reached for her free hand and she squeezed his fingers, like she used to when they were mute children.

"I wonder what Connacht is like now," he daydreamed.

"I wonder is Mary still alive. And the others."

"I hope my mother is. I hope everyone is."

"Listen to us! Out to sea for a few years and acting as if one hundred have passed!"

Seanie took the emerald from Emer's hand and held it out in front of them. Something about it made them both sigh and feel happy. Something universal, like music or love. Without words, without even looking at each other, their plan was forged.

# .34.

# Dreams Come True (Part 2)

As I waited for everyone to go to bed, I packed and walked through my plan. After I did that a hundred times, I sat and looked at the two bags I'd bought that morning, which would soon be full of treasure. How could I possibly pull this off? How could I possibly get away with it? I felt such a mix of fear and anxiety that I found myself stuck in the same old wish. Oh, to be a dog again! Oh, if life was as simple!

On top of everything, Emer Morrisey's feelings ate me whole. I longed to kill everyone. I longed for someone to love me. I longed for treasure. I felt like a sniveling idiot.

When the time came to leave my room, I was shaking. I waited until the roots were turned off, for the cook to close the kitchen for the night, and for Hector's bedroom door to close. Then I heaved my small backpack over my shoulder and quietly slipped down the stairs and along the dark road. A thumping bass, from the tiny dance hall bar next door, echoed off different landmarks as I walked, and I felt scared and full of jumpy adrenaline. As I neared the glass house, the high-pitched buzz from frogs in the nearby pond deafened me.

When I got to the fan-shaped bush, I took a long, deep breath and tried to relax. I jumped the fence, snagging my foot in the wire at the top, but wiggled free. By the time I reached the tree line only fifty paces from the road I was sweating harder than I ever had. I wiped my face with my shirt, crouched down, and walked slowly—counting—through the grape trees. I found my other landmarks and continued on into the dark forest until I could see the light coming from the house. It was television light, flashing and twisting the background of the grove into a psychedelic hallucination. I stopped and caught my breath.

I aligned myself with the patio door and with a tree I remembered from that afternoon, but somehow I was in the wrong spot. I walked slowly toward the house, careful not to make a sound, but the Doberman heard me and barked. Then, I heard his big pointy nose sniffing toward me. When he got there, I stroked his chest and he licked my ear.

"Where is it, boy?" I asked.

He kept licking my face. I cleared leaves from the ground where we were and moved the sand with my hands. The dog understood. He got up and trotted toward the correct spot, five feet away. He sat patiently while I started to clear the ground and pull out the first sapling. Trying to be quiet while pulling whole trees from the ground was tricky, and I stopped a few times to make sure I could still hear the television sounds coming from Fred Livingstone's house.

I finally pulled the shovel head from the ground, and stopped to marvel at how well it'd kept. Then I put it to the side, unfolded my father's army shovel, and started digging as fast as I could.

After a few minutes, the dog seemed to understand what I was doing. He centered himself along the opposite edge of the hole and started digging, too, tossing pawfuls of beach through his legs into a pile behind him. We maintained a rhythm—his paws, my shovel, and our piles growing behind us. For each of his eight beats I made one, and we continued on for a span of time until I felt I needed to rest, by which time we had already cleared two feet of sand and dirt.

I stopped and leaned against a tree, inspecting our progress. The dog's side of the hole was like a ramp. My side was more like a cliff.

By the time the hole was deep enough for me to stand in, time had passed in bucket loads. I had two blisters and a sore wrist, and the light flickering from Fred Livingstone's house was gone. The sky brightened to a predawn blue and I panicked. I had never thought about running out of time. Now I would have to fill in the hole and start all over again.

I was muttering jumbled disappointments, just about to give up, when I heard Mairead's voice in my ear. *Keep digging, Saffron. Dig!*

And then my shovel hit something hard.

And wooden.

Something hard and wooden. Like a crate.

"Holy shit."

# .35.

## The Dust of One Hundred Dogs

Emer spent her last day aboard the *Vera Cruz* packing. There were only a few things she wanted to keep from her evil life on the high seas. She pulled her neatly folded stack of embroidered capes from the shelf, rolled them tightly, and placed them into a satchel. She retrieved her small sewing box and her ivory and silver thimble, a spare pair of flare-legged trousers, her two pistols, and a snuffbox she'd retrieved from a sailor killed on the *Emerald* and tried to get them all into the satchel, too, but it was too small. So she turned to her crates of swag and removed all the bland black packing fabric, replacing it with her capes.

Emer stopped and admired her best cape before wrapping it round the oversized emerald and then placing it in the box. It was over now. The running, the killing, over. When she was finished, Seanie nailed the lids on tightly and they stacked up their luggage next to the door.

They all decided that once they got to Port Royal, they would cash the treasure and split it. David insisted on some time alone in the sparkling cargo hold first, to pick a few rare things for himself before they sold it.

"For my future wife, aye. She won't know what to do with a ring the size *I* give her!" he explained. He looked toward Emer, but she didn't seem a bit bothered.

She handed him the key. "Take what you like."

The next morning, when they docked in Port Royal, Emer turned to David before he went ashore. "We'll buy a new frigate for the trip to Europe. You're welcome to anything we leave behind. The *Vera Cruz*, the whole fleet if you want it, the maps we got from that Dutch frigate last year, the rest of what's in my cabin. If I were you, I'd start with those maps! You never know what's buried at the red *X*. And you should get far away from here for a while. Safest, aye."

"So this is goodbye?" David's mind wandered back to the first day he'd met her, on Foley's sugar run.

"Can you blame me?" she asked.

"I reckon I can't," David answered, looking at Seanie on the dock standing next to the two crates and the satchel.

Emer hugged him and whispered a million thank-yous into his ear. It was like saying goodbye to a brother. And in thinking that, she was reminded of Padraig and fought back tears.

Eight hours later, she and Seanie boarded their new ship. Seanie went to work choosing a few lads to sail it toward Ireland, and Emer retired to their cabin to rest her foot. She fixed a warm salt bath and soaked it for a half hour, the way the doctor had prescribed.

As they sailed from the Port Royal docks into the sunset, Emer went above deck to wave goodbye to her last Caribbean port—her last stinking hive of whores and drunkards—and recognized a face on the dock. She ducked down and turned away from him, but not before he had a chance to recognize her as well.

"Curses!"

Seanie heard this. "What's wrong?"

"It's that goddamned French bastard!"

"I thought he was dead."

"So did I," Emer said.

Having substituted cannons with food and marines with rum, Emer knew her ship was inferior. She slipped back below deck and peeled an orange.

At bedtime, Emer ordered the man in the crow's nest to alert her if *any* ship approached from *any* direction at *any* time of the night. She hoped to fool the Frenchman by going the long way round Jamaica, when most ships would head for the Windward Passage. It was her only option, once she'd left dock, to lose him.

A knock came at the door in the middle of the night.

"A ship behind us, sir," a voice said. Emer rose and dressed. She limped up the steps and stood at the stern with a telescope. It was as if she were gazing into a mirror—the

Frenchman stood at the bow of his ship, looking right back at her with his telescope.

At the rate he was gaining, there was only one possibility of escape. She and Seanie would have to make a run for it in a rowboat and hope that the Frenchman would continue to follow the frigate. She turned to her new first mate. "Prepare the rowboat. I've got to get ashore without that bastard seeing me."

"Aye, sir."

"Steer as close as you can. I'm going to collect my things," she said. Before she went below deck, she fetched the first crutch she could find—a short-handled shovel— and used it to relieve the pressure on her aching right foot.

"Seanie," she whispered, shaking his arm. "Seanie, wake up."

"What is it?"

"We have to go. He's found us."

"We can kill him, then," Seanie answered, still half asleep.

"Seanie, come on. Get up. Help me move these crates to the rowboat. We've only got a few minutes."

Seanie got up and dressed, picked up the crates, and followed Emer and her shovel-crutch up the steps again. She pointed to the rowboat and Seanie secured the boxes.

"Just continue west," she said to the first mate. "Don't slow down."

"And when he catches us, sir?"

"Surrender. Pretend you're the captain—just shipping rum and food. Innocent."

"Aye. And will I return to pick you up?"

"We'll meet you back in Port Royal. Dock and wait."

Seanie helped Emer into the rowboat and gave the order to lower them. They tried to hit the water as softly as possible, but the frigate was moving at a hardy pace and their landing was rough. Once they cleared the frigate's wake, they paddled slowly toward the Jamaican shore, toward the darkest spot. Emer prayed aloud.

"Please, God, just one more favor. Just one more escape."

They dragged the boat ashore, hid it under the canopy of grape trees, and began to walk through the dark forest along the shore, dragging their luggage. Emer stopped to see if the Frenchman's ship had slowed to notice them and saw it sail by, still in hot pursuit of her frigate.

After an hour of walking, the two were exhausted. "Where the hell are we going, anyway?" Emer sighed. They sat on a sand dune to rest.

"I don't know," Seanie answered.

"These crates are too heavy to carry back to Port Royal, and this foot won't make it much longer."

"Let's have a rest," Seanie suggested, and held his arms open for her to lie in. She propped her foot up on a crate and cuddled up to him.

"Why don't we leave them?"

Emer shook her head. "No, no. It's all I've got to show for all that blood."

"Then why don't we bury them here and come back for them later?"

Emer nodded in agreement, but stayed safe in his chest for ten minutes. She nearly fell asleep there, until he shifted.

"Okay," Seanie said. "Let's get these in the ground,

then." Leaving the crates with Emer, he walked over to a small clearing in the trees, counting his steps, and began to dig with her well-selected crutch. She listened to the rhythm of his digging and accidentally nodded off. When she woke, he was shoulder-deep and sweating.

"You should take a break," she said.

"You were starting to look pale," he said. "You need to take care of that foot."

He finished. Returning with the shovel, he stuck it upright in the sand, peeled off his wet shirt, and leaned down to her. He kissed her, and she grabbed hold of his hair and held him there until he nearly lost his balance.

"I won't be long," he whispered, turning toward the sea.

Emer watched him walk into the surf, splashing water on his face and chest to cool off. She imagined him on his dream farm with his dream children and his dream wife. It seemed only fair that God granted her this after so many years of hardship—it seemed only just that she would now have a chance to be truly happy. As Seanie walked back into the firelight, she smiled and tilted her head, feeling deep love twist her innards.

And then, a loud report. Seanie stumbled toward the shovel and fell onto it. He clenched his teeth, clutched his bleeding side, and collapsed.

She leapt to Seanie's aid, throwing herself down next to him on the cool night sand. He coughed three or four times, gurgling, and then stopped breathing. Emer cradled his head and hugged and kissed him, her face frozen in grief.

She heard someone walking on the beach. Reloading. She scrambled to her feet and hobbled into the trees behind her. Reaching for her flintlock pistol, she loaded it and waited.

The Frenchman approached slowly from the east, his gun scanning the beach for more enemies. He walked toward the two curious boxes and Seanie's limp body. First, he stopped at the dead body and wiggled it with his foot. Then he took two steps toward the crates, and leaned down to open the lids.

Emer aimed her pistol from the trees and fired.

With one last, almighty roar, the Frenchman fell to his knees and died. When the smoke cleared, Emer kicked him to make sure he was dead. Bent on one knee in the moonlight, holding his head with her left hand, she took a marlinspike and removed his right eyeball with relative ease. She rolled it in the sand next to his head and shoved the spike deep into his empty socket.

She placed her pistol gently into her waistband and looked toward the sea.

"I curse you!" she screamed at the dark water. "I curse you for all you gave me and for all you pilfered! I curse you for the journeys you begin and the journeys you end! I curse you until I can't hate you anymore! And I scarcely think I will ever hate you more than on this wretched day!" Her fair hair stuck to her face, wet with sorrow and surf, and her hand-embroidered cotton blouse clung to her, stained with her lover's blood.

Turning again to the two dead bodies, she retrieved the shovel from underneath Seanie—Seanie, her first and only love. She limped back to the clearing. Looking around to make sure no one was watching, she sat down on the edge of the hole and talked to herself.

"There was only one reason to stop all of this poxy business." She turned and looked at the distant dead. "What worth is a precious jewel now? Damn it! In all these years, over all this water! And I end up a fool with a lap full of precious nothing."

She dragged the two crates into the hole and began to cover them quickly, concerned that the Frenchman's reinforcements would arrive at any minute. She buried the shovel last, on top, and used her hands to fill the remaining depression, covering the sand with sticks and dead leaves.

Returning to the scene of the dead men, she lay down beside Seanie, placed her head on his chest and sobbed.

"It's like two different lives in the same bloody day."

Through her sobs, Emer heard footsteps. A voice boomed from the darkness, making her jump. She scrambled to her feet and reloaded her pistol.

"Foul bitch!" he began, in island-accented English. "You have meddled in my life for *too many* years! I'm sure you didn't know every whore in these islands heard him scream your name a thousand times! And me, too! Now look at him! Dead!"

Emer saw the man emerging from the tree line, his hands hidden. She had seen him before, on Tortuga and on board the *Chester*. The Frenchman's first mate.

"You will *see!*" he yelled, jumping from the brush. "You will see how true love lasts! You will *see* how real love spans time and distance we know nothing of!"

He rushed forward then, shaking a small purse toward

her. From it came a fine powder that covered Emer's hair and face. She reached up and wiped her eyes clear, confused.

"What are you at?" she asked, spitting dust from her lips.

He stood with his arms and face raised to the night sky. "I curse you with the power of every spirit who ever knew love!" he screamed. "I curse you to one hundred lives as the bitch you are, and hope wild dogs tear your heart into the state you've left mine!" He began chanting in a frightful foreign language.

Still brushing the dust from her hair, Emer took aim with her gun and fired.

As she watched the man fall, she felt a burning prod in her back and stumbled sideways—long enough to see that the Frenchman had miraculously not been all dead, and long enough to see that he was covered in stray pieces of the strange dust his first mate had thrown at her.

She tried to fall as near to Seanie as possible, and managed to get close enough to reach out and grab his cold hand. She took her dying breath lying halfway between her lover and her killer, covered in the dust of one hundred dogs, knowing she was the only person on the planet who knew what was buried beneath the chilly sand ten yards away.

And not knowing she was about to become a French Poodle puppy, two thousand miles away from the Caribbean Sea, with her memory completely intact.

## DOG FACT #8
### *Learning to Be a Happy Dog*

Dogs don't need much to be happy. Your dog will most likely be content with the basics. Food, water, exercise, companionship. You don't need to give him warmed gourmet meats or hugs every ten minutes.

Moderation is the key.

The same goes for discipline. A beaten dog behaves no better than a spoiled dog who's never been scolded. A dog must be taught what's right and what's wrong and learn from his mistakes. This goes for humans too, of course. Though dogs can't argue about their mistakes, which is where humans waste so much of their time.

Take the American Civil War, for example. It's hard to believe there was a time in U.S. history when people thought it was okay to enslave other people. It's hard to understand why, when confronted with ideas of equality and progression, people fought instead of changed.

At the time, I was a Yankee dog living in Gettysburg, Pennsylvania. My owner was an abolitionist who helped move slaves north to become free. He would meet them in the local wood, then bring them to our root cellar to hide until they were rested and fed enough for the next leg of their journey.

Trouble started in late June. My owner sent his wife and girls, on his best horses, to his brother's house many miles northeast, up by the Susquehanna River. As night fell on the county, Confederate cavalry moved in by the thousands.

Five days later, the fields of Gettysburg were littered with more corpses than the war had seen so far. I found my master there, bloated and wet from the hard rain, missing half of his torso. The view from the top of the hill was unbearable. The smell was worse. Dead horses and soldiers were laid out like carpet on a hot July afternoon. Men buried the dead, and piled up the distended horses and burned them for days, causing the entire town to swim in an ocean of thick, deathly stench which made every creature ill.

All of this for slavery. All of this for a white man's right to own a black man. To own wives and children and mothers. All of this stinking death for the right to deprive other people of their own rights.

Crazy, isn't it?

And yet the war continued for two more years. And it took another one hundred years to give those freed slaves' great-great-grandchildren basic rights. In fact, the microwave oven was invented two decades before a black man could sit where he wanted on a bus in some parts of America (the land of the free).

If dogs ran the world, there would be endless food, water, walks, and humping, but not much conquering. Humans want to conquer everyone they can, and buy everything they see. I think this is because humans have forgotten how to be happy. It's not their fault—it's not easy figuring out how to be happy in these days of anything-but-moderation. But it's possible.

Step one: Start with the basics.

Step two: Try not to make the same mistake twice. ❧

# .36.

## Fred Livingstone's Grave

I dropped to my knees in the hole and cleared the surface of the crate. I exposed the corners and dug my fingers into the cool, compacted soil, then rocked it back and forth. It started to come loose and then, suddenly, jerked up toward me. As I scrambled to catch myself, my brain noted that the crate felt far too light. The lid was cockeyed, and only half attached with rusty nails. When I landed on my butt, the box on my lap, it opened all the way—revealing only a bit of deflated black fabric.

My heart sank.

I rummaged through every corner of the box, finding nothing but three of Emer's capes, damp and full of small brown beetles.

I flung the box and capes to the side and explored the hole's walls for a sign of the second crate, but couldn't find one. Had Emer buried it next to the first? Or had she buried it on top? I closed my eyes and ran the old film in my head. I saw Seanie digging the hole, then lying dead. I saw Emer shooting the Frenchman and taking his eye out. I heard the rustling of leaves—but then I realized that this rustling was not in my memory. It was right above me. I looked up just as Fred Livingstone appeared through the foliage.

"Looking for something?"

He was out of breath and sweating. His thin, greased-back hair fell in a straight line on his forehead, and his foot was wrapped in several layers of bloody terry cloth. He smelled vaguely like Listerine.

"I said—are you looking for something, you stupid little bitch? Answer me!" He held out a thick hunting knife and shook it.

*Stupid little bitch?* What happened to the guy who invited me to dinner? And why did he have a knife? I was so scared that my hands and feet went numb. My heart was jumping in my chest and I could feel my sinuses clear.

Fred moved to the edge of the hole and squatted down to eye me closely. He had a look I can't quite explain on his face. A mix of surprise and glee. He even leaned above me and sniffed the air. Almost seeming amused, he muttered to himself, "My God. It's her." Then he said, "Shut up!"

He stood up again, still muttering a little, and looking at me as if he'd just realized who I was and why I was here. "Answer me!" he barked.

I moved my mouth to say something, but nothing came

out. Where the hell was Emer Morrisey now? Couldn't she see I needed her? He stood, waiting for an answer. Since I couldn't find one, I continued to dig out handfuls of dirt, in search of the second crate.

As I did, my index finger bashed against something solid, and I pried the second crate from the grip of damp earth. Fred circled me, limping, mumbling, and laughing. When I finally freed it, it too was lighter than it should have been. And when I opened it, I found the rest of Emer's capes, but not one dagger. Not one gem. The Emer within snarled.

"Where is it?" I asked.

"Where's what?"

"You know." *Did he? Could he?*

He put his finger to his lips and feigned deep thought. "Oh! You mean your puny little collection of worthless shit?"

I stared at him, incredulous. *He knew?*

"It was garbage," he said. "Didn't get me more than a few hundred thousand."

"You're lying." Emer was hopping around inside my skin. I looked down at the capes, now strewn across the bottom of the hole. "You spent all of it? All of it?"

"It was rightfully mine, wasn't it? Just like you?"

I stared at him, my head cocked.

"Don't you remember our nights in Tortuga? How we loved each other, my sweet Irish girl?"

I blinked. Was it really *him?*

I snatched my two woven bags from the edge of the hole while Fred continued to limp around, muttering under his breath. He seemed insane, like he was arguing with himself.

Was he cursed too? From the dust that night on the beach? Had he just lived the lives of one hundred dogs like I had?

Emer took control of me. "If it wasn't for the daylight, I'd kill you right here and eat your eyes for breakfast!" I screamed, stuffing the capes into a bag.

"Ah yes, my eye. Bad manners, entirely! But wasn't I able to kill you, despite that? Just after I killed your little cabin boy? Honestly," he said, twirling the knife around his wrist, "I never thought you'd be stupid enough to come here."

"I want what's mine." I tossed the second empty crate to the side. "I want my life back!"

"Isn't that what you have? Isn't *this* your pathetic little life?" He splayed his arms to accentuate my situation. "And didn't I leave you enough to be happy about? Those stupid cloaks. You used to prance around like you were some enormous hero. Like you were in charge!"

"I *was* in charge."

"Not when I had you, you weren't."

I stared at him so hard that I bored a hole through his skull. I didn't know what to say, but Emer moved my mouth. "You never *had* me, asshole." I snatched my father's army shovel from the ground and climbed out of the hole, ready to beat him to death.

He faced me.

"Is that you, Fred?" someone called from the road.

Neither of us had heard a car stop, but now a taxi sat there, revving, and a plumpish Jamaican man stood there, the rising sun behind him, peering into the trees. We both froze. Every Saffron-atom in my body said, *Run*. And every Emer-atom wanted to kill both of them before they killed me. But once I thought about it, it didn't seem worth it. Everything was spent. The whole crazy thing was over. All that time, I'd been calling on Emer to give me courage, and now that she'd finally come to help, I had to make her go away again. I didn't want to kill anyone. I just wanted what was mine. And now I knew—there was nothing. The only thing left to do was get out of there before Fred Livingstone did something crazy.

As I moved away, Fred limped after me. "Just where do you think you're going?"

"I'm going home," I said.

"What about me?"

"What about you?"

"Aren't you going to fight?"

"No." What could he give me, anyway? He couldn't give me what he once took away.

"Fred?" the Jamaican called, now standing at the door of the condo, looking into the tree line. "You in there?"

"Oh damn," Fred muttered. He seemed suddenly distracted and confused, like part of him wanted to crawl back into bed.

He pointed the knife at me. "You can't just walk away!"

I shrugged and took a step toward the road.

Fred Livingstone was not used to being blown off.

"I'll kill you!" he yelled and came at me, aiming the knife for my chest. I dropped the bag of capes and swung my dad's shovel at his head like a baseball bat. I hit him square in the ear, knocking him off his feet.

Next thing I knew he was falling, head-first, right for me. I leapt out of the way and let him fall into the hole. He landed awkwardly, on one of the crates, and the knife tumbled out of his hand into the dirt. My bag fell in after him, and landed to his left. He was passed out and floppy like he'd broken his neck. Sand sprinkled onto his head from the steep side of the hole, and blood trickled from a deep cut on his balding forehead.

"Fred, mon! No games, yanno. You there?"

I panicked and didn't know what to do, so I jumped into the hole with him. When I peeked out, I saw the Jamaican creeping slowly toward me, holding the jumpy Doberman by his collar. Who was this guy? History couldn't really repeat itself, could it?

"No kidding, Fred," he said. "I need some cash for the taxi man."

The taxi honked. I was paralyzed, so Emer took over. She moved my legs toward Fred and bent my body over him. She made me reach down toward the stuffed bag, and that was when I smelled his breath. It was the same. The same breath from the cave on Tortuga, and from the Bahaman prison, and from right there on that cursed beach, the night Emer died.

On the dirt, just inches in front of me, was his knife. To my right was the bag, stuffed full of capes. I looked at the knife, then at Fred, and then at the bag. And even though I knew Emer would want me to kill him, I couldn't. He was too pathetic. It was a different time, now. The bag was calling for me. It was telling me to grab it and get out of there. When I grabbed it, I saw the red knotwork and the embroidered eyeballs, and I remembered the gems. All the tiny gems.

The Jamaican reached the hole. "Who dat?" he said. The dog jiggled and jumped to get free.

"He's not dead," I said, feeling caught and stupid, my one hand moving toward the knife, just in case.

He smiled and put his hands up. "You don't need to kill me too."

"I don't?"

"Nah, mon." The taxi honked again.

The dog came down to lick my face. He sniffed Fred's crotch, and then nudged me until I scratched under his ears.

"You go on. I'll take care of Fred."

I picked up the bag and shimmied myself sideways, with one eye on Fred's limp body the whole time.

"Go on," he said, walking past me, lowering himself into the hole.

"But…"

The taxi man yelled something in patois. The Jamaican rummaged around in Fred's pocket for his overstuffed wallet. He handed me a wad of cash and patted my wrist warmly.

"Go on, now. Go."

The dog walked me to the road. I leaned down and gave him a rough cuddle and stole one more glimpse of Billy's Bay behind me. The beach was empty, the water was calm, and the Jamaican was pacing the hole, holding my dad's army shovel and looking down at Fred, singing something to himself under his breath.

As I plonked myself into the taxi's back seat, I felt a weight like two ton of shot lift off my back. Emer was gone. Three hundred years' worth of emotion floated into the atmosphere. Three hundred years' worth of loneliness and hate and fear and anticipation evaporated, and I was left staring at a complete stranger in the rearview mirror. Me.

The Montego Bay airport was crowded. The line for the ticket counter was about twenty-five minutes long, and I waited with my eyes closed, the shock and fatigue finally catching up with me. I must have looked like an idiot, slouching there with my eyes clamped shut. But I just couldn't face the string of facts laid out before me. I was leaving Jamaica without my treasure. I was about to arrive in the Hollow Ford trailer park with nothing more than a few moldy capes and a handful of whatever was sewn into them. I was as pitiful as the rest of my family. A failure.

I paid a hundred dollars (of Fred's extra cash) to change my ticket, and then, after passing through security, I walked slowly to the gate area and sat in an uncomfortable plastic chair. I stared out the window at the airport workers moving luggage on the tarmac until I realized that I'd have to bum a ride from the Philadelphia airport with whoever in my house was sober enough to drive. I walked back through the concourse to the airport shop and bought a bottle of water and a phone card, and dialed the pay phone that was next to the flickering departures board.

The trailer park phone rang and rang. After eighteen rings, someone I didn't know answered sleepily. I asked for Sadie Adams and the guy said something like, "I don't know any Sadies." I asked him to go and knock on the trailer for me, and he told me that #34, our trailer, had been burnt out two nights before.

"Was anyone killed?"

"All I know is that it was trippy, man. Flames everywhere."

As I stood there, trying to retrieve my sister Patricia's phone number from my memory, I saw a young man watching me from the outdoor smoking area, beyond the security check. He was smiling so warmly, like he knew me, that I looked behind me to see who he was looking at. But I was the only one there. And when I looked back, he was gone.

When I got ahold of Patricia two panicked minutes later, she told me that Mom and Dad were fine and staying with some friends in a nearby trailer. Then she told me that Junior started the fire. I didn't know what to say, so I just said, "That figures."

When I hung up, I felt like the universe was trying to tell me something. In the same day that I'd broken free from Emer's three-hundred-year-old grip, I'd been set free from my wretched family, too. I looked at my boarding pass and realized that I'd just bought a ticket to a place where no home was waiting for me. A ticket to nowhere.

But before I had a chance to change my mind, they started boarding call and my brain muddied up. I should go home to make sure my parents were okay at least, I figured, and then go from there. Anyway, it was only fair. My parents had raised me, hadn't they? And where else did I have to go? I waited in line, showed my boarding pass, and walked down through the tunnel into the plane. Rather than stow my small, stuffed backpack overhead, I kicked it under the seat in front of me. Something about the air inside the plane made me instantly sleepy, so I adjusted my papery airline pillow, leaned my head back, and closed my eyes.

"Excuse me," someone said. "I think you're in my seat."

A sunburned lady in a Hawaiian shirt held her hand up to apologize for waking me.

I reached in my back pocket for my boarding pass. "Are you sure?" My seat read *12A*. She showed me her pass. *12A*. I shrugged.

We summoned a flight attendant, who spoke to the ticketing desk on a walkie-talkie from the crew area. I gazed out the window at the busy airport workers on the tarmac. I looked past the runway to the skyline, and then back to the airport. Before I looked away from the view, I spotted the young man from earlier—looking at me from another gate's window.

I squinted. He had wavy dark hair in need of a trim and wore a red T-shirt. His tanned legs stopped at a pair of worn, rugged hiking boots. His eyes seemed sincere, even at a distance. He was staring at me and smiling, just as he had when I was on the phone. He looked familiar, and I tried to figure out where I might have seen him before.

A bunch of the landing crew came in then, eager to close the door. The flight attendant approached me, shaking her head, seeming troubled. I looked back at the man in the airport window. He was still smiling. And then he raised two fingers and moved them from side to side, like Seanie had all those years ago.

I felt something in the core of me tighten. I waved back. He smiled and I smiled. He waved again, and I waved again. Our eyes locked.

I shivered. Every ounce of me knew what I had to do. I didn't know how. I didn't know why. I wanted to question and doubt, but no matter how I tried, my three-hundred-year-old nose would not let me complicate something so simple. Why not believe what was right in front of me— rather than look toward the future all the time? Why trade a chance at real happiness for a misery I already knew?

I pulled my backpack onto my lap and stood up. Before the flight attendant could tell me the bad news, I moved to the aisle and told the lady to take seat *12A*.

"It's okay," I said. "I'll take the next flight."

## Acknowledgments

This was my first published book after fifteen years of hard work writing novels. I owe thanks to many people for support over those fifteen years and the ten that have followed, but one name stands out: Thank you, Andrew Karre, for asking that one question— "Have you got anything weird?"—and for your support of everything I've done since. You are the best editor a writer could ask for, a good friend, and a good human being. You teach me things I never knew I wanted to know. For that, I am continuously grateful.

Thanks also to Michael Bourret (best agent alive), my friends and family, my writers groups over the decades, and to my adult literacy students in Kilkenny City—without whom this book may have never been written.

*The Dust of 100 Dogs* was a ten-year-long bestseller at my favorite independent bookshop, Aaron's Books in Lititz, Pennsylvania. Thanks to Sam and Todd for supporting this story and every book I've written since and for being so kind to my family over the years.

And thank you to every bookseller, librarian, teacher, book blogger, podcaster, booktuber, and fan who shared my work with other readers. Your support means the world to me, and my gratitude is galleon-sized.

Keep reading for an excerpt of

A. S. King's newest novel

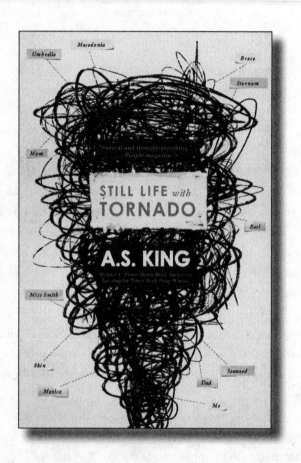

Nothing ever really happens.

Or, more accurately, nothing new ever really happens.

My art teacher, Miss Smith, once said that there is no such thing as an original idea. We all think we're having original ideas, but we aren't. "You're stuck on repeat. I'm stuck on repeat. We're all stuck on repeat." That's what she said. Then she flipped her hair back over her shoulder like what she said didn't mean anything and told us to spend the rest of class sorting through all the old broken shit she gets people to donate so we can make art. She held up half of a vinyl record. "Every single thing we think is original is like this. Just pieces of something else."

Two weeks ago Carmen said she had an original idea, and then she drew a tornado, but tornadoes aren't original. Tornadoes are so old that the sky made them before we were even here. Carmen said that the sketch was not of a tornado, but everything it contained. All I saw was flying, churning dust. She said there was a car in there. She said a family pet was in there. A wagon wheel. Broken pieces of a house. A quart of milk. Photo albums. A box of stale corn flakes.

All I could see was the funnel and that's all anyone else could see and Carmen said that we weren't looking hard enough. She said art wasn't supposed to be literal. But that doesn't erase the fact that the drawing was of a tornado and that's it.

Our next assignment was to sketch a still life. Miss Smith put out three bowls of fruit and told us we could arrange the fruit in any way we wanted. I picked one pear and I stared at it and stared at my drawing pad and I didn't sketch anything.

I acted calm, like I was just daydreaming, but I was paralyzed. Carmen looked at me and I shrugged like I didn't care. I couldn't move my hand. I felt numb. I felt like crying. I felt both of those things. Not always in art class, either.

When I handed in a blank paper at the end of class, I said, "I've lost the will to participate."

Miss Smith thought I meant art class. But I meant that I'd lost the will to participate in anything. I wanted to be the paper. I wanted to be whiter than white. Blanker than blank.

The next day Miss Smith said that I should do blind drawings of my hand. Blind drawings are when you draw something without looking at the paper. I drew twelve of them. But then I wondered how many people have done blind drawings of their hands and I figured it must be the most unoriginal thing in the world.

She said, "But it's your hand. No one else can draw that."

I told her that nothing ever really happens.

"Nothing ever really happens," I said.

She said, "That's probably true." She didn't even look up from the papers she was shuffling. Her bared shoulders were already tan and it wasn't even halfway through April. I stood there staring at her shoulders, thinking about how nothing ever really happens. Lots of stuff has happened to Miss Smith. I knew that.

My hands shook because I couldn't draw the pear. She looked up and I know she saw me shaking. She could have said anything to me then. Something nice. Something encouraging. Instead, she repeated herself.

She said, "That's probably true."

So I stopped going to school.

It's true about the letters they'll send when you stop going to school. After a week or so they come after you and make you meet with the principal. But that's happened before, just like tornadoes, so it didn't impress me. My parents escorted me into the school building and they apologized a hundred times for my behavior but I didn't apologize even once.

I couldn't think of one reaction to the meeting with the principal that was original. Apologizing, crying, yelling, spitting, punching, silence—none of those things are original. I tried to levitate. I tried to spontaneously combust like a defective firework.

Now that would be original.

I'm at the bus shelter two blocks from school and it's raining and I'm pressed back as far as I can be into the shelter and I'm not doing or thinking anything original. I am on my way to City Hall to change my name. Still not original, but at least I won't be Sarah anymore.

Dad was perky this morning. He said, "I wish you'd do something constructive with these days. You could paint or sculpt or something. At least you'd be productive." He didn't hear the spaces between those words. He didn't hear the rests between the notes. "But I know you're going to school today because we have a deal, right?"

*Deals.* That's what life with Dad is—a series of deals. He thought I was going to school on the bus and I did go on the bus, but I didn't get to school. I got off one stop early to catch another bus, like I've done for the last eight school days. I could be shooting heroin or dabbing or smoking meth. I could be flirting with boys after school like normal girls do. I could be pregnant. Of course, none of those things are original, but they would be constructive and productive, which is what Dad seems to want. Right now, I'm going to City Hall.

I still don't know what name I'll choose. I have twenty minutes until I have to decide. I catch my distorted reflection in the windows of the passing cars, and I think about how people elope to City Hall and get married without telling anyone. I'm doing that, but I'm doing it by myself. I will elope with the new me. I will come out with a new name but I'll still have the same face and everyone will call me Sarah but I'll really be whoever I decide to be. I will confuse the Social Security Administration. My number will now match the wrong name. I will not tell my parents what my new name is. I won't even tell myself.

A woman walks up and sits down next to me in the bus shelter. She says hello and I say hello and that's not original at all. When I look at her, I see that she is me. I am sitting next to myself. Except she looks older than me, and she has this look on her face like she just got a puppy—part in-love and part tired-from-paper-training. More in-love, though. She says, "You were right about the blind hand drawings. Who hasn't done that, right?"

I don't usually have hallucinations.

I say, "Are you a hallucination?"

She says no.

I say, "Are you—me?"

"Yes. I'm you," she says. "In seven years."

"I'm twenty-three?" I ask.

"I'm twenty-three. You're just sixteen."

"Why do you look so happy?"

"I stopped caring about things being original."

When the bus comes she gets on it with me, and to prove she's really real she stops and slots a token into the machine. There are two Sarahs on this bus. We are going to City Hall.

"We're eloping," she says.

I'm conflicted. Is this what eloping with the new me looks like? Riding to City Hall on a bus with myself? How will I ever fool the

Social Security Administration if there's a witness? Even if the witness is me? I try to concentrate on names I like. Wild names. Names that surprise people. I can't come up with any names. I just keep looking at twenty-three-year-old Sarah and my brain is stuck on one name. *Sarah. Sarah. Sarah.* I can't get away from myself.

I'm stuck on a bus with Sarah who is twenty-three. She has a snazzy haircut and highlights. My hair is still long and stringy like it always has been. It doesn't stop people from staring at us like we're identical twins. She's comedy and I'm tragedy. Even that thought isn't original.

She says, "You're not really going to change your name, are you?"

I say, "You tell me."

She smiles again and I want to tell her stop smiling so much. We have an ordinary smile and it annoys me.

She says, "I'm still Sarah."

"I'm still going to City Hall," I say.

"Fine with me."

"I don't want you to come with me."

She smirks. "You can't even change your name yet. You're only sixteen."

"I'm practicing," I say.

She rolls her eyes. "I guess."

When the bus nears the next stop, I repeat myself. "I don't want you to come with me."

"Suit yourself," she says.

She gets off at the next stop, and as the bus pulls away, I watch her walk up 12th Street and see she still has our favorite umbrella.

Maybe I'm snapping. Maybe I've already snapped and I'm coming back to real life. Maybe this is some sort of existential crisis. I couldn't tell you right now whether my life has meaning or value. I don't even know if I'm really living. Either way, I'm going to City Hall. Either way, I'm changing my name.

As the bus goes east, we pass through the University of the Arts campus. This is where I say I want to go to college. Except I'm skipping school, so I probably won't get to go to college. Or maybe I will. I'm not sure. Going to college doesn't seem original. Not going to college doesn't seem original unless I plan to do something original instead of just not going to college.

I thought being an artist would be the right thing to do. Since I was little, everybody told me I was good at it. Every year on my birthday Dad gave me something a real artist should have—a wooden artist's model, a set of oil paints, a palette, an easel, a pottery wheel. When I was nine, he woke me up every summer morning saying, "Time to make the art!" And I made art. Sometimes I made great art and I knew it because people's expressions change when they look at great art. When I was ten, after we went to Mexico, he stopped waking me up that way, but I still made the art. Right up until Miss Smith and the pear. It wasn't the pear's fault. It was building for months because sixteen is when people stop saying great things about a kid's drawings and start asking questions like "Where do you want to go to college?"

I just don't think college is where artists go. I think they go to Spain or Macedonia or something.